AT DEATH'S WINDOW

A Selection of Titles by Jim Kelly

The Detective Inspector Peter Shaw Series

DEATH WORE WHITE
DEATH WATCH
DEATH TOLL
DEATH'S DOOR *
AT DEATH'S WINDOW *

The Philip Dryden Series

THE WATER CLOCK
THE FIRE BABY
THE MOON TUNNEL
THE COLDEST BLOOD
THE SKELETON MAN
NIGHTRISE *
THE FUNERAL OWL *

* *available from Severn House*

AT DEATH'S WINDOW

Jim Kelly

CRÈME de la CRIME

This first world edition published 2014
in Great Britain and the USA by
Crème de la Crime, an imprint of
SEVERN HOUSE PUBLISHERS LTD of
19 Cedar Road, Sutton, Surrey, England, SM2 5DA.
Trade paperback edition first published 2015 in Great Britain
and the USA by SEVERN HOUSE PUBLISHERS LTD.

Excerpt from 'Medieval Glass-Making in England' by R.J. Charleston reproduced
with kind permission from Broadfield House Glass Museum, Dudley MBC.

British Library Cataloguing in Publication Data

Kelly, Jim, 1957- author.
  At death's window. – (A Shaw & Valentine mystery)
  1. Shaw, Peter (Fictitious character)–Fiction.
  2. Valentine, George (Fictitious character)–Fiction.
  3. Murder–Investigation–Fiction. 4. Police–England–
  Norfolk–Fiction. 5. Detective and mystery stories.
  I. Title II. Series
  823.9'2-dc23

ISBN-13: 978-1-78029-068-3 (cased)
ISBN-13: 978-1-78029-550-3 (trade paperback)
ISBN-13: 978-1-78010-598-7 (e-book)

All Severn House titles are printed on acid-free paper.

Severn House Publishers support the Forest Stewardship Council™ [FSC™],
the leading international forest certification organisation. All our titles that
are printed on FSC certified paper carry the FSC logo.

Typeset by Palimpsest Book Production Ltd.,
Falkirk, Stirlingshire, Scotland.
Printed and bound in Great Britain by
TJ International, Padstow, Cornwall.

For Eric Boyle
A champion of books

ACKNOWLEDGEMENTS

This is a work of complete fiction. While all the characters in this story are the product of my imagination, enthusiasts of the north Norfolk coast will note that I have also created an entirely fictitious village in Burnham Marsh, the location for much of the action in *At Death's Window*. Shaw and Valentine both work for West Norfolk Constabulary, which does not exist.

I have, however, taken some pains to understand the arcane art of glassmaking. I would like to thank Kari Moodie, curator of Broadfield House Glass Museum, Dudley, for her help, and permission to use a passage from R.J. Charleston's paper 'Medieval Glass-Making in England'. Jasmine Allen, curator at Ely Cathedral's excellent stained glass museum, was also very helpful. Any errors on this topic are entirely mine.

I would also like to thank my agent, Faith Evans, my editor at Severn House, Kate Lyall Grant, and Sara Porter, for all their work and support. Jenny Burgoyne, as always, brought her eagle eyes to the manuscript. My wife, Midge Gillies, has again provided an 'on site' referral unit in all matters to do with plot, character and writing.

ACKNOWLEDGEMENTS

ONE

The first killing frost of the year struck on the night of the first of October; then, the following day, the skies cleared and the sun rose, burning off an autumn mist which clung to the beaches. Thermometers began to climb into the sixties, and then the seventies as a classic Indian summer took hold. For eighteen days in a row the noon air crackled with heat and electricity along the north Norfolk coast and thunderclouds billowed at sea, mushrooms of boiling, billowing, humid air. Thunder rumbled and jagged lightning crackled, but the rain held off. Trippers and second homeowners made the most of the heatwave for a week, then two, until even they had to go back to work, leaving the sands to grey-heads and couples with pre-school toddlers. The locals simply waited for the weather to break. The water was green and choppy, white with spray: a winter sea under a summer sky.

DI Peter Shaw sat on the back terrace of the Old Ship Inn – one of the coast's burgeoning collection of gastropubs – looking out over Brancaster Marsh, his wife, Lena, beside him. They sat in wicker chairs beside a glass-topped table, a bottle of white wine in a chiller. The plate before Shaw was porcelain, the two scallops chargrilled, each with its accompanying orange 'coral'. The detective used his knife to separate what he knew to be the mollusc's brightly coloured ovary from the rest of its body. There was something visceral about the vivid flesh which made his throat contract. He concentrated on the three new potatoes, which had been shaken in lovage, and the sprig of green samphire, the local 'sea asparagus', picked from the marsh and dusted with sea salt.

High tide was an hour away, and the sound of the surf breaking on the distant, unseen beach was a clear, methodical drum roll. The channels and creeks of the marsh were filling up to the brim like silvered mirrors. Lightning flashed once out at sea and the cutlery and glasses pulsed, as if intermittently charged with neon.

'God's fireworks,' said Shaw. The detective had a quiet, musical voice, which suggested an ability to hit a note at will. One of his eyes was blue – almost colourless, like tap water falling. The other was blind, the iris simply a moon-like white disc. Shaw pressed both eyes tightly shut and saw the forked lightning shape behind the right lid only. Five years earlier he'd been blinded in an accident involving toxic waste on the beach, but he never tired of testing his disability, pushing his remaining senses to the edge of what was still possible while monitoring the performance of the one vital remaining eye.

'This weather,' said Lena, stretching out long, lean legs. 'Can you promise me it'll be like this every year?'

'Sure. Every year. No problem.'

Lena was Jamaican, her black skin glowing after a summer spent working on the beach. The English weather to her was a constant source of real horror. Rainy days in June and July clouded her mood; a long grey English winter left her depressed. Living on the north Norfolk coast had always been a gamble. Sometimes she wished she'd never taken the risk.

'Odd term: Indian summer,' she said. 'Colonial, I suppose – another echo of the Raj?'

'For once you're wrong. Not everything's about the Empire,' said Shaw.

The coast, its moods, its shifting atmospherics, was one of his obsessions. Lena imagined him researching online, worrying away at the origins of that odd couplet: Indian summer.

'Nineteenth century, I think, from the Great Plains of America. A *Red* Indian summer, do you see? Not very PC. It gets worse: the Indian summer usually followed a Squaw's Winter – that's the first frost. We used to call it a St Martin's Summer – the feast day's November the eleventh, so presumably it can last till then. It's good news wherever you're from, because it shortens the winter. Less months to eke out the harvest grain. We love it because it lengthens the summer.' Shaw scratched his skull through close-cropped fair hair.

'You're telling me we could have *another* month of this sublime weather?' she asked. Lena's face was made up of a series of ample curves, as was the rest of her. Shaw thought she resembled an animated African mask, like the ones hanging in a museum of ethnology: Lena didn't so much show emotions as broadcast them.

Thunder rolled, buffeting the tables, making the wine glasses and cutlery tinkle. A woman sitting further along the terrace on her own let out a cry of alarm. Each table had a gas heater like an industrial hairdryer set to one side. Several were on, the flame-heated elements glowing like coals, giving an illusion – if little else – of extra heat as the afternoon waned.

'Here's to table heaters and global warming,' said Lena, lifting her glass. 'That's one thing we can do without.' She touched the metal stanchion of the heater beside their table. 'I'd prefer to see our customers wrapped up. We could provide blankets – I've seen that done. Tartan. How about open fires, in braziers? The Plough does that. A bit of heat, but it's a psychological trick. You just feel warm if you can see flames.'

Lena ran a beach café on a stretch of sand between Old Hunstanton and Holme, five miles to the west of where they sat. They'd bought the Old Beach Café for £8,000 six years earlier, having fled London. There was no mains power, no water, and no vehicle access except along the sand in a 4×4. Beside the café was the Old Boathouse, and behind it a small cottage. They'd converted the boathouse into Surf!, a shop selling everything from seventy-pence beach windmills to £3,000 wetsuits. They'd taken the café upmarket, symbolized by a gleaming Italian coffee-maker which looked like a vintage motorbike. This last summer, armed with a licence in Lena's name, they'd started staying open late, serving wine, bottled beer and snacks. The gentrification of the East Coast, spreading north from its heartlands in Suffolk, was bringing new money into a local economy which had once relied on old money.

Lena planned a big extension to the café, turning it into a pub and café, maybe even – eventually – a restaurant. She had in mind a beach bar she'd seen in Cornwall one summer's evening, which had been packed with nearly five hundred thirsty, hungry customers.

Shaw wondered what the hell they were doing. They'd moved to the Old Beach Café from the capital because they loved the solitude, the bleak beach, the dunes. And it was Shaw's childhood home – he'd played on that very beach, swum off the wide sands. They'd left the gritty greyness of the suburbs to give their daughter some space to grow. Shaw was happy to help Lena realize a dream – but one day soon he'd have to tell her that hundreds of trippers on his beach at sunset was his idea of a nightmare.

They'd agreed to spend the winter checking out the opposition along the coast, the dinner bills offset against tax. Lena wanted to write a business plan before approaching the bank for a loan. This was their first recce, and Shaw had chosen the spot. He rather hoped Lena would see that the market was already well served and that most customers wouldn't walk a hundred yards for their Pouilly Fumé and Brancaster mussels, let alone a mile of deserted sand. The downmarket outlook was no better, in his opinion. If people just wanted a pint and a packet of cheese and onion crisps they'd want to park by the door, not walk a mile along the beach.

'This is a world record, of course,' he said, skewering one of the scallops. When they'd first moved up from London they'd got six scallops on a plate. Then, very slowly, the number had begun to go down. All the pubs and restaurants seemed to follow suit, enthralled by just how few scallops could qualify as a meal. So far the lowest total on a plate was three. Two was a new north Norfolk world record.

'Needs a posh name,' he said. 'How about a duo of scallops? It chimes with a trio of fishes.'

Lightning crackled again like an old-fashioned flashbulb. Lena looked at her husband's face in the stark, flickering light as he stared out over the marshes: a nomad's face, wide and open, an outrider perhaps of the Mongol horde – broad, tanned, the skin stretched between cheekbones, the eyes always searching a distant horizon.

'I love this stuff,' he said, sucking the salty green flesh off the finger-like fronds of samphire.

'Glad to hear it,' said Lena. 'I checked out the main suppliers online – thirty-five pounds a kilo. Most of it gets eaten on the King's Road, of course. It grows out there . . .' she said, pointing at the marsh, '. . . and costs nothing to pick. That's one hell of a mark-up.'

Her eyes widened and she parted her lips to reveal pearl-white teeth. Shaw could see what those eyes saw: a packed bar, tables on the sand, food being ferried by a small army of staff. He was good at reading faces. His own was immobile – a handsome mask. Poker faces ran in his family. He'd had to learn as a child to read emotion, character or intent into the smallest of mannerisms: the precise invasion of personal space, the retreat of a chin, the mid-focus glance. Peter Shaw had emotional intelligence the way bats have sonar.

Lena's plate held six oysters caught off Brancaster, two miles west. She held each to her nose, breathing in the ozone, before tipping back the shell with a sharp twist of her wrist.

'So when are you going to tell me why we're really here, Peter?'

It had been a struggle to get Shaw to agree to the winter schedule of checking out the opposition. His day job took up most of his waking hours, heading up a CID unit at King's Lynn, the town twenty-five miles along the coast. Getting him 'off duty' was a feat. Oddly, he'd been positively eager to check out the Old Ship Inn.

'Tell me what you see,' said Shaw. He stretched his six-foot-two-inch frame out straight, touching the chair only at his neck and the back of his thighs. An hour sitting down was beginning to tax his nerves. It was one of the dynamic tensions within his character, that the immobile face was twinned with a body which did not sit still. Lena knew he'd be thinking about his evening run now: the straight mile along the beach to the café, the time chalked up on the blackboard in the corridor to the cottage, each one comfortably under five minutes.

Lena, on the other hand, was often still. When she played 'statues' with their daughter, Fran, she never lost.

She tried to concentrate on his question. What *did* she see? For the first time she studied the landscape. Brancaster Harbour: a maze of tidal channels between islets clogged with weed and reeds, filling up to flood point. In the next hour islets of reed would slip under the surface. Boats at their moorings in the channel were making that unmistakable sound of ropes against masts in the light breeze. Further out, old houseboats lay at angles in the black mud, a few now wrecks, bare timbers exposed like whalebones.

Lightning lit the scene, this time very close. The thunderbolt made their wine glasses jump on the metal-mesh tabletop.

'I see Brancaster Harbour, close to high tide. What do you see, Peter?'

'Crime scene.'

She couldn't keep the disappointment out of her face. Lena had a slight cast in her left eye – an odd echo of Shaw's own moon-eye – and when she blinked the lid occasionally seemed to stick, so that one eye was slower to blink than the other. It could mean tiredness, exhaustion, or a sudden fall in mood.

'Sorry,' said Shaw, spotting the tic.

'It's OK,' she said. 'But promise me we aren't limited to eating out within sight of the latest serious incident on the CID logbook.' They tried to keep Shaw's career – the everyday, sordid, details of it – out of their home life. The A10 had taken them out of London, through the grimy suburbs, precisely to escape the capital and its crimes. Lena had been a lawyer for the Campaign for Racial Equality in Brixton. Between them they'd seen enough of the dark side of human nature to throw a shadow over a host of angels. Shaw was still a copper, but they always hoped they'd left behind the hard heart of crime.

He picked up a sprig of samphire.

'This is a wild crop, OK? There's not many of those left. All of it grows in tidal marshes, all of it between the high-tide mark and the sea. So it's anyone's. As you have discovered, it's thirty-five pounds a kilo online. A year ago it was ten pounds a kilo. Next year – who knows? Supply is pretty much static, demand rising geometrically. Even I can do the math. Fifty pounds? A hundred? Suddenly it isn't something that a fishmonger can just chuck in with your piece of cod, or your scallops, or your mackerel.

'Along this coast there are probably half-a-dozen serious commercial pickers of samphire. It's a secret world. They don't say where it grows. Some certainly don't tell the taxman. Over the years the business has gone from father to son – along with the geography – in here,' he said, tapping his forehead.

'It's not a full-time job, of course. Just one of those little secret sidelines that can keep a fisherman alive, or a poacher, or a shipwright.'

He leant forward and refilled Lena's glass. This, for the monocular, was a real challenge – one of the many skills he'd had to learn since losing his eye. He picked up the bottle and tipped it forward while holding Lena's glass in his other hand, then let the bottle rest on the lip. He raised his elbow to pour the wine.

'There's fifty places like the Old Ship Inn along this stretch of coast alone. All of them want samphire when it's in season. And they're happy to freeze it too. Then there's the smart London restaurants, and the trendy Manchester restaurants, and the supermarket deli counters. It's big business. The inevitable has happened. Someone's moved in, from London.'

Lena looked out over the marsh. The light was fading gently. Sunset would be about six, so they had a few hours left of the day, but the sun was low and the shadows long.

Lena shrugged. 'It's a wild crop – who's to stop the locals picking it? I don't see much mileage in straight competition. It must be down to local knowledge. You're telling me there's a bunch of cockney wide boys wandering around the marshlands looking for sprigs of samphire? Del Boy in green wellies?'

'Hardly. There's a specialist outfit at Billingsgate – name of Green Gold. They collect all along the Essex marshes, Suffolk, as far as Cromer. But they outsource, getting local collectors on board. This time it didn't work like that. Someone in Lynn – a gangmaster – stepped in and made a better offer. He'd be the middleman, running the local operation and getting the stuff down to London for Green Gold.'

'Chinese?'

'No, a local thug from the Lynn estates, name of Stepney. Known to the police as John Jack Stepney.'

Lynn's post-war estates were full of East Enders who'd moved north out of sub-standard housing. They were no more inclined than the locals to commit crime; it was just that there were 80,000 of them, and once they'd got to their new homes the port promptly closed, robbing most of them of any chance of making a decent living. The result was the kind of poverty the government's statistics said didn't exist, and crime, often embellished with that nasty urban edge they'd fled London to avoid.

'In many ways this Stepney character is as much an outsider as a gangmaster from Guangzhou. An entrepreneur too, if twice as ruthless. Stepney put on his whistle-and-flute and went down to Billingsgate to make them an offer: he'd meet their targets and he'd get the stuff down to market. Then he looks at his problem: how do I harvest it? There's a Polish club in the North End at Lynn. There's a Polish club for everything but this one's for sea fishermen, not trawlers – inshore small boat-fishing for pocket money. So he pops along and asks how'd they like to earn a few bob running boats along the coast and picking weeds? I reckon he roped in one of the original local pickers to mark up a decent map with the best locations of samphire and to lead them to it, at least on the first trip. The season starts in June. So did they. It didn't help that they just ripped it up. Thing is, you're supposed to snip off the green fronds of the plant and leave the woody stem in the sand.' Shaw made a scissors movement with two fingers. 'The locals have to come back next year. It's a wild crop, but that doesn't mean it can't be nurtured. This lot did considerable damage in the first month.'

'So . . . bad blood.'

'Yup. The locals hit back. A week ago someone broke into John Jack's garage off the Tuesday Market in Lynn and slashed the tyres on his fleet of vans. So he did what any decent psycho-path would do when attacked – he hit back too, only harder.'

'It's like the mafia.'

'And his enemies will sleep with a trio of fishes.'

They interlocked their feet under the table.

'How did he hit back?'

Shaw produced a pocket telescope and scanned the distant dunes and the sea beyond. To the far west he could see a wind farm off the Lincolnshire coast; directly north, three white sails in an arrowhead formation. 'Local uniform at Morston, time-server called Accrington, says the harbour master there found two of the locals' boats keel-up, with a hole hammered through the fibreglass hulls. No crime report, which is always a bad sign, because it means they think this is a problem they can solve themselves.'

He focused on a buoy in the harbour channel, bucking at its chains as the tide flooded in.

'To be fair, Accrington was thorough. He tracked down one of the boat owners and went to visit him at home in Binham.

Finds him in bed, all the fingers on his right hand broken and his fist in a cast. So he's not harvesting samphire for a while, is he?'

'How did that happen?'

'He fell down the stairs, apparently.'

'Not very convincing.'

'You said it. He lives in a bungalow.'

Lena, shivering for the first time, fixed her eyes on the water, which was now churning and swirling into all the pools and creeks in the marsh.

'How long is a samphire season?'

'You pick in June and July – six to eight weeks. This time of year they'd usually just go out to check the beds, but otherwise it's downtime. The late summer extended this year's season. It's pretty much done now, though.'

'So why the interest?'

'John Jack Stepney has hired more men. He's trained the ones he's got not to rip up the plants. Next summer he'll be back in force.'

'You're the guardian angel of the coast, are you, Peter?'

'They'll be back. They made money, Lena. That's what this is all about. The question is what next? I predict fishing trips. Year after next he'll have the ice-cream vans. Then the amusement arcades. Slot machines. A bit of contraband, perhaps. In ten years' time he'll run the coast. Who knows – maybe pubs, restaurants, fag machines, drugs for the rich kids . . .'

Their plates were cleared and Shaw ordered coffee – a double espresso – while Lena went for chocolate brownies.

When the waiter had left, Shaw leant forward and looked Lena in the face. 'Nobody owns this coast. I can't let that happen.'

Sensing a change in the air pressure, he looked up: a single branch of electric-white lightning zigzagged down and seemed to strike a point on the distant dunes. Shaw's good eye blinked at the moment of impact, while the shockwave seemed to pulse through his chest. Then raindrops began to fall, the size of paperweights. Lena stood, a hand on the rail of the terrace, her face turned up so that the water began to roll over her skin.

'Here it comes,' she said, smiling. She loved rain on the beach, walking in it and the sound it made, as if the sea was whispering.

Shaw's RNLI pager buzzed. He was on the crew of the lifeboat at Old Hunstanton and pilot of the inshore rescue hovercraft. He grabbed it quickly as it performed its waggle dance, like a bee trying to indicate the way to the flowers.

The message made his heartbeat triple: 121212 – the code for an emergency call-out for the hovercraft.

They paid in cash and ran for Shaw's old Porsche. As he swung it out on to the coast road they felt the visceral thud of the maroon going up from the rocket station on the cliffs at Hunstanton, and then ahead, rising up over the coastal marshes, the sudden purple synapse of the signal blazed in the sky.

TWO

Leo D'Asti had always felt uneasy about owning a second home. To be brutally honest, it was, technically, his third home. Or, given the company flat in Paris, his fourth. In all the years he had tussled with the moral and political questions involved with multiple ownership, however, he had never actually thought owning a second home would kill him. But now there was a very good chance it would indeed lead to his untimely death at the age of just fifty-one. A betting man, he calculated that the odds were, perhaps, thirty to one *against* him surviving the next hour.

He was standing on a sandbar called Mitchell's Bank in the wide estuary marked on his OS map as Overy Creek. The tide was still rising. Being a fine swimmer (two of the houses had pools), the situation was not, on the face of it, inevitably lethal. The problem was that he was not alone. His held his daughter, Lucilla, by her right hand – she was eight and could swim a width of the Serpentine Lido. By his left hand he held Paulo, who was six and couldn't swim. And Paulo held the hand of the toddler of the family, three-year-old Cornelia. She didn't really like paddling. If Leo had taken her advice when they'd set out they would not now all be in this appalling situation. They'd be eating ice cream.

They were stranded on Mitchell's Bank. To the north the creek spilled into the North Sea through a narrow gap, which boiled with white water. The water around them was choppy; a maze of whirlpools, whorls and wavelets. Out at sea, thunder rolled along the horizon like an empty barrel.

It had all looked very different just half an hour earlier. He'd driven up to the house in nearby Burnham Market the day before with the children, leaving his wife to run her business – a florist's on Upper Street, Islington. Leo was a banker, a distant scion of the Asti family of Piedmont – a very junior scion, it had to be said. His father had been sent to London after the Second World

War to learn the business and had gone quietly to seed 'watching the shop' in an office on Lombard Street. Leo had inherited this unchallenging brief. The family spent the summers in a house they'd inherited in the foothills above Lucca. Autumn and spring was north Norfolk – crabbing with the children, sitting in pubs eating too much, and watching wood burn. They let the house to friends on 'mates rates' because Leo had seen what could happen if properties stayed empty all year. His ancestral home was a three-storey pile on a hillside above Brindisi, in a village now entirely inhabited by sheep. At Christmas the kids loved to play hide and seek in its warren of staircases and rooms, while the grown-ups fed wood into a stove the size of a small car.

Each house had its own routine. Today, Leo had driven the 4×4 to the quayside at Burnham Overy Staithe, half a mile inland from Mitchell's Bank, and they'd walked up the riverbed, past the crumbling houseboats, the clinker-built yachts, the two or three small trawlers. They'd done it a hundred times before: a predictable hike, shot through with mild peril. Leo had collected driftwood and he'd brought a firelighter and matches. They'd build a fire on the sand, catch some unlucky crabs then wander back and have an early evening meal in the Red Lion at Stiffkey. Or Stewkey, as the locals called it. Although Leo suspected you'd struggle to find a local to ask in summer.

The walk out to Mitchell's Bank was supposed to be an adventure. It certainly was now.

Things had gone wrong almost immediately once they'd set out across the wide black mud flats. The kids loved to get close to Scolt Head Island, which formed the western bastion guarding the narrow outlet to the sea. Paulo had discovered Enid Blyton's Famous Five, and particularly Kirrin Island, and told his sisters all the stories – of treasure, thieves and ruined castles. Their destination was Mitchell's Bank because it was an island too – although not a full-time one. It had steep, glistening sides, and they had to form a human chain to reach its lowly summit. Leo said the pinnacle must be ten foot high and he always let Cornelia plant a plastic flag at the spot to mark their ascent.

Once they were up they would look around and see how Mitchell's Bank had changed since their last visit. The tide was like an invisible sculptor, remaking the landscape each day, moulding it with salt-water hands. Today, they found that a channel had been cut across the heart of Mitchell's Bank – a rivulet, cut deep into the black mud. It was partly flooded because the tide was already running in fast. Leo was certain that this muddy crevasse had not been there on their previous outing the day before.

It was Lucilla who saw the body first.

'Look,' she said, as cold-blooded as any child. 'There's a drowned man, Daddy. Can we see?'

Out of breath, carrying Cornelia, he squinted in the direction his daughter was pointing, expecting to see a dead seal or driftwood, but instead the air flooded out of his lungs.

The corpse was mud-black, stretched out and stiff, as if he'd dived into the water and been instantly preserved in that falling, elongated shape. Floating, but only just, with his feet towards the sea, a ship's rope taut round his ankles, taking the strain, attached to something heavy which had sunk into the gloopy mud.

What could Leo do? Telling the kids not to look seemed bizarre. There was nothing else on Mitchell's Bank. So they gawped. Then they all got closer, and gawped again. They were ten feet away when Leo set Cornelia down and told Paulo to hold her hand. Paulo complained because his hands were full, clutching his model sailing ship – the *Endeavour*. Paulo lived for ships and boats, but now he obediently set the toy down on the mud and took his sister's chubby fingers in his own.

Leo edged forward, stepping over the channel, and knelt down in the yielding ooze. It was luck, of course, but he thanked God for it. The wound was on the far side of the head, hidden from the children. It looked like someone had taken an axe to the neck, nearly severing the skull. Mud had filled the wound and the blood and flesh was dull red, like old meat. Lightning flickered overhead and the dead man looked alive, as the shadows on his face switched from grey to black and back again. For a second it looked to Leo as if the pale white death-mask had flinched.

'Stay there, kids,' he said, astonished at how natural he could make his voice sound.

He made himself touch the skin, just below the ear, feeling

for a pulse. The flesh was solid, cold, unyielding. The face looked
up at the sky, the eyes full of mud, which was a blessing. The
water in the deep-cut rivulet was rising quickly – a funnel into
which the tide was rushing. The body was bucking and pulling
on the rope, attached to its unseen weight. Leo still didn't know
what to do. He checked his mobile phone but he knew what he'd
find: no bars.

He decided, almost too late, that he should try and identify the
dead man. Placing one Wellington boot in the water he unzipped
the man's windcheater and looked for a wallet, but there was nothing
in the inside pockets. He couldn't make himself force a hand into
his trouser pockets, but they looked empty too, although they seemed
to be oozing mud. So he stood back, struck again by the unnatural
pose: the diver, each bone aligned to its full extent, as if he'd woken
up in bed and this was the first stretch of the day.

The wound gaped. Leo looked back at the children, his eye
going beyond, tracing their footprints back towards land. The
tide had risen, and it looked as though they might already be on
an island. If he'd acted then – instantly – they'd have been safe.
It was only two or three feet of water. But he kept thinking that
if he slipped he might get washed away and then the kids would
be alone, and he couldn't allow that to happen. Juliet, his wife,
would never forgive him. She wasn't a judgemental person, but
she had a shrewd eye for Leo's slightly flaky decision-making
under pressure. So, instead, he ordered Paulo and Lucilla to
quickly reconnoitre their new kingdom. The children ran to the
edges – north, south, east, west – and reported back. They were
trapped, it seemed, and then it really was too late.

The children didn't panic. Cornelia had started crying when
she'd seen the corpse but had quickly recovered. Paulo was
fascinated, excited even, while Lucilla just watched, as she always
did, taking it all in. The realization that broke Leo's heart was
the knowledge that their lack of fear sprang from confidence in
him: that he would get them all safely back to the 4×4 and then
drive them off to a nice warm pub for fish and chips and sticky
toffee pudding. So the children didn't panic. But Leo did. He
made an elaborate ploy of examining his mobile phone as if it
held the secret to walking on water.

Then Lucilla said a woman was waving from the bank near

Gun Hill – the sandy hill at the eastern edge of the outlet to the sea, the counterpoint to Scolt Head. Relief flooded through Leo's veins like heroin. They all waved back and bellowed: 'Help!' Stupidly, they were so relieved they were all smiling and laughing, and Leo was tormented by the thought that the woman would think they were having fun. She returned the wave, then ran, walked, ran, walked along the towpath back towards Burnham Overy Staithe. She'd have to find a phone – a landline. Leo checked his watch: 3.08 p.m. The chalk board by the harbour had said high tide was 2.45 p.m., but Leo was no day-tripping fool. Winds and air pressure often combined to bottle up the water; drive the tide in with extra force. Tide tables were useful, but all the locals said you had to use your eyes.

Twenty minutes later the water had reached Leo's knees and he could feel the current tugging at his trousers. Another few inches and his own weight would be sufficiently diminished to the point where he'd be unable to keep a foothold. His muscles were shaking quite badly now, and he kept readjusting his legs to hide the tremor from the children. He briefly let go of Paulo's hand and was dismayed to see the first flash of fear in the boy's eyes; but he needed the arm free to pick Cornelia up, because the water was at her chest. Once he had her on his hip the boy could wrap both arms round his father's thigh. Lucilla squeezed his other hand and he realized with a desperate sadness that she was trying to comfort *him*.

Thunder rolled over them from a bank of clouds which had formed as if by black magic right over their heads. Scenarios flashed like newspaper headlines before Leo's eyes: all of them dead, the children saved but him dead, and worst of all – all of them dead *except* him.

He checked his watch: thirty-one minutes had passed since the woman had waved from Gun Hill.

'OK,' he said, and this time his voice was an odd half-octave too high so that all the children looked at their father. 'Let's just have a plan. First of all – Lucilla.' He forced himself to look at her. She was still clutching a see-through plastic bucket full of the murky outlines of muddy crabs. 'All this water is pouring in – see? It's flooding down towards the village. You can swim. When the time comes I'll take your coat and wellies, and you need to just float away. Let the tide take you in, Luce – all right, sweetheart? Don't fight it – float until you come aground, like a bottle with a message in it.'

Lucilla's eyes flooded with tears. 'What message?'

'Just get yourself safely on dry land and then find someone as quickly as you can.'

He turned away because she didn't move a muscle in response. 'Paulo,' he said.

The boy had his head buried in his father's waterproofs. 'I can't swim,' he said.

'I know,' said Leo. 'That doesn't matter. People float. You can't stop yourself.' He forced himself to chuckle. 'Honestly, once your feet leave the bottom you'll bob like a cork. Just stick with me and Cornelia.'

The waves had been breaking just out to sea, beyond the gap, but now one didn't break, it rolled over the submerged sandbar at the harbour mouth and carried on, so that they all had to step forward, accommodating the sudden swell. Cornelia screamed.

The wave went on to break in the reeds beyond them.

'What about the man, Dad?' asked Paulo.

They all had their back to the floating corpse, but Leo had been stealing glances. Because of the rigor and the tethering rope holding the feet down, the body was upright as it rose in the pit of the channel, and the outstretched hands and arms were now sticking up out of the water, the head appearing then disappearing with each wave. The heavy skull flopped on its shattered neck. It was an unnatural sight, and disturbing, because it looked as if the man was striving to rise out of the flood – like one of those nuclear missiles, bound for the sky, or a God of the deep ascending, like Poseidon.

A fresh wave broke around them and Leo pulled them all to him, his plan disintegrating. He was too scared to pray, so he just kissed Cornelia's hair.

Which is how Peter Shaw first saw the D'Asti family – a circle of silent figures, half submerged, in mid-stream, the man bending down with that strange bird-like pecking motion which signals a kiss. The picture was etched on his retina thanks to a blinding flash of white lightning.

THREE

Flyer was doing twenty-six knots – close to top speed – and had just cleared Scolt Head, so that Overy Creek now opened out to view, a tumult of choppy milky-green water. The emergency call, made thirty-two minutes earlier via the police control room at Lynn, had come from a domestic landline on Burnham Overy Staithe, at the Hero public house. It reported a family of three, knee-deep, apparently stranded on a sandbar. At a distance of a hundred and fifty yards Shaw could see that the male adult was holding a small child, so that made four. Using the hovercraft joystick he reduced power to the two rear propellers, and dipping the port ailerons brought *Flyer* round in a wide arc to approach the family against the tide.

The earpiece in his helmet buzzed: 'Target sited fifteen thirty-one hours. Sea state moderate. Over.'

With a four-man crew *Flyer* still had room for six passengers. Henderson, the navigator, had charts open in the cabin. His voice was next on air: 'Targets standing. Water here now four foot to four foot six. Touch down not on. Repeat: not on.'

Shaw now had the *Flyer* facing north, seawards, edging towards the stranded family. The water surface was exceptionally difficult to navigate. A sharp on-shore wind had blown up as soon as the waves had started clearing the submerged sandbank at the harbour bar. The sea was pitted with troughs and white horses, the spray blowing free in the air. The dashboard gave Shaw a sea temperature reading of ten degrees Celsius – closer to the summer average than the winter; a factor which had probably saved this family their lives. The adult male – presumably the father – was waving with his free hand and holding a child with the other. The two other children were holding on to his legs.

Shaw's single eye scanned the seascape ahead. The big danger was *plow* – running the superstructure of the hovercraft into an oncoming wave. This could pitch them all forward violently and it would cut the speed drastically, possibly spinning *Flyer* off course. A touchdown was impossible, so he'd have to bring the hovercraft alongside and hold her position in moving water.

He weaved through the oncoming waves, increasing the speed to twenty-eight knots, searching for that crucial moment when he could achieve a dynamic equilibrium, matching the forward thrust of the engines against the force of the floodwater funnelling into Overy Creek from the open sea.

The two standing children had their heads pressed against their father's leg, a free hand over exposed ears, trying to cut out the noise. Even with his flight helmet on Shaw could hear the high-pitched whine of the twin turbo-diesel engines. Increasing the power incrementally, he edged the hovercraft forward until he was ten feet from the family. Henderson joined crewmen Griffon and Cotteril at the rail, and they each reached out over the inflated sponsons to grab a child – the youngest last, straight from her father's arms.

As soon as his children were safe something cut out in Leo D'Asti's nervous system: his right knee gave way, the leg folded, and he slipped into the current, so that Shaw was just able to glimpse his head as the body swept past on the port side. Despite the noise of the engines he heard the man call out as he slipped past on the port side: 'Help me, please.'

Shaw swung *Flyer* round in pursuit.

There was a flash of lightning and an immediate thunderclap. The bolt shook the instrument panel and the intercom buzzed with static. Henderson brought the children into the cabin and strapped them quickly into a low steel bench with bucket seats. Shaw kept his eyes fixed on the man ahead in the water, swimming, his head ducking, arms floundering. His torso position was very upright so that his head was clear of the water, and Shaw guessed that his legs might be deadweights, dragging him down.

Full throttle, with the wind behind, he reached thirty knots, telling Griffon and Cotteril to get a light rescue net to the side and to cast it when they were alongside. Shaw lost sight of the man's bobbing head and then saw the net cast against the blue-black sky.

'He's missed it,' Griffon said on the intercom.

Henderson was on the prow, his boots up against Shaw's windscreen, so he was able to lunge out with a rescue pole and hook. D'Asti surfaced once, thrust an arm out and caught the loop. With his safety harness attached to the forward rail, Henderson was able to lean out over the water, lifting D'Asti by the shoulder and swinging him over the sponson, where Cotteril and Griffon gathered him in.

'Swimmer secure,' said Henderson.

They took him down the side and on to the rescue deck. In his side mirrors Shaw saw the man's face: blue, stretched but unnaturally animated. He swung round in the pilot's seat to face the children. 'Your dad's safe. See?' All three twisted in their seats to look through the glass along the deck. Their father lay like the dying Nelson in the arms of Cotteril and Griffon, but they already had a bottle of water to his lips, which would revive him.

Shaw took *Flyer* on an elliptical path towards the coastal dunes below Gun Hill and ran her up the slight incline of the beach, cutting the engine before the forward motion was spent, allowing the hovercraft to sink into its skirts. The silence, the knowledge that they were off the water, was like a magic spell on the D'Asti family.

Within minutes they were all sitting together in a huddle with hot drinks, under a single blanket.

The father kept saying he was sorry: 'Really. It's crazy – I know what it looks like. Some idiot dad taking his kids crabbing in a tidal surge. But it wasn't like that.' He stopped, tears welling up in his eyes. 'We'd have been back on the bank in time but we saw a body – out on the sand. So we had to see. And then it was too late.'

Shaw had his eye on the sonar, tracking the electric storm as it drifted along the coast. 'A man's body?' he asked, swinging round in his seat.

The children chimed in, agreeing with their father. The windscreen was covered in sea spray so Shaw set the wiper going and the scene cleared. The cloud cover was almost complete and late afternoon light made all the greys bleed into the inky blacks.

'He was tied down to a weight, something under the mud. Right on top of the big bank,' said Leo. 'As the water came in he sort of stood up. Last time I looked you could still see his arms. There . . .'

Shaw unclipped the locks on the windscreen and tilted the glass out so that they had a perfect, uninterrupted view. A grey world of rippled sea, low hills and the reeds.

A hundred yards distant Shaw *could* see something. He took the binoculars mounted on the dashboard and used them to hone in on the spot with his good eye, over the water.

He saw two hands, streaked with black mud, held aloft, as if in surrender.

FOUR

The Silent Lawyer stood beside the floodlit medieval London Gate, the old entrance through the walls into the port of Lynn from the south. King's Lynn to the outside world; Lynn Regis for centuries – the dusty, down-at-heel capital of West Norfolk – gateway to the northern coast. By way of welcome the pub sign showed a man lying in a coffin, still decked out in his courtroom finery of black frock coat, white lace collar and dusted wig. The gate itself, a massive double bastion of brick faced with ashlar stone, was bathed in the amber glare of a floodlight set up in the town cemetery, just beyond the old walls. The spikes of the portcullis showed as shadowy teeth in the narrow archway.

Lynn could be a rough town, and the London Road was its roughest street. Pubs like the Silent Lawyer had a standing order with the glaziers: every Sunday morning they'd send round a van, plate glass stacked to the outside gantry, to repair the damage from Friday and Saturday. A reputation for Wild West saloons glamourized the neighbourhood's seedy urban problems: prostitution, alcohol and street crime. Further down the road the pubs had no windows at all, just blackout boards.

DS George Valentine had lived off the London Road most of his life. These were his streets and his pubs, which was why he'd agreed to meet in the Silent Lawyer. There was one window seat, to the back of what had once been the public bar, commanding a view of the two doors to the street. In position at least twenty minutes early, with a pint of IPA, he'd sat and considered the rest of his Saturday night: cards in the Artichoke, a curry, *Match of the Day*.

Gordon Lee, chief reporter of the *Lynn Express*, was on time. As the frosted-glass door swung open Valentine heard the maritime clock on St Margaret's chime the hour; the medieval clock face showed stars and the moon, and indicated the turn of the tide, and although Valentine hated water, and especially seawater, it had helped regulate his life for the best part of half a century.

Lee was a Londoner, part of the great sixties exodus from the East End – early fifties, bald, short, bustling, almost heroically awkward. As he advanced on Valentine his trailing raincoat caught a glass which fell to the floorboards and smashed. Five minutes later the barman had swept up the shards and Lee was sitting with a pint in front of him, a whisky chaser in his fist.

'Cheers,' he said, downing the spirit then readjusting the pint on its mat. 'Thanks for showing up. Like I said, we need to talk.'

Valentine had known Lee since his first days on CID in the seventies. Their equally lacklustre careers had tracked each other like falling stars. Looking at him now, Valentine had to remind himself why he actually liked the journalist. When Valentine's wife had died of cancer, aged forty-two, very few people had bothered to knock on the door of the house in Greenland Street, even though they all must have known that he was inside and alone. That first night Lee had called, and insisted he walk to the Red House on the corner. No story, no agenda, just an hour talking about nothing. It had pretty much saved George Valentine's life.

'So, Gordon, if I understood your message, you've had a letter from some bloke who won't give his name about some burglaries on the coast?' asked Valentine, looking away to the flat-screen TV to catch a corner being taken at the Emirates on Sky Sport. 'Did you really need to drag me down the pub on a Saturday night for that? It's my keep fit class, and I never miss it.'

The implicit irony in this remark was obvious. DS Valentine was fifty-eight, a lifetime smoker, who if required to run a mile would have clocked a time nearer four hours than four minutes. His skull was like a hatchet blade, oddly two-dimensional, so that if he moved his chin a little left or right, his head presented a different aspect; it swung back now to Lee, bored with the TV.

Lee put a cigarette between his teeth. 'It's a bit tastier than that, George. Shall we take the air?'

The yard was concrete with a brand-new picnic table which held an umbrella branded CANCER RESEARCH.

Valentine took a light from the reporter.

'Like I said, George. Letters. Note the plural. Same bloke, three times. Well, same writing. Otherwise anonymous.'

'Who they from?'

'Very funny, George.'

Lynn CID was currently engaged in a major inquiry into thirteen related break-ins along the north Norfolk coast – all at second homes. So far there had been a complete, and successful, media blackout on any details. Nothing had leaked out. The decision to keep the whole thing under wraps had been personally authorized by the chief constable. When Valentine had got Lee's text stating that the paper had been tipped off about this mini crime-wave, he'd talked the implications through with his boss, DI Peter Shaw. The best way forward, they decided, was a chat over a pint. Privately, they had both lobbied the chief constable to lift the media blackout anyway. Shaw had put his views in writing in a private note to the chief constable's office. Gordon Lee didn't know it yet, but this was one of his lucky days.

'Just so we understand each other,' said Valentine. 'I'm not confirming we've had any burglaries, OK? I'm just listening. You're just talking.'

'Three letters so far, George. Weird stuff – I can't let you see 'em. Bartlett's on some kick about reader confidentiality.'

Bartlett was the editor, newly appointed, a whizz-kid from Liverpool, barely old enough to vote. Early retirement was Gordon Lee's favourite subject of conversation as a result. He had Valentine's complete sympathy. One of the less attractive features of growing old was being told what to do by children.

'Weird in what way? Green ink? Rhyming couplets?'

'Political. The writer claims the burglaries are politically motivated. That this is all just the start of a violent campaign aimed at second homeowners. Apparently they leave slogans daubed in the houses – GO HOME, RICH SCUM – I don't know, stuff like that. It's a fucking good story, George – you know that as well as I do. Bartlett wanted to just print them, running a story on the front. I said I'd have a word first. I owe you that.'

Lee's inherent decency did not preclude him operating as a seasoned hack. There was no way the paper would run the story without some form of corroboration – or denial – from the police. Equally, there was no way that Valentine, or any official police source, could deny the allegations in the letters. The burglaries *were* politically motivated: fact. At least this way they got to control the story.

They went back inside and Lee bought the second round. Valentine noted that he didn't treat himself to a chaser.

A group of underage drinkers was playing pool on a blue table. Otherwise, the bar was empty, save for a man at the bar with two Alsatians on leads, dribbling through muzzles.

Valentine put a folder on the table and extracted a brown envelope containing an A4 scene-of-crime picture. It was stamped with a reference number and date, and signed by the head of the St James' forensic unit, Tom Hadden, and the chief investigating officers, DI Peter Shaw and DS George Valentine. The sight of his own signature made Valentine pause. Taking in a quick lungful of air he nearly choked on the thin thread of skunk he detected. Looking round the bar he found the source – one of the kids playing pool had a spliff rolled behind one ear.

He put one finger on the print, the nail clipped and clean.

The picture showed a large sitting room in a period cottage. There was evidence of attempted burglary: the drawers of two tallboys were pulled out, sheets hanging out of one. Several ornaments on the mantelpiece had been knocked over, and there was smashed crockery on the carpet. The picture over the fire – a landscape of Holkham Beach – hung at an angle.

But the most striking feature of the room was the slogan written on the wall in what looked like a spray-can red, over two lines:

GO BACK TO YOUR
FIRST HOME

'And this,' said Valentine, producing a second picture. This was an outside shot of what looked like a Victorian rectory, surrounded by extensive gardens. One of the windows on the frontage had been smashed and the wooden sash was broken. Daubed in black under this window on the whitewashed plaster was the slogan:

BANKERS GO HOME

'And – the final exhibit.'

This was a garden wall, about sixty yards of weathered local brick, running in front of a medieval farmhouse painted pink. The letters, in black, were about a foot high, all capitals, and as neat as a schoolteacher's instructions for homework:

THIS HOUSE COULD BE HOME TO FIVE
LOCAL FAMILIES – NOT A COUPLE WHO TURN
UP TWICE A YEAR

A sheet hung from one of the house's upstairs windows.

Lee held the picture up to the light. 'This is a photocopy, right?'

'Correct.'

'Copied where?'

Smart question. Photocopiers were as individual as fingerprints.

'A print centre off the ring road. It's not traceable.'

'Quality's crap.'

'You're not getting originals. They've gone to the Home Office.'

Lee drank the rest of his pint but he didn't take his eyes off Valentine: 'What's in this for you?'

'Control. If the story's going to break we'd like it to include certain facts. Primarily – and you'll see this if you read the file – we have a description of one of the burglars from an eye witness. It's hardly compelling, but it's a start. We need publicity, Gordon. This crowd know what they're doing. We've had nearly fifteen break-ins and no forensics. The only way we're going to catch them at this rate is luck. That's not a very convincing Plan A, is it?'

'Why the blackout up to now?'

Valentine got the third round.

Back in his seat he filled his lungs. Forty cigarettes a day for thirty years had taken its toll on George Valentine. Long sentences were getting harder to finish. 'The chief constable wanted the existence of these slogans, left at the scene at the burglaries, kept under wraps. You can see his point of view. These slogans are being left for publicity. Note the absence of any obscenity: they could run in any paper, on TV, anywhere. That's the point. It's a political campaign. The chief constable takes exception to being used.'

Lee made a face. 'Why hasn't someone locally seen the slogans and broken the story?'

'They've all been inside buildings, or on private land, and in each case they've been whitewashed over or removed, admittedly with the owners' consent, but not many people are willing to deny a police request, especially when they're trying to deal with the emotional impact of having their home violated.'

'Good story,' said Lee. 'Doesn't matter which side you're on. There's six thousand second homes in the circulation area – at an average of three hundred thousand pounds a pop. A lot of businesses would close down without incomers. On the other hand, there's plenty of people who don't mind having a good moan about the Chelsea set, right? Coming up here, taking our homes. They're like Poles with money.'

He played with a new cigarette. 'What they pinch then? Usual stuff?'

'Sure. Jewellery, art, computers, gadgets, mechanical stuff, white goods. Booze. Anything they could sell on.'

'And the chief constable orders a blackout on the lot just because he doesn't like being dicked about? Really?'

Valentine leant forward over his pint, his hatchet-like head extended forward on his neck like a praying mantis. This was the bit that really had to be off the record.

'Between you and me, Gordon . . .'

'Yeah, yeah. We never talked.'

'The chief constable's problem is Wales. Specifically, Wales in the seventies. You'll recall that Welsh nationalists bombed nearly two hundred properties in an effort to make the principality a no-go area for the English – particularly the London rich. They objected to the English getting Welsh water, taking away their language, and then buying up property. Max Warren, chief constable, thinks if we let the story run we'll have copycat burglaries, vandalism, arson. Do I need to paint the picture further?'

'Sounds like Warren could do with an introduction to the real world,' said Lee. 'This is north Norfolk – not Kurdistan. Does he really think there's a People's Front of North Norfolk out there? What's their ultimate goal – independence, with a capital in Little Pisspot? Mind you, I don't understand most of the locals, so presumably they do have their own language. George – this is fantasy.'

'Fantasy? Maybe. I didn't tell you this, but you might like to look back at Warren's CV. The chief constable was a DC in the Met in 1969. On the first of July that year he was seconded to Caernarvon for the investiture of the Prince of Wales. As you can imagine, the security was tight. At five-thirty a.m. that day a bomb went off near the railway station – two Welsh nationalists were killed planting the device. It's one of those startling facts which gets forgotten. Violent Welsh nationalism died out, so we've airbrushed the history. But it did happen. DC Warren was detailed to organize clearing the scene. It was – according to press reports – a butcher's shop on a railway line. Fantasy, or nightmare?'

The pool player with the spliff miscued and the white ball jumped from the table, crashing to the bare boards, accompanied by an ironic cheer from the spectators.

Valentine took out his mobile and put it on the tabletop. He was on call, the noise levels were rising, and he didn't want to miss a text.

'Warren came up here for a quiet life from the Met twenty years ago,' he said. 'They eventually made him CC because the bloke they really want is tied up with the Home Office in Northern Ireland – he'll be free in two years. Warren's keeping the chair warm. He wants a quiet life. He wants a knighthood. Only one thing can ruin that rosy scenario – this fucking story. This story, and its implications – which have not been lost on the Home Office either, it has to be said.'

Lee looked blank, so Valentine spelt it out.

'Who is north Norfolk's most high-profile second homeowner, Gordon?'

Lee's eyes went out of focus, then snapped back to look the DS in the eye. 'Oh, fuck. Right. Got it.' He actually licked his lips, as if he could taste that front-page byline.

'Exactly,' said Valentine. 'Her Majesty. Not so much second home as fifth, I think – or maybe sixth. It's an interesting take on the whole question, of course – the country house. Nobody complained about them when they employed a hundred servants below stairs. And not just HM. Part of the Sandringham Estate has just been refurbished to provide a new home for Prince William, his wife Kate and their baby George.'

'Anmer Hall.'

'Correct.'

Anmer was a one-horse village in the hills just north of Brancaster Staithe. The house was a late Georgian pile with an indeterminate number of rooms which the royal couple had indicated was inadequate for a family of three by proposing an extension.

Guarding Anmer Hall and making sure its new occupants led a carefree life was Max Warren's number one policing priority.

Valentine's mobile danced a tight circle on the Formica tabletop.

The text read: *Murder Inquiry. SOCO leaving Boal Quay in 15 minutes. Shaw.*

Valentine read it three times while Lee studied the pictures.

'I have to go, Gordon.' He pushed the pint away.

Lee held up a hand. 'One question. Same question. Why me?'

'I need you to tell Bartlett a lie about the origins of the story. These pictures were sent to the Home Office. They've asked to be kept abreast of developments, which is clearly adding to the pressure on the chief constable. Havelock's still on the *Guardian*, yes?'

Steve Havelock had been a junior on the local rag before heading south for Fleet Street.

'I want you to tell the newsdesk that you used contacts at the *Guardian* to get through to the Home Office. Back channels – whatever you call it. That's the deal. The details, the photocopies, all came from the Home Office, via the *Guardian*. I don't want my name to appear in the list of possible sources, let alone the probable ones.'

As Valentine left he put his CID business card on the blue baize of the pool table by the elbow of the kid with the spliff.

FIVE

They put up the scene-of-crime tent on Mitchell's Bank at nine-thirty p.m. that evening: a cube of white light in the darkness of Overy Creek. It looked as if a giant's Chinese lantern had come to rest on the north Norfolk coast. At low water Mitchell's Bank would no longer be an island, but linked by a damp, muddy path to the shore. Shaw had decided almost immediately that they couldn't wait that long. Even as the tidal waters closed over the tethered victim he'd used the RNLI radio to put a message through to the Ark – West Norfolk's forensic laboratory, at the St James' HQ in Lynn. They had six hours in which mud, beach and reed would be exposed, before the next tide began to turn. They couldn't afford to let the night pass.

The police launch arrived on the scene shortly after dark. Shaw had flown *Flyer* back to Old Hunstanton. The D'Asti family were taken to the Queen Elizabeth Hospital in Lynn, care of a flying doctor helicopter trip from the beach in front of the lifeboat house. The father was suffering from shock and would remain overnight, while his wife was driving up from London to be with the children.

Shaw returned to the scene of crime in the RNLI's Atlantic 75 – an inshore fibreglass rescue boat. When he rounded the point by Scolt Head he could see that the waters had retreated enough to allow Hadden's team to put up the forensic tent at the summit of Mitchell's Bank. The night was moonless, clear and cool, so that the sandbanks and channels, the dunes and reeds, seemed to be illuminated solely by the wheeling planetarium of the stars, revealing a world of nearly-sea, threaded with nearly-land. The scene ahead of Shaw's boat appeared to shimmer and change with each minute of the slowly falling tide, revealing sandbanks, islands, cockle beds, the brown, fibrous stumps of an ancient wood and the bones of a shipwreck under Gun Hill.

Shaw cut the twin Yamaha seventy-five horsepower engines and let the boat skim up the leading edge of Mitchell's Bank.

He wore a full winter wetsuit and a safety helmet with a head-lamp. His passenger wore a gabardine raincoat, black synthetic slip-ons and a lifebelt; DS George Valentine was not in his element. His discomfort levels had peaked when Peter Shaw had handed him a wetsuit outside the lifeboat house. George Valentine wasn't even comfortable in his own skin.

While Shaw ran a mooring rope to a black-and-white marker buoy, Valentine sat watching, immobile, until a match flared and the cigarette smoke drifted in the night like a ghost.

'When you're ready, George.'

Shaw was scanning the scene, his feet set wider than his shoulders. His father, Jack Shaw, a DCI back in the seventies, had teamed up with a young DI called George Valentine. In ten years as the force's crack detective unit they'd made a name for themselves – before it all came tumbling down with their last, ill-fated case. Shaw Senior had bequeathed his son a handful of working maxims, indispensable to the up-and-coming detective. Rule Number One: memorize the scene of crime, everything you can see, all you can touch, smell and hear, so that for the rest of the inquiry you can carry it around with you, as accessible as the family photo in your wallet. When his father had died, an invalid in the wake of the case that had broken his body as well as his spirit, Shaw had cleaned out the bedside table in the family home and found his wallet. It was no surprise to find he'd hadn't carried a family photo.

Valentine put a foot on the sand and the water welled up and over the lip of the slip-on. His first full step produced an obscene noise as water squirted out of the shoe in a series of miniature fountains. The DS swore under his breath, expertly keeping his cigarette in position in the left-hand corner of his mouth. He wasn't happy. He didn't like the seaside, hated boats, couldn't swim, and had been looking forward to *Match of the Day*. He'd grumpily given Shaw a résumé of his interrupted meeting with the reporter. They'd agreed that the chief constable could be safely kept in the dark until the story broke. In fact, he could *stay* in the dark after the story broke.

The DS's raincoat flapped around his narrow thighs. 'Where's that?' he asked, pointing at lights reflected across the water.

'Burnham Marsh – nearest village.'

'I thought we got the call from Burnham Overy Staithe?'

'We did. That's back inland along the towpath . . .'

Shaw pointed directly south where they could see another cluster of lights a mile distant.

'Burnham Marsh is much smaller – and the only way you can get there from here is by boat. Unless you want to pick your way over the sands at low tide. It's a dead end. Pretty, picture-postcard and all that, but about as much life as a dead whelk.'

Shaw was going to dismiss the thought of Burnham Marsh but he had long learned that Valentine had a genius for spotting the obvious.

'However, now you mention it, George, we better think about house-to-house. If and when you can get a signal on the mobile let's get the team together in the morning on the quayside at Burnham Marsh. Mobile incident room – the full works. I think we can be pretty certain our victim didn't die of old age given D'Asti's statement.' He snapped his fingers. 'Get Paul Twine, in fact – he can be point.'

'Point' was a key position in any murder inquiry. The officer chosen had to act as a central gateway for all information. It required a first-class brain, an ability to work without sleep for long periods, and excellent organizational skills. Twine, a grad-uate-entry fast-tracker, was the obvious candidate.

Valentine looked at his feet. 'I sent Paul a text when I had a signal, before we left the lifeboat station, back at Hunstanton. He's sorting the incident room now. Team will be on the road by six.'

Shaw took a deep breath but couldn't quite make himself say sorry. Before being busted down a rank – after becoming embroiled in Jack Shaw's last, disastrous case – DI Valentine had a spotless CV boasting more murder inquiries than Shaw's did GCSEs. Shaw really did need to learn to trust his right-hand man.

'I've got Fiona and Mark too,' said Valentine. 'We'll knock on a few doors early on. Most of 'em will be second homes anyway; it's not like anyone's got work to go to in the morning.'

Shaw's torchlight beam lit Valentine's face. The DS's skin was sallow, slightly grey in natural light, as if cigarette ash had caught in the folds.

'I know a lot of people with money are crooks, George. But be careful. Some of them worked for their money. It'd be pretty dull up here on the coast without the Chelsea pound.'

'Sir.'

Shaw gave him an old-fashioned look. He'd known George Valentine for thirty years. He'd worked with him for six. He was a friend of the family, if a cantankerous one. The 'sir' dripped with irony.

They approached the forensic tent, following a line of flags set on a path left by the SOCO team. As Shaw pulled aside the flap to enter, his heartbeat picked up. The sight of death was always a solemn moment, because Shaw felt the victim, despite death, still had the same rights as the living. Seeing the corpse as a mere assemblage of forensic evidence was the first step to the kind of corrosive cynicism that had produced George Valentine. And Shaw's father. It was a fate he had promised Lena he would do everything in his power to avoid. For him the dead were owed urgency and respect.

Inside they found two men: one dead, still held in the stiff pose of a diver, caked in the drying face-pack mud, while at his head knelt Tom Hadden, head of West Norfolk's forensic science unit: strawberry blond, but losing his hair, with a slight lesion on his forehead where a skin cancer had been removed two years before. A former Home Office specialist based in Whitehall, Hadden had come north to escape a messy divorce, and to indulge a passion for coastal bird watching. It occurred to Shaw that he'd probably stood on Mitchell's Bank before, watching the migrating geese fly over in D-Day formations.

'Peter, George. Make yourselves at home.'

Shaw prowled around the narrow space. If he did stand still he moved his head rapidly from side to side, a technique he'd learnt during occupational therapy after he'd lost the sight in his eye. The skull movement allowed his brain to get a series of images of the same objects, from different angles, through a single lens, helping his brain build a three-dimensional picture. He was a human blackbird, eyeing an emerging worm before the kill.

Valentine held his snuffed out cigarette between thumb and finger, fishing a plastic evidence bag out of his raincoat. His eyes

were focused on a point about three feet in front of his nose,
anywhere in fact that was not the victim's face. We all have an
appointment with death, but George Valentine suspected his was
closer than most. Fear of death did not haunt him. He'd stood
over a hundred murder victims in a thirty-year career in CID. It
was just the thought that if his own death came now even he
would have to judge his life a failure.

Hadden watched Valentine stash the cigarette. 'Next time I do
an autopsy on a lung cancer victim I'll give you a bell, George.'

'Don't bother, Doc.' Hadden wasn't a medical doctor and
disliked the appellation, which encouraged Valentine to use it.
'What's the point, anyway? I could give up then find myself like
this bloke. I'm only guessing, but I don't think the immediate
cause of death is a daily intake of forty Silk Cut.'

Hadden was using a metal spatula to lever the dead man's
head from left to right. The bones of the spine grated slightly
and Valentine looked up at the stretched white polyester ceiling.
In the autopsy room back at the Ark – the force's forensic lab
– he always watched the clock when they opened up the corpse.
Here he had nothing to rest an eye on – just four white walls, a
white ceiling. The way in which his eyes just slipped off the
reflective surface was beginning to make him feel sick.

'OK. You'll want to know when he died, Peter, and – as ever
– I won't be able to tell you. Justina might, but only after an
autopsy. A guess? Rigor's passing. The water temperature is ten
degrees centigrade. I think he's been dead *at least* twenty-four
hours.'

'Why's he like that – stretched out?' asked Valentine, licking
his upper lip, wishing he could have that cigarette back.

'If the body was here, on this spot, twenty-four hours ago,
then the intervening tide would have lifted him off the mud. His
feet are roped to a lead net weight. We'll get it out once we move
the corpse. Once underwater his limbs have floated up, the arms,
the hands, reaching up, as it were, for the surface. Rigor set in
then – hence the diver's position. It's wearing off now.'

'George?' asked Shaw. 'Thoughts?'

'I'd give him eight point nine on style and eight point eight
on degree of difficulty. But let's face it: he's not going to do any
better next round, is he?'

Shaw let the silence stretch out, just so that Valentine knew he'd gone too far.

Valentine coughed. Then straightened his back. 'Something's not right,' he said. 'Cut the rope and the body would be out in the North Sea on the first ebb tide. Would we find it? Probably not. Would someone find it? Maybe. Dutch coastguard. Thames River Police. Take your pick. Why tether the victim?'

'Indeed,' said Shaw. 'What're we saying on timing, Tom? This time last night?'

'Working hypothesis – yes. But nothing more than that. As I say, the pathologist will be with us soon. It's her stiff, Peter. You know that.'

Shaw held up both hands. 'Last question. We're saying the blow to the neck killed him?'

'Christ, Peter. You think he could survive *that*?'

In the end, then, Valentine had to look. The guy was dead meat, cold dead meat at that, but there was no ignoring the brutal nature of the wound. Valentine didn't let on but he'd passed the eleven plus with flying colours. His favourite subject had been English – especially Shakespeare. Not the drama, just the language. He rolled it round sometimes in his head, but never out loud. He knew immediately the word that applied to this kind of head wound, delivered in battle by a swinging axe which *cleaved* the head from the body.

'But it's not the only wound,' conceded Hadden. 'There's a bad bruise on the left side of the skull above the hairline. I'd say it was bad enough to leave him unconscious, but nothing like bad enough to kill him.'

'He was out here on this sandbar all today – in broad daylight?' asked Valentine.

'Looks like,' said Shaw. 'We're in a gully – so you can't see it from the side that easily. There's no visitors about, the Scolt Head ferry isn't running, no fishing boats out in winter – in fact, I'd guess no one left the harbour all day. So, yes. He's been out here looking at the sky all day.'

Hadden used gloved hands to tilt the skull. 'As to murder weapon, Peter. Justina will read you through the medical assessment, but if you want somewhere to start I'd speculate it was a spade, edge first, which isn't very nice, is it? Or a machete. But

as we're in Norfolk, I'd go for the spade. The wound's about
four inches deep, which is good going, given it's had to smash
through the neck, spine, muscle. We're talking maximum force.
Traumatic impact. He'd be senseless immediately, dead within
seconds.'

'And the lesser head wound?'

'Blunt object – not metallic. Wood, I'd guess. A decent bit of
timber.'

A small crab appeared in the victim's curly black hair. Hadden
plucked it out with a gloved hand and added it to a murky plastic
bucket which stood beside his forensic tool kit.

'When we've got pictures, and Justina's had a look, we can
clean his face for you. But for now we'll have to stick with the
mud-pack.'

The eyes were open, some of the mud washed away, but not
wide open, so the iris colour was impossible to pinpoint, although
they looked brown. He could have been any age between eighteen
and thirty. But as Valentine had pointed out, he wasn't going to
get any older.

Shaw looked at the facial structure: wide cheekbones, broad,
flat forehead, heavy jaw. A boulder skull, close-cropped hair,
deep eye sockets. He looked like a Halloween pumpkin without
a candle to light the eyes.

Faces were Shaw's special subject. The DI was one of less
than twenty officers in the UK qualified as a forensic artist. Art
at Southampton – his chosen degree – had included a year out
at the FBI college at Quantico, Virginia; an option he had not
shared with his father, who had encouraged him to pursue any
career of his choice *except* the police force. Back at Southampton
Shaw had added a Home Office diploma in facial reconstruction.
By the time he'd left the Met he was able to build a face from
an eyewitness account, age the face of a missing child, tease key
details out of reluctant witnesses and construct a wide range of
ID pictures – from the traditional photofit to a subtle three-
dimensional pencil portrait.

If they failed to find an ID for the victim Shaw would be
called on to 'revitalize' the corpse's face for a picture to be
distributed to the media: a pencil sketch of what the victim might
have looked like before that traumatic blow had knocked the life

out of him in a single, brutal second. British newspapers in the twenty-first century rarely ran photos of the dead, unlike their Victorian forerunners. Using the work of a forensic artist was the only way to broadcast an image acceptable to the public.

Looking at the face now, Shaw decided he'd have to begin work with the eyes – opening them right up to reveal the colour. The human iris was less than twelve millimetres in width – a constant throughout life – but often the most significant facial feature, part of the 'lifelong look' which gave every face its unique imprint. Within minutes of death eye colour fades, often obscured by a smoky white film. Shaw would have to rely on the pathologist to assess the original colour and hue.

'Anything on ID?' asked Shaw.

'Not really,' said Hadden. 'Unless there's a chance this is a Mrs T. G. Grainger.'

He tipped the halogen lamp so that they could see a Visa credit card on the top of the evidence box.

'No wallet – at least, nothing I can find. That was in his shirt top pocket.'

'Odd. We need to check her out fast, George. A relation? Theft?'

Valentine made a note, copying the numbers standing out and throwing minute shadows on the silvered card. He saw two things the others had missed but said nothing: the leading edge of the plastic was worn, and the expiry date was 2011.

'Pockets were empty but for these,' said Hadden. He'd vacuum packed a pair of kitchen scissors. 'Outer pocket of the waterproof. With this . . .'

A second vacuum pack, this one containing a single woody sprig of samphire.

'Now we're talking,' said Valentine, stepping closer. In Shaw's experience his DS's principal failure as a detective was a need to find a theory before he'd assessed the facts.

Pointedly he turned to Hadden. 'Tom – any ideas? Facts. That's what we need at this stage. But are there any?'

Hadden was too good an operator not to have a hypothesis. His sphere of competence wasn't just the body, but the wider crime scene. His team had got here with twenty minutes of light still lingering in the sky, so whatever picture he'd managed to assemble was multifaceted. That was Jack Shaw's Rule Number Two: listen to the experts.

'Cheap synthetic clothes, although the shoes are brand new and good quality. Poor teeth, with evidence of sub-standard dental work. Hip flask in the breast pocket contains whisky – not malt. Fingers on the right hand show evidence of nicotine. He's not a relation, is he, George?'

'Can't ignore the obvious,' said Valentine, rearranging his feet, largely to conceal the fact that he suddenly needed an extra lungful of air to complete his next sentence. 'Samphire wars: locals vandalize the London mob's vans, so the newcomers hit back by stoving in the skull of some poor sod who collects weeds for a living. Which would mean mud-man here is local, and his killer's probably already home, thanks to the A10.'

'For a start it's *not* the samphire season,' said Shaw. 'The plant vegetates in winter, so that's not right. Plus it might cost you thirty-five quid for a punnet online but it's not heroin, is it? Is murder a proportional response to a few slashed tyres?'

'I don't think the average East End scumbag knows what a proportional response looks like,' said Valentine. 'If they get angry enough they're quite capable of swinging a spade at some-one's skull – usually from behind.' Valentine went to spit on the sand, then remembered where he was.

Outside they could hear the last of the water trickling out to sea down Overy Creek.

Valentine ploughed on: 'Plus it's a theory that fits the one fact that really stands out – if we're talking facts. Someone's attached the victim to a lead weight, deliberately arranged for the corpse to stay put and be found, which sounds like a warning to me. Unless anyone's got any better ideas.'

No one had any better ideas, so they stepped outside.

The air was still, balmy, the temperature somewhere in the fifties. A sliver of an old moon had risen over the north Norfolk hills so that they could just see the thin creek running in its deep, muddy bed.

Hadden's eyes flitted over the shadowy landscape and Shaw had a sudden intuition that he was searching for birds.

'We've taken pictures of all the footprints,' said Hadden. 'But don't hold your breath. The body's been attached to the buoy, then inundated by high tide, so all those prints are lost. Then it's been discovered by the D'Asti family, so that's four sets all over the place, and then we've had another high tide. That means there's very little left, and certainly no print patterns.

'One stroke of luck. The tide *before* the one that washed over our friend here on the night he died was a spring tide, second highest of the year so far, so that left a clean slate on the beaches. Any prints below the spring tide mark, but above the last tide, on the flat sand, have been left in the last two days. We came over on the launch from Burnham Marsh and there's a single set from the staithe leading out this way for about twenty feet. I got a cast.'

'Just one set?'

'Yup. So it could be our victim. Or it might be somebody with nothing to do with the crime, or it just might be the killer. When was the last time we were that lucky, Peter?'

SIX

Peter Shaw's toes floated free of the mud: weightless, he enjoyed the moment, sensing the slight seaward tug of the current. The winter wetsuit was double-insulated, but he could still feel the chill of the sea, which was cooling his body, working inwards from the hands and feet to the core of his chest. When he let the wavelets slap his face the shock of it made him gasp. Water was Shaw's medium; on land he always felt the compulsion to run, to expend energy, in order to dissipate tension. In the sea he felt quite different because it was moving all the time and he had to struggle to be still. So he could use up nervous energy by trying not to move; he could just *be,* living in the moment, like a child. One of his first books had been *Through the Looking-Glass*. His favourite character had been the Red Queen, who had to run on the spot just to stay where she was.

He let his body tip forward, its centre of gravity sliding towards his chest, then his waist, so that he fell into a swimming position. For a moment he lay outstretched, looking down into the darkness before making two rapid arm strokes and slipping away from the edge of Mitchell's Bank. The crescent moon and stars lit the surface of the sea, while what lay beneath was unseen: a black, fathomless element. In daylight there was always a degree of transparency, but not after sunset, when the sea was transformed into a medium within which something hid. Treading water he turned in a circle, his diver's headlight a lighthouse beam on the water. He thought about his legs hanging down into the depths, as if he were a very large piece of fisherman's bait. Unable to resist the uneasy fear this image brought, he hitched his knees up and let the point of buoyancy tip him back again, so that he lay looking up into the sky.

Midnight: the next three hours until high tide presented a clear opportunity in the investigation, and Shaw was determined to seize it. It was still possible there was evidence on the beaches from the night of the murder. Hadden's team already had a set of footprints leading out towards Mitchell's Bank from the village of Burnham Marsh. Were there other tracks to find? *One* set of prints begged several questions. Shaw needed to beach-comb, and he needed to do it quickly, before the evidence was washed away. On his back he had a diver's wet-bag, with camera, tape, torch, map and notebook.

Swimming across the channel he reached the sands beneath Gun Hill and emerged in twenty brisk steps, each one adding incrementally to his weight as his buoyancy diminished. Standing still, his feet in an inch of water, he let his breathing return to normal, unzipping the top two inches of the suit to let out the heat generated by his own body. Sticking to the shallows, he ran two hundred yards along the water's edge and then retraced his steps, playing a torchbeam over the flat sand further up the beach, searching for prints.

After fifty yards he spotted an old campfire. Slipping off the thermal glove of the suit he tested the ashes: cold, damp too. There were no footprints. The surface of the beach was a desert, each half-buried razor shell with a 'tail' of sand left by the north wind. He spotted a barbecue tray, some cans of beer and a condom, but again the sand, between the water and the spring tide mark, was free of prints.

A crab scuttled, leaving its hieroglyphics among the light-weight prints of birds' feet. Lugworms created bubble domes in the wet sand at the water's edge, as if the earth was a gently deflating balloon. Worm casts appeared as he watched, morphing into miniature organic castles. But there were no forensics. No footprints. No one had arrived or left this beach after the spring tide of two nights earlier.

Over on Scolt Head Island, across the narrow gap through which the sea was still pouring into Overy Creek, he heard a seal bark, then a chorus of others, like a pack of dogs greeting a midnight postman. Slipping back into the water he struck out across the mouth of the creek with as much power as he could summon, his toes at one point brushing the submerged sandbar which lay mid-stream. A trailing hand brushed the sandy bottom and so he stopped and stood up, facing the sea, the incoming tide split on either side of him, making a small wave at his waist.

In the summer a ferry ran to a wooden jetty on the island from

Burnham Overy Staithe, bringing visitors out to the National Trust reserve. Scolt Head drew bird watchers, hikers, adventurous families. Camping was banned, along with fires, dogs off leads, bikes and litter. The island comprised two and a half miles of rare habitat and nesting grounds, a warren of marram grass, sandhills and wind. The best time to explore was winter, but the maze-like trail through the shallows was treacherous. Every winter the lifeboat had to make several rescue visits, picking up stranded ornithologists, loaded down with zoom lenses and hiking sticks.

He swam on, emerging from the water beside the landing stage. To his right a pathway led round the point towards the open sea, glowing in the dark, its serried ranks of white water sweeping in, the wind strong enough to hit the constant, mournful note of winter. A faint, ghostly luminescence lit the falling, foaming water. He turned left, inland, along the south shore of the island, which faced the marsh and Mitchell's Bank, the illuminated cube of the forensic tent still at its summit. The wind died as he fell within the lee of the sandhills which formed the island's backbone. After five hundred yards he'd found nothing but the wrecked remains of some lobster pots, a pair of seal trails, and a few broken wooden staves of old oyster beds.

On the point of turning back he saw footprints. Two sets, crossing the flat sand below the spring tide watermark. From his wet-bag he retrieved his iPhone and took a set of pictures: not admissible as forensic evidence, as no court would accept a digital image, but a record nonetheless. The prints stood in sharp contrast to the moonlit sand, one line coming ashore, the other retreating. Parallel sets, as if the walker had used the first set as a guide to firm ground. The set coming up the beach were deeper than the set going down to the water. Obvious inference: someone came ashore carrying something heavy, then left without it. The prints were sharp enough for Shaw to take measurements: ten inches by three and a half at the navicular bone. A small man, an average woman or a child? Both sets made by the same sized boot. What he couldn't see, and never would now the tide had risen, was whether they'd come ashore by boat, or waded in at low water.

He stood back from the double line of prints, moving his head from side to side, trying to see the evidence within the landscape

– trying to imprint a photographic image in his brain of the
setting. Instead, he saw two other trails – not footprints, but thin
cuts, as if someone had drawn parallel lines to the footprints
using a discarded lolly stick. Not a continuous line, as it came
and went in a regular pattern, every three to four feet.

His brain constructed a moving picture: the killer, walking, a
short spade in one hand, swinging it by the handle, touching it
down with each stride. Was this spade the murder weapon? Or
had the killer come ashore with it to bury vital evidence? Or
both. Shaw realized he'd made an assumption. He'd been building
a picture in his head: the murder out on the mud, the rising water,
the killer slipping over to Scolt Head, perhaps in a small boat,
to bury evidence. But the double set of footprints could tell
another story: what if the walker had *left* the island empty-handed,
and then returned carrying something? They could have buried
vital evidence on the island. They could still be on the island.

Shaw scanned the long ridge of marram grass set against the
stars. The footprints disappeared once they crossed over into the
rough sand above high water, but the general direction of travel
was clear: directly north, over the ridge, towards the sea. Shaw
climbed the hill, zigzagging between clumps of tall grass, until
he reached the summit. A *tour d'horizon* revealed the sea to the
north, marsh to the south, Mitchell's Bank now slipping underwater, the forensic tent encircled by the tide; and finally the coast
itself, stretching east and west – a white line of surf in the night.

The wind came out of the north with just a hint of Arctic ice.
His face stung, crusted with salt, but the wetsuit still retained its
warm layer of blood-heated water. Jogging down the face of the
sand cliff like a skier, turning his heels left, then right, then left,
he ran out on to the beach itself, over thousands, millions, billions
of crushed and shattered shells. The glittering sand crunched like
shattered glass under his bare feet.

A thin moon shadow stood out on the white beach, thrown by
a pile of stones, maybe a foot high, conical, made of concentric
circles of pebbles in diminishing layers, tapering to a miniature
peak. The cairn was plainly man-made. Its most remarkable
quality was, however, unseen. As he knelt, the skin on his cheeks,
chilled by the night air, detected a palpable wave of heat. Slipping
off his thermal glove he touched the summit. It was hot, as were

all the stones, not glowing, but radiating, a constant almost magical heat. A fire then, recently doused. But when he carefully dismantled the pyramid, all signs of the fuel – ash, wood, charcoal or flotsam – were missing, while the brittle, blackened sand itself radiated an unnatural heat.

SEVEN

The tombstone, harshly illuminated by the orange flood-light, read:

Julie Valentine
1953–1994
Asleep

George Valentine sat on the bench he'd paid for the day she died. It had been one of a dozen mindless tasks with which he'd filled the hours after returning home from the hospital. Then he'd gone to the Red House with Gordon Lee. That had been the first night he'd found it impossible to go straight back to the house on Greenland Street. Wandering the streets of the North End, he found a bench on the towpath. At last orders he'd bought himself forty Silk Cut so he just sat and smoked them all. At dawn he'd tracked the sun as it rose over the cannery at West Lynn. Then he'd gone home to make himself a cup of tea. He wasn't desperate, or suicidal, or distressed, just keenly aware that this was the first day of the rest of his life.

Now he often walked after going to the pub, and usually ended up here. Tonight was no different. He'd driven home from Old Hunstanton in the battered Mazda, the car chasing leaves down narrow lanes. North Norfolk went to bed early, especially on an autumn night, and he'd sped through villages in which no light showed. His mind ticked off the list of duties completed: DC Paul Twine would organize a mobile incident room for Burnham Marsh the next morning, complete with a cable internet link and generator. Several other officers had been contacted to be on site by six to organize the uniformed unit due to conduct house-to-house inquiries. Shaw had left him with a list of jobs to do at St James' the next morning before he too was set to join the team at Burnham Marsh. Hadden and the rest of the forensic team would work through the night at the Ark – the force's forensic lab. Valentine had driven home, content that another murder inquiry had begun, dimly aware that his life was in some ways illuminated by the deaths of others.

When he'd got to his front door on Greenland Street he fully intended to go up the stairs – carpetless now as they had been for a decade – and throw himself across the double bed. He needed to be fresh for the morning, and he knew the hour spent by Julie's grave was self-indulgent, slightly pitying. But a last draught of nicotine beckoned, so he'd walked to All Saints. He'd brought a small shell and crab's claw he'd picked on Mitchell's Bank and placed them on the top of the granite headstone.

Now he was there, looking at her name in stone, he knew what he'd come to say.

'It just seems disloyal,' he said, out loud, but not shouting. 'I didn't want you to think I didn't miss you any more.'

He laughed, looking away, up at the dark east window of the church. All Saints, the lost member of the town's trinity of great medieval churches, lay surrounded by an eggbox sixties housing development of heroic ugliness. The graveyard was a playground for dossers. A can of Special Brew stood on the tombstone next to Julie's.

He lowered his voice: 'She'll probably tell me to chuck my hook anyway. I'm old enough to be her father.' He rearranged his raincoat to cover his crotch. 'You'd like her. She's good at listening too.'

He threw a cigarette away still lit. 'Anyway – it's just a drink. Not a date, not as such. Like I said, she'll stand me up. Just like you did the first time.'

Valentine's mobile throbbed in his pocket with a message from Shaw.

See you at St James. Body on way to Ark. Autopsy 2 p.m.

That was something to look forward to. It might be him one day, if he contrived to die unexpectedly, unnaturally, or even violently. Julie had told him many times that he wasn't going to make old bones.

One more cigarette. Looking for the lighter he found a set of unfamiliar keys in his pocket. The vicar of All Saints had given them to him only that morning in case, on his nightly visits, he'd care to check the church. Vandalism had always been a problem

at all the town's churches – especially here at hidden-away All
Saints – but there had been a fresh twist this autumn. Someone
with an air rifle had been taking pot shots at the stained-glass
windows. So far there had been three attacks on St Margaret's
and one at St Andrew's. Valentine, who'd taken on the case, had
dropped by to warn the vicar at All Saints, who'd agreed to keep
the floodlights on all night. Two lamps burned, one at the east
end, one at the west. The light was weak and sickly, like Tizer,
but it was better than leaving All Saints in the dark.

The church crouched in the shadows. The original stonework
had been plastered over, the tower had fallen a century ago –
dilapidated, forgotten – while the glass was lost behind heavy
metal mesh. Once All Saints had rivalled the town's other great
churches – St Margaret's with its celestial tide clock, and the
soaring St Andrew's with its vast interior built for the merchants
who made the town rich. Now it lay hidden, unseen and
overlooked.

Valentine felt sleep slipping further away. Restless, he stood,
and walked to the church doors, unlocking the padlock on the
wire mesh outer screen, and stepping into the porch. The inner
wooden door needed two keys, and then fell open under its own
weight. The smell of All Saints was quite distinct – that damp-
ness of unread prayer books, and a hint of polish, but also
something of its own, because the stone floor was lower than the
graveyard, and it seemed that the rich aroma of decaying soil
had slipped in through the door.

The grandeur of the interior came alive when Valentine threw
the master light switch. All Saints had been the heart of the
maritime community of Lynn for centuries, and stood less than
a hundred yards from the old wharves upon which the whalers
had unloaded their bloody cargo, the blubber boiled in open vats
along the riverbank. The walls of All Saints were sea-salt white,
the lead in the windows strips of shell. Like all ports, Lynn held
the promise of the foreign lands its ships served. It could have
been a church in Lerwick, Hamburg, Riga or Den Haag.

Valentine sat in the wooden choir stalls, pulling down a miseri-
cord on which to perch: he always chose the same one, three
seats along the line, with a carved hare on the underside of the
tipping seat. He lit a cigarette, enjoying the sense of sacrilege,

balanced against the knowledge that he was a custodian, with special rights: a guardian angel on forty Silk Cut a day. It was this thought that made him look up to the east window, which he recalled showed at its apex a single angel, with high, muscular wings and golden hair.

In daylight the window blazed with medieval light. At night it was cluttered with mesh and lead, the glass itself only dimly seen. Tonight was different, because the floodlight outside electrified the images: a glimpse of Jonah's whale; Christ casting his net on Galilee.

But the angel had gone.

No – the angel's face had gone, and in its place was a small opening through which the orange light flooded into the roof space above. It seemed that the vandals had finally found All Saints. Valentine felt an almost personal sense of violation.

He walked the length of the nave until he stood directly below the window. Some pieces of shattered glass lay on the stone, but one piece, three inches square, had survived the fall. Picking it up, he examined the pale yellow glass upon which the medieval artist had drawn an eye. He thought of Shaw's moon-eye, the ghostly white counterpart to the blue of the other, then slipped the shard of glass into his pocket.

EIGHT

Mitchell's Bank, the scene of crime, appeared strangely spectral: a drying whaleback of mud at low tide, grey waters rippling around it like a tablecloth. A mist still clung to the marshes beyond. The police launch, beached at an angle, was moored to the distinctive black and white navigation buoy which marked the exact spot where the D'Asti family had come upon the victim. The only colours, other than the assortment of greys, were the pulsing red and green navigation lamps on the launch.

The image refreshed, remaking itself digitally from the top to the bottom, and Shaw leant back in his chair, stretching out until he realized he was mimicking the position in which they'd found the victim – the diving man in reverse, rising up from the sea. The picture he was looking at was NT WEBCAM 6 – the camera fitted to an automatic weather station mast on Gun Hill. He'd found it after twenty minutes of trawling through north Norfolk webcams, most of which were installed to help weekend sailors and holidaymakers time a dash up to the coast.

This 'live' picture, online thanks to the National Trust, was remade every thirty seconds, and the next image revealed a transformation. The sun had broken through, the water for the first time taking on a blue sheen, and the steel fittings on one of the boats off Burnham Marsh glowed like underwater gold.

The image wiped, blacked out, and then returned.

DC Mark Birley appeared at Shaw's door, which was permanently wedged open by a pile of paper supplies used for forensic art reconstructions: reams of A4, A3 and tinted Canson Mi-Tientes paper, ideal for pastel work, allowing Shaw to recreate skin tone. Plus reams of rough paper for witnesses to sketch on – especially children, who always responded to the freedom of the blank page, and matte acetate overlays, foam core board for courtroom displays, and finally quality vellum, for preparing finished work as evidence. A large easel stood to the side of the window, a dustsheet covering whatever lay beneath.

Birley, a rugby player, fifteen stone and built like the Tate & Lyle sugar-cube man, always seemed on the verge of bursting the seams of his suits. Ex-uniform, meticulous, with an ability to maintain focus for long periods of time, he'd joined Shaw's team five years earlier and was now an experienced evidence sifter: pictures, video, CCTV. The visual image seemed to be his medium of choice.

Shaw swung his screen round so that Birley could see the webcam image.

'Scene of crime – on film,' said Shaw.

Birley's eyes bisected the screen, searching, establishing the frame of what he was seeing. 'Paul's got me up to speed,' he said, saving Shaw the wasted effort of double-briefing. Twine's team role as 'point' for the murder investigation meant it was his job to be the communications hub, to keep everyone informed.

Shaw tapped the screen with his pencil rubber. 'The webcam's on top of Gun Hill. National Trust owned. Takes a shot every thirty seconds. We think the victim died after dark the night before last – but who knows, we could be wrong by three hours, which would just get us into daylight. So far three sets of foot-prints on or near the scene: one going out to the sandbank from Burnham Marsh, one going up the beach on Scolt Head Island, one coming back. Or possibly the other way round. I've marked the spots on the map outside – can you bring it when we transfer down to the scene? George and I are off in twenty minutes. Meanwhile, Mark—'

'I'll get through to the National Trust,' said Birley. 'Big question is, do they keep the film, and if they do keep it, for how long? Scientists tend to keep data. The Trust's doing a lot of work tracking seal colonies. Well, it's providing the data. So we've got chances, sir. Good chances. Next question – do they let the camera run through the hours of darkness? Most don't. Some do. We need to be lucky.'

Birley crossed his fingers and turned away, back into the 'room', CID's open-plan main office. George Valentine's desk was out there too, but the last time he'd been seen sitting at it was at the New Year's Eve party when he couldn't stand up.

The Mitchell's Bank killing wasn't the only major case on Lynn CID's patch. At the far end of the room a whiteboard had been set up with suspect pictures, maps, family trees and SOCO shots. Acting DS Fiona Campbell was talking to the team assigned to tracking down the source of adulterated drugs being sold on the streets of the town. Three local dealers had been arrested and charged, but none was prepared to name their original source of the adulterated cocaine. Several addicts had been admitted to A&E suffering from the side effects of the supply. One had died. The supply to the street had stopped, but that might not last. Campbell's team was working twenty-four seven to try and trace the origins of the drug before more users died.

Shaw, standing at his door, let his eye rest on a full-length mortuary shot of the victim – the left arm below the elbow jet black where the skin had died, while the rest of him had still been alive. This symptom, known as necrosis, was a telltale sign that cocaine was being mixed with Levamisole – a drugstore medicine used to help control cancer. The problem with Levamisole was that it could wipe out white blood cells, leaving the extremities to 'die' while the patient fell sick. The resulting necrosis – of hands, feet, arms – was so characteristic of drug abuse that very few of its victims would willingly present themselves for treatment at A&E, preferring to suffer instead, hoping against hope the skin would rejuvenate. It never did. Dead skin was dead skin for life.

Shaw tore his eyes away and back to his screen. He'd recommended Campbell for promotion to acting DS, and he had to let her run her own inquiry. Delegation was a key skill. He just hoped Campbell didn't let him down, mainly because he didn't want to see another corpse disfigured by necrosis, but also partly because he'd sensed Valentine's discomfort at her elevation. Playing second fiddle to Shaw on a murder inquiry was never going to be George's idea of job satisfaction, and he'd have relished the freedom of running the drugs inquiry, but Shaw needed him: he had a murder inquiry to run, alongside the highly sensitive investigation into the second-home burglaries. And besides, he knew George Valentine well enough to realize that he only really came alive when the victim was dead.

He sent his DS a text even though he could guess he was only fifty feet away – on the top floor, in the canteen.

I'll pick you up.

Shaw left his door open and took the fire exit steps up to the canteen. Valentine had a favourite table right by the door so that he could enjoy a cigarette outside. The wire mesh platform was littered with cigarette stubs.

On the table, which was long enough to seat ten officers, the DS had arranged what looked like a jumble of shattered stained glass. There was also a large oval plate reserved by the canteen staff for the fabled St James' full English breakfast. A clean plate, save for a smear of ketchup. Shaw had a sudden image of three scallops, a sprig of samphire and a lone new potato.

Valentine sat at the table, but standing at its head was a woman Shaw didn't know. Petite, almost gamine – a street urchin in suede boots and jeans. Her face was symmetrical, like a computer hero's, but saved from being anodyne by a wide bone structure which seemed to stretch her skin. Shaw knew enough about the psychology of faces to know he was attracted to this woman's because it was a feminine reflection of his own. She was drinking from a bottle of spring water and had ignored Shaw's arrival, her eyes focused down on the coloured glass.

Valentine leant back in his chair. 'DI Peter Shaw,' he said. 'Sonia Murano – glass expert. She's helping us with the case.' He indicated the shards of shattered window.

The smile was warm, almost a full beam, but she shut it down too quickly, as if she'd swapped a pair of Greek theatre masks. Joy for sorrow. There was a sadness in her slightly crumpled body language, the nervous rearrangement of her short blonde hair, and the intense academic focus. Even now, a few seconds after being introduced to Shaw, she was examining a piece of the shattered red glass with an eyeglass as if it was the only object in the room.

Valentine, getting up and shrugging himself into his raincoat, passed Shaw a single piece of yellow glass punctured by a single hole.

'What's the story, George?'

'Not much of one. Some kid with an air rifle's wandering round town in the small hours taking a pop at church windows. This one's from All Saints. Town night squad's got the case files.'

The night squad was a unit of uniformed officers responsible for the medieval town centre after dark. They had an office on the Tuesday Market which was lit up like an all-night kebab bar. Shaw knew All Saints, and that Valentine spent hours on a bench beside his wife's grave, chatting to the dead. Julie Valentine had been a shadowy presence in his own childhood, closeted away in the kitchen with his mother, while the men talked shop in the front room over whisky and cigarettes.

'They've tried to keep a bit of glass from each church to help ballistics,' said Valentine. 'So we know it's an air gun, low velocity. A popgun really. Couple of times the pellet's hit the lead – see . . .'

He showed Shaw a piece which was almost solid lead, depicting a crown of gold, the pieces of glass just slivers for jewels. The impact was marked by a crater in the soft metal.

Valentine held up an evidence bag, the flattened pellet visible inside.

'Ms Murano's been appointed by the diocese to do the repairs. I asked her to bring the stuff in – I thought it would help, and it has.'

'Lucky to have an expert on hand . . .' ventured Shaw.

'I've got a shop in Burnham – glassware,' she said, her voice much lower than Shaw would have guessed. 'But my degree's art history – MA in medieval church glass. It's a hobby really, and I'm too busy, but I couldn't say no. Lynn's glass is second to none. Look . . .'

She held up a single piece of blue glass so that it caught the light.

'We have to fly,' said Valentine. 'Thanks for bringing it all in. How long can we hold on to it?'

'A couple of days. I've set aside some time this coming weekend – I need to get a kiln going at the house at Holme. I buy in a lot of glass but the trick is getting the colour right, and adding the details by hand. I make a little too – using medieval methods. I'm going to try and tackle all the replacement pieces in one session. I'll ring when I'm sorted.'

Valentine offered a hand. 'Thanks.'

As she packed gloves away in a neat leather satchel, Shaw wondered about the house at Holme. The village was one of the most exclusive on the coast, nestling behind a spectacular beach which looked out across the Wash towards distant, misty Lincolnshire. It wasn't millionaire's row, but it was a prime slice of north Norfolk real estate. A glassware shop in well-heeled Burnham Market clearly turned a penny.

She nodded at them both, and fled.

Shaw held up a piece of glass containing a painted face. The airgun pellet had missed the drawn eye by a few millimetres. He felt a sympathetic pain within his own blind eye and massaged the muscle at his temple. Valentine looked away. The DI's good eye was tested every three months by St James' medical staff to make sure he was fit for duty. What they didn't know was that Shaw's good eye had shown worrying signs of deterioration, possibly as a result of his decision not to have the injured blind eye removed. He didn't want the standard glass eye: the milky moon-eye had become part of his past, part of who he was. Technically, Valentine should have reported any sign of decline in his superior's eyesight. (He had been invited to report such matters by at least one senior officer keen to see Shaw's otherwise sparkling career derailed.) His decision to turn a blind eye – as it were – had forged an unspoken bond between DS and DI.

'St Margaret's, St Andrew's, All Saints,' said Valentine, indicating each cluster of colourful fragments in turn. Shaw edged closer. Each collection of shards told a common story: the yellow glass reserved for flesh, the elliptical heavenly eyes, the delicate feathers of wings.

'I just thought I'd try and track this joker down,' said Valentine. 'After all, there can't be that many people with a grudge against angels.'

NINE

Sea mist, drifting in off the Wash, was the default weather forecast for the Darnall Estate. This morning's *haar* was resisting the early morning sun, still just a pale disc hanging over the Sky dishes, so that the maze of cul-de-sacs which formed the estate was still marked out by pearl-like strings of amber street lights, orbs suspended magically on invisible lampposts, like St Elmo's Fire – the legendary will-o'-the-wisps which hovered around the masts of sailing ships, harbingers of electrical storms. These lights were false sirens, because yesterday's lightning had moved on, striking three offshore wind turbines before fizzling out in the North Sea. The radio weather forecast, however, predicted their return by dusk.

The Darnall had been built in the early sixties to help accommodate London's overspill: thousands sent north from the blighted bombsites of the East End to find jobs and modern homes in the Norfolk port. The estate still reeked of the age of the council estate, but most of those who judged it harshly had forgotten just how pleased its original tenants had been when they'd first arrived: the Darnall offered indoor toilets, insulated roofs, galley kitchens, spare rooms, and back and front gardens. It was pretty much paradise in 1963, except that in heaven you didn't get a serving hatch between your kitchen and dining room.

Time had dealt harshly with the Darnall. The target population had been five thousand, but the money had run out in the mid-seventies and the streets were interspersed with stretches of wasteland, each one graced with the suffix *park* – as if that alone could transform what the locals called *rough lots* into Kensington Gardens. Daily life on the estate was blighted by a small number of thugs and a handful of so-called 'families' – remnants of the East End's underworld aristocracy, shipped out of the capital alongside the workers. The estate had no special reputation for street crime – that was reserved for the entire town – but the Darnall had its own particular vice, its specialist event, so to speak: car crime. Vehicles of all sizes and makes were stolen for joy rides in Lynn, then dumped on the Darnall before being ceremoniously set alight. The merry flicker of flames beyond net curtains was something the locals had come to live with, along with the anxiety prompted by the inevitable question: how much petrol was there in the tank?

Shaw swung his Porsche 167 off the main drag, a dual carriageway called Jubilee Way, which wound its way around the heart of the Darnall like a hangman's noose. Shaw had chosen the Porsche because of the narrow A-bar – the stanchion between the windscreen and the side window. The Monocular Society, a self-help group set up in London, had a list on their website of cars suitable for those without stereoscopic vision, and the Porsche was top of the list. Modern cars had thick A-bars, designed to improve safety, but which amounted to a considerable barrier to the single-sighted. Shaw loved the car for itself too: the slightly antique lines, the sheer panache of the design. It looked classy, even on Jubilee Way, and even with George Valentine in the passenger seat.

They were entering New Darnall – the council's latest attempt to save the neighbourhood from decline to full-blown sink estate status. Here the tarmac had been colour-coded to match new speed limits, sleeping policemen installed across every road, CCTV posts added at junctions like alien invaders from *The War of the Worlds*. Finally, an aesthetic touch; each of the terraced houses had been painted a different poster-paint colour: blue, yellow, green and red. The locals had dubbed the area Balamory, after the popular children's TV programme, which had been one of Fran's favourites, and which Shaw had come to loathe due to its incessant good humour.

Shaw and Valentine were both keen to get out to the scene of crime. They'd tackled the paperwork at St James' – murder created red tape like no other crime. Shaw had endured a ten-minute interview with the chief constable, who had taken the opportunity not only to demand a quick and speedy arrest of the culprit, but also to remind Shaw that his other priority was to swiftly bring to a close the hunt for the second-home burglars – or Chelsea Burglars, as he called them. Shaw had resisted the urge to point out that the concept of two priorities was a linguistic

nonsense. He had also declined the opportunity to tell his superior
officer that the case was about to hit the local media – probably
in Monday's evening paper.

Meanwhile, Valentine had rung round the rural police stations
and mustered a squad of twenty uniformed officers to undertake
a fingertip search of the coastal path, the Overy Creek sea wall
and the outskirts of Burnham Marsh itself.

It had been Valentine's idea to fit in one last bit of routine
police procedural foot-slogging before they left town. While he
would never admit it to Peter Shaw, he was just as likely to recall
DCI Jack Shaw's maxims as his son, and near the top of the list
was: *Don't forget the obvious.* It was all very well sifting through
the forensics, but nothing galvanized a police murder inquiry quite
as potently as interviewing a suspect on his own doorstep.

The body on Mitchell's Bank was either linked to the trade
in samphire, or someone wanted them to think it was. The
victim had samphire in his pockets, and a pair of heavy-duty
scissors – the tool of choice for the professional harvester. John
Jack Stepney ran the van fleet which took the crop down to
Billingsgate every day. His arrival on the scene that summer
had sparked confrontation and violence. If they had to name a
suspect *right now*, it was Stepney. Valentine had fixed the
interview on the basis that they wanted to discuss the criminal
damage to the vehicles at his garage. With luck he'd know
nothing about the body on Mitchell's Bank – unless he was
responsible for the killing. Either way, it would be instructive
to watch his reactions under questioning.

John Jack Stepney lived at 54 King George Close. Valentine
had phoned at 6.05 that morning and Stepney sounded chipper,
as if he'd been at his desk for hours. Happy to discuss the vandals'
attack on his fleet of vans, he asked only that the interview be
moved to his daughter's house – 56 King George Close. Number
54 was pink, number 56 green. Unless they wanted to meet later
in the day, in which case he would be on his boat at Wells-next-
the-Sea: a twenty-seven-footer by the name of *Highlife,* moored
on the town quay. Valentine, who loathed boats and the people
in them, had opted for a meeting on dry land.

The Porsche slid into the curved kerb. 'You're banking on it
still having tyres when we get back, right?' asked Valentine,

levering himself out of the passenger seat, his spine emitting a plastic click as he achieved the vertical.

Shaw had a clipboard with the West Norfolk Constabulary's crest on it which he set up on the dashboard.

'That's nice,' said Valentine. 'Nothing like an incentive for the local thugs. Double points for a copper's car.' Suddenly breathless, he covered the moment by putting a cigarette between his lips, then transferring it behind one ear.

The garden was just grass, but neat enough, and they stood in the cold mist of morning listening to the doorbell echo inside. The two houses were twinned semis. Shaw wondered how difficult it was to wangle that arrangement if you wanted to keep the family close at hand.

A young woman opened the door in tight shorts and a T-shirt. 'We're off to Tenerife,' she said, as if that explained everything.

'I'm Emilia,' she added, which was a surprise. Shaw thought it was a beautiful name. 'Dad's upstairs. He's not coming – he just buys the tickets, thank God.'

They heard a child squeal from the front room.

'Just go up – like, it's not *Downton Abbey* – you'll find him.'

The stairs were carpeted, spotless and newly hoovered, but littered with children's toys. On the landing stood a single one-armed bandit, a modern digital model, plugged in, and winking at them images of apples and oranges and pears, with all the usual paraphernalia of NUDGE and HOLD. Shaw loathed the machines because they reminded him of being at the seaside in the rain, rather than on the beach in the sun. Whenever he saw a slot machine he could smell damp coats, and feel wet sand between his toes.

Stepney was at his desk, perched on an office chair. Shaw always thought there were two kinds of desk – the sort people pose at, and the one that people work at: this was the second variety. Two MacBook Airs stood open and working (both on Face-to-Face and showing talking heads). There were two other desks, four mobile phones visible, plus a speaker. In the corner was a Lavazza coffee machine in brushed chrome, and a wall-mounted pair of Hi-Fi speakers.

Stepney, fifty according to his police file, looked ten years younger, biceps pronounced without the whole iron-pumping swell, a cut-away gym top revealing a tattoo of a bald eagle. He had close-cropped salt-and-pepper hair which made his scalp look like he'd have a spotted coat, like a dog, if he let it grow.

'Gents. I don't do seats for visitors – sorry. I like to encourage brisk business. Give me a second.'

There was something wrong with the accent, and Shaw and Valentine exchanged glances. They'd been expecting Estuary English and they'd got classless BBC, with no regional burr. His file had listed a perfunctory education at a primary in Poplar and a secondary in Bow.

Stepney wound up his two digital conversations and then stood, perching himself on a desk edge. Out of the window, which had blinds set open, Shaw could see down into the misty garden, and a child's climbing frame, in red and blue.

'Thanks for meeting here,' he said, unprompted. 'I like to keep work separate. Emilia's got a spare room and the wife likes her privacy. Anyway, fire away.'

After six years of conducting interviews together, Shaw and Valentine had evolved several effective techniques to unsettle interviewees. This was their standard double act: Shaw asked questions – on this occasion about the tyre-slashing of Stepney's vans in the garage off the Tuesday Market – while the DS took notes. Then Valentine would start to chip in, while Shaw took time out to listen and think. After that they fired at will.

Stepney was happy to talk about the business. The contract with Green Gold, the Billingsgate wholesalers, required them to supply 150 punnets of fresh samphire a day in season: mid-June to mid-October. That required two vans on the road every morning at two a.m. The fleet consisted of three new Vivaros, each with a 1,100-kilogram payload. Stepney paid six boat skippers on contract to run up and down the coast picking direct from the beach. They in turn hired pickers – mostly migrant workers – who worked as sub-contractors.

'You don't employ any pickers directly then?' asked Shaw.

'Nope. Why get my hands dirty, eh? It's a rough trade. Too much like hard work, if you ask me. "Halfway down hangs one that gathers samphire – dreadful trade!"'

'Fan of *EastEnders*, are we, sir?' asked Valentine.

'It's Shakespeare,' he said. 'Although, to be fair, that's rock samphire – this is the marsh variety.'

Valentine asked a series of routine questions about the night the vandals targeted the vans.

Shaw thought about what was behind Stepney's curiously lifeless grey eyes. Physically he radiated energy, but those eyes hardly emitted light, let alone emotion. The pretence was obvious enough: the entrepreneur in his office, the veneer of education, the easy manners. Valentine had summarized his previous convictions on their journey out to Balamory. Two counts of GBH, six of ABH, five of burglary. One of the more serious charges involved Stepney kicking a 'business associate' more than thirty times while he lay in the gutter outside a pub in Lynn town centre. One witness described how Stepney had called out a number after each blow: from thirty, counting down. The damage this attack had done to his victim's internal organs had resulted in a long stay in intensive care, his condition causing enough concern for files to be prepared to support a murder charge. He'd got four years for that offence, and had not been in trouble since – a clean sheet of nearly eight years. Shaw felt certain this meant he had not been *caught* for eight years.

Stepney's patience with Valentine's questions finally snapped. 'Look. What is this about?'

'You said it was a rough trade,' said Shaw. 'How rough a trade, precisely?'

'I think I got my question in first, Detective Inspector. What is this about?'

The doorbell rang and they heard Emilia calling up the stairs: 'Bye! I'll ring from the flat.'

Stepney didn't move a muscle. They heard the taxi driver's voice, then the child crying, then the door slamming.

'She likes to get away. Problem is, when you get back, it's still the Darnall. There's a sixties protest song – "The Eve of Destruction" – that has a great line in it: "You may leave here for four days in space, but when you return it's the same old place". Escaping isn't as easy as it looks, is it? Place like this pulls you back down every time.'

Shaw ignored this piece of philosophy. 'The fishing boat captains you hire on contract are all Polish, Mr Stepney. How do they know where to find samphire in season?'

'First rule of business, Detective Inspector. Market intelligence.

I recruited the knowledge. A fisherman works out of Wells called
Slaughden – Painter Slaughden, they call him. He knows every
inch of the coast and takes each of the boats out for a recce in
early summer. Next question?'

Any pretence that this was anything but an adversarial interview
had evaporated.

'Any idea who slashed the tyres?' asked Valentine, sensing
Shaw wanted a time out.

'I think that's your job, answering questions like that. My
guess? Some of the old samphire pickers trying to scare us off.'

'Did you retaliate?'

'In what way?'

'Did you retaliate?' repeated Valentine.

'Nope.'

'A man has been found dead in the marshes at Burnham Marsh.
Murdered,' said Shaw.

'Nothing to do with me, or mine.'

This mock-mafia ideal of family was often used in Lynn to
justify crude violence. It sickened Shaw.

Valentine made a note. 'Where were you on Friday night, sir,
between eight and midnight?'

'Do I need a lawyer?'

'Depends what the answer is,' said Shaw.

Anger twitched at the edge of Stepney's eyes – at the tail of
the eye, where the skin tightened.

'At the warehouse. That's the one the vandals broke into so
they could slash the tyres on my new vans. That's the crime
you're supposed to be investigating. Insurance claim is one thousand eight hundred pounds, by the way. I'm guessing you don't
care. Since the damage was done to the vans, one of us stays
over at the garage. That night it was me.'

'Alone?' asked Valentine.

'I got a takeaway delivered at nine from the Bengal. They
know me. And the drivers clock on at one o'clock.'

'But it's out of season for samphire, right?' said Valentine.

'The vans are business assets. You need to sweat your assets
to stay in business. I run organic veg down to New Covent
Garden. Just about covers the costs, but beats letting four new
vans sit on their tyres all day. Especially slashed tyres.'

'And what do your Polish fishermen do all winter?' asked Shaw.

'That's not my problem. I hire them for three months – that's it. If they were on my books I'd get them to run cockles. They're never out of season. Cheap labour, high mark-up – especially if you can get the produce out to Spain. But like I say, that's their lookout.'

'I'd like their names, please. And the port registration numbers of the vessels,' said Shaw.

Stepney shrugged and called up details on one of the MacBook Airs. Valentine added them to his notes and they all went downstairs to the front door. Outside the fog was lifting, revealing a stretch of waste ground opposite, in the middle of which was a burnt-out car. Strands of mist floated from the wreck, as if it was still smouldering.

'You *can* escape, of course,' said Stepney. 'I've got two sons, they're at St Felix's near Lincoln. Emilia wouldn't have it – so she's going to pay the price. She'll never get out. Mind you, my boys are fucking strangers to me. Me to them. Least they're still scared of me, so that's something.'

'Quite a philosopher, sir, once you get going.' Valentine lit a cigarette, and Stepney's smile slipped off his face like an iceberg calving.

'Concept of escape seems very important to you, Mr Stepney,' said Shaw, stepping a foot closer, right into his personal space. Shaw's voice, which normally held an almost musical quality, buzzed with menace. Valentine had seen Shaw do this before but every time it made the DS's scalp prickle – the switch, from calm, methodical inquiry, to the edge of violence. Not for the first time he recognized in this second voice a ghost of his old partner, DCI Jack Shaw.

'If I recall,' continued Shaw, 'you served your four jail terms as a model prisoner. I'd hate to see your new-found business empire curtailed by a further prison sentence. Doesn't matter how many vans you've got on the road if you're banged up in cell sixty-nine, does it? Which – to resort to the local patois – translates as this: if you've told us less than the entire truth I'll have you back inside, Mr Stepney, before you can say *King Lear*: Act Four, Scene Six.'

TEN

I t was the locals' favourite pub quiz question: how many Burnhams were there in north Norfolk? The widely accepted but often contested answer was seven. But there was never any doubt about which stood as the capital of Chelsea-on-Sea. That was Burnham Market, or more accurately Burnham *Up-Market*: a small town straight out of *Country Life*, with its super-posh pub, its old-fashioned traditional butchers, fishmongers and bakers. Add to that the discreet Bentley dealership, the independent bookshop, the half-dozen restaurants, three cafés, an art gallery, and an estate agent's specializing in the million-pound-plus market.

The clichéd façade hid something else: a real village, local old money as well as families of agricultural workers and fishermen, and a stretch of fine East Anglian farming country. Not to mention the second homeowners who'd decided to retire, sell the first home, and make the place their real home. Since the war, incomers' money and tourism had kept the coast alive.

Beyond Burnham Market lay the six other Burnhams – Deepdale, Norton, Thorpe, Overy Town, Overy Staithe, and Westgate. But there was one last Burnham on the map, always forgotten, always overlooked, and, thanks to its exclusive position, invariably overpriced.

Shaw slowed the Porsche and checked that Valentine's Mazda was still in the rear view before turning off the main coast at the signpost that read Burnham Marsh.

The distance was put at one mile, but it was a country mile. The village lay on a peninsula between Overy Creek – the estuary of the River Burn – and Norton Creek, which wasn't a creek at all, but the tidal channel that separated the mainland from Scolt Head Island. The old houses, Georgian and Edwardian façades on older medieval ranges – lay along a sandy sea wall built by the Romans. Behind this barricade of clay lay a few modern buildings, mostly built in the forties and fifties, before the planners realized they had something to protect. Each of these villas was worth a fortune, but nothing like the fortune you'd need to buy one of the old houses with their views out across the sandy estuary, towards the gap between Gun Hill and Scolt Head, and the open sea beyond.

That view today encompassed the St James' police launch moored off Mitchell's Bank, and the black and white scene-of-crime buoy flashing an amber light despite the bright autumn sunshine.

The staithe itself, the village's old harbourside, was of stone, about fifty yards long, and broken by a slipway. The wharf's one iconic structure was an old ship's crane for lifting cargo directly out of the water, a remnant of the 1920s, in rusted iron, with an arm stretched out at three o'clock from a large flywheel. The village church, St John's, lay in ruins on the shore, half inundated by sand. Offshore, lying in the mud at low water, were a dozen small fishing boats, and – in summer – a small fleet of yachts, moored to three ranks of red buoys.

As soon as Shaw got out of the car he could tell there was something very odd about Burnham Marsh. No barking dogs, no curtains twitching, no distant static of digital music or radio, no lawn mowers, no engines idling, no smoke drifting from chimney pots, no washing flapping, no drains gurgling: nothing, not even the whirr of aircon, or the sudden nagging tone of a mobile phone. If he didn't know better, he'd guess that Burnham Marsh was in shock. So far he'd seen only one resident – a woman at an upstairs window hanging out a rug, as a uniformed PC knocked at her front door.

DC Twine had got the team together for a briefing. The sun was climbing and the heat building to an unseasonal seventy Fahrenheit, so they stood out in the sea breeze. A digital printer juddered away inside the mobile incident room, which rocked slightly on its springs. Twine gave out a one-page summary of the evidence so far: just facts, times, dates and tides. Shaw took his copy and made an effort not to check it. There was nothing to be gained by eroding the DC's authority on the first day of what could be a long inquiry by studiously editing the handout.

'OK. Listen up,' said Shaw. Silence fell instantly. He'd chosen most of the squad personally, and they were all ambitious, knowing that rapid promotion relied entirely on results.

'Paul's given you the facts. So what don't you know? George and I have just interviewed John Jack Stepney – who effectively runs the samphire outfit which has moved in along this coast, ousting the locals. If this is all about a squabble over turf then we need to identify the victim as a priority – then we'll know which side he was on, and which our killer might be on.

'We can leave house-to-house here in the village to uniformed branch. Mind you, finding someone at home's going to be a challenge.'

Despite the fact they were standing at the heart of the village, in broad daylight, in mid-morning, they hadn't seen a single pedestrian, car, van or bicycle. The place was dead, picturesque certainly, but with as much movement as a picture postcard. It felt unsettlingly like standing on a film set waiting for someone to shout 'Action!'

'We may be lucky,' said Shaw. 'He's somebody's son, some-body's husband – you know the cliché. They may come forward. If not I need to do an artist's impression from the corpse. George and I will attend the autopsy at the Ark this afternoon. Once I've completed the image we need to get it out and about: TV, local papers. Meanwhile, let's dig down into the samphire trade. George has a list of the local pickers and the Poles Stepney uses for the trade. And we need to track down the local picker who marked Stepney's card, showed him where the pickers should go. Name of Painter Slaughden – out of Wells.

'My guess is our stiff is local – but it's just that, a guess. I don't want to be standing here tomorrow relying on guesswork. So let's get busy.

'We need to hit missing persons. Radio's best: anyone not turned up for work, not been seen at the corner shop, you know the routine. We need to be fast, thorough. I've got a feeling this will break quickly. Mark's looking through some CCTV of the scene, so we might even have the killer on film. But only from five hundred yards away, and at night. So let's not get our hopes up. If you were planning a night out this week, cancel it. We need to run at this one. Questions?'

'So we're saying people have started killing each other over salad?'

'Yup. George often says he could murder a Savoy cabbage.'

It got a laugh but actually it was a very good question, and one that had been worrying Shaw since Hadden had shown them the sprig of samphire in the victim's pocket.

The officer who'd asked the question was DC Jackie Lau, in her standard leathers, wrap-around sunglasses, jet-black short-cut hair. Lau had worked for a decade at her father's taxi firm in Lynn before joining the force. She spent her spare time stock-car racing, and her Megane, with spoilers, airfoils and go-fast stripes, was parked alongside the squad cars. In the team she was known for a penchant for meat, lots of it, and an open disdain for vegetarians. She wanted to be West Norfolk's first female DCI, and with Birley assigned to the CCTV footage, and Fiona Campbell running the drugs inquiry, she was the most senior member of the team on the ground after Valentine.

'Is this really sufficient motive for murder, sir? A murder like this: a ritual killing, the head nearly severed then the body deliberately left in a position where it would be exposed. It doesn't seem to add up. Sir.'

'If it was just the samphire trade then cold-blooded murder looks unlikely – I'll give you that,' said Shaw. 'Although it's worth doing the maths. At thirty-five pounds a kilo, and two vans running a day, I make that a retail value of something like two thousand quid *a day*. I know the pickers won't make that, but it gives you some idea of what it might be worth, and that's for three months, every year. And your costs are minimal. But you're right, Jackie, this can't just be about the samphire.

'What if it's just the opening skirmish in a much bigger confrontation? I think Stepney wants the coast like that . . .' Shaw showed them his hand balled into a fist. 'There's plenty of scams running from Hunstanton to Cromer – and a lot of wealthy people waiting to be parted from their cash. I think Stepney thinks this is his manor. It isn't. All right?'

Nods all round.

'The truth is someone's certainly happy for us to think this is about samphire. That's why they left the sprig of the stuff on the body, along with the clippers. It's the obvious motive, and that's why we're going to deal with it, but we have no real idea what we've got here yet. So keep an open mind – all of you.'

A uniformed PC appeared at the open door of the mobile incident room. The house-to-house team had radioed in and wanted a member of CID to attend at Marsh House, one of the 1950s villas beyond the sea wall.

ELEVEN

Shaw and Valentine, armed with a large-scale map courtesy of Paul Twine, walked the lane to the flood bank, climbed a sharp incline by an elegant war memorial, and then dropped down into the reclaimed marsh on the far side. The newer houses were in a variety of styles, from mock-Tudor to baronial. Outside one, a brick-built villa, they saw an elderly man leaning on an old-fashioned mower talking to a uniformed PC.

The call had come from a classic neo-Lutyens pile; a grand suburban villa, with double bay windows on the second floor which must offer a stunning vista across Overy Creek. It stood behind a wide gravel turning circle and a garden of shrubs and trees so perfectly pruned and tended it looked like a submission for the Chelsea Flower Show.

A PC was at the door, which was oak and embellished with iron studs, and a small copper nameplate reading MARSH HOUSE.

'Constable Boles,' said Shaw, recognizing one of St James' regular foot-sloggers. 'What we got?'

'One moment, sir. There's this,' said Valentine's voice behind them – the 'sir' a ritual nod to Shaw's rank when they were with the team.

Valentine stood beside a BMW parked on the drive; Series Eight, with leather interiors. Down on one knee, Valentine was examining the back rear wheel. Shaw retraced his steps and saw that the rubber of the tyre had been marked with a chalk mark at the apex of the circle – 'noon' if it had been a clock.

'Burglar's trick,' said Valentine. 'You pretend to deliver some mail, or just knock. If no one answers you mark the tyre. Come back a few days later and check it. If the chalk's still at the same point you know they've not used the car. Chances are the house is empty.'

PC Boles licked his lips. There was very little quite as annoying as being upstaged by CID, especially on scene-of-crime observations, more especially when he'd been standing at the door looking at the BMW for three hours.

'We knocked and got no answer,' said Boles quickly. 'It's a big house so one of the boys went round the back. Rear French windows were locked but he could see inside – evidence of burglary, pictures off the walls, papers and ornaments on the floor.

'Owner's away, but we tracked down a mobile from the newsagent in Burnham Market and spoke to a member of the family. The windows and doors are alarmed, but there's an old cellar for coal and it looks like they got in through that. There's a key safe here . . .' He indicated the small metal box bolted to the brickwork inside the porch, below it six rolling number wheels like a padlock on a bike. 'They let it out to friends, apparently.'

PC Boles showed Shaw the Yale key in his hand, attached to a wooden paddle etched with the name *Marsh House*.

'Anyone been inside?' asked Shaw.

'No, sir. There's an alarm keyboard. I've got the code.'

Shaw turned the Yale and swung the door open, stepping into the house. Boles followed him in and deactivated the alarm system. The hallway was panelled; a copper electric lantern like a church thurible hung over their heads. Shaw stood still for a moment as if memorizing details, whereas in fact he was reassessing the entire inquiry: what kind of inquiry? Burglary, murder or both?

'No post on the mat,' said Valentine behind him. There was a cherrywood table and the letters, free sheets and advertising fliers were neatly arranged in piles.

Shaw was aware of a radio playing: Radio Four, the measured BBC tones inimitable.

The kitchen could have accommodated Hugh Fearnley-Whittingstall and Rick Stein and their respective film crews. There were three bowls out for cats and all had fresh food in them. The blinds were up and the hob light on.

'And the owners said the house was empty?'

'Sir. They said they had someone who came in to feed the cats, check the place out. *Keeps an eye* – that's what they said.'

A door led into the house's main room, a mock medieval dining hall. The central table was polished wood and Shaw estimated its value at the best part of the national average wage. The roof had faux beams, and wooden shields with heraldic devices. Two walls – the end and one side – had a series of arched Gothic windows, while the other walls were solid. The largest blank wall was whitewashed stone and contained a Hollywood-scale fireplace with iron dragons holding up the grate. Over it had been daubed a slogan in black paint:

NEXT TIME YOU'LL COME HOME TO A REAL FIRE

'Subtle,' said Shaw. 'But hardly surprising. I wonder if arson is their next move, or just a threat. Forensics need to be here, and we could do with a complete set of pictures. Let's contact the owners and tell them what's happened. While we're on, get me a name for the friendly neighbour who pops in.'

'Pretty sophisticated,' offered Valentine. 'Lights on, radio – all standard anti-burglar stratagems. Hardly your average neighbour-hood watch.'

'Hardly the standard neighbourhood. Perhaps they do for each other,' said Shaw.

Boles lifted his lapel mike to his lips just as it buzzed with an incoming call. The hall filled with static, so he went outside to take it, leaving Shaw and Valentine alone.

'Thoughts?' asked Shaw.

'I don't believe in coincidences,' said Valentine. 'Nor did Jack.' It was a rare direct reference to Shaw's father. Valentine had known Shaw's father better than his son ever would.

'Still, coincidences happen,' said Shaw. 'Why would a bunch of house burglars-cum-political activists stray into murder?'

'How far precisely is it from Mitchell's Bank to this house?' asked Valentine. 'A thousand yards? This is north Norfolk, not Baltimore. There are three hundred burglaries a month in the whole of Norfolk. The entire county. And less than eight hundred violent crimes. And we're saying they both happened, on the same night, and there's no link?'

'There's no proof of a link, George. So for now we keep an open mind.' Shaw bent his neck back, craning to examine the heraldic shields carved into the roof beams. 'But to answer my own question, why burglars turn to murder, it's worth thinking through *their* motives. Are they local political activists who take the opportunity to lift some valuables, or are they burglars who can't resist making a political point? It seems to me there's an inherent tension between those two aims.'

He locked eyes with Valentine. 'Question is, George, is there enough tension to warrant murder? Did thieves fall out?'

Boles reappeared. 'Second break-in, sir. Next door.'

TWELVE

The Old School House, built after the sea wall was strengthened in 1948 – according to the plaque on the façade – had been converted into a seaside getaway. A grass field to one side was as smooth as a snooker table. Shaw could see, through the large, full-length original classroom windows, a lounge set around a Swedish wood-burner. Inside, the old parquet flooring rattled slightly under their feet as they made their way down a long corridor and into the main room, at one end of which hung a panelled board listing the head teachers of St John the Baptist's Junior School from 1901 to 1967.

Sgt Bill Cooper, the senior uniformed officer on site, was waiting for them by the stove, a boot up on the grate as if he owned the place.

'Bill. Place empty?' asked Shaw, checking his mobile for an elusive signal.

'We're trying to trace the people,' said Cooper. 'They didn't have anything delivered from the shop in Burnham Norton – that's the nearest. We're trying to track down the postman. The alarm's been disabled – wires cut. Council offices open in an hour, so we can always trace them from the council tax roll if all else fails.'

Second homeowners paid less than the full council tax, Shaw recalled, getting a discount of five per cent – although it had once been a whopping fifty per cent. The only way, it seemed, was up. Shaw wondered if the council would one day start charging *extra* for second homes. It seemed unlikely given that all the major parties strained to remain aspirational. Labour, he recalled from the last election, wanted a flat, equal rate.

'OK, Bill. Let Paul Twine know you're on it. Thanks. We'll just nose about.'

Dismissed, Cooper left them to it.

The room contained several items of memorabilia from the original school. A handbell on a rope hung from a metal stand.

Two wooden settles placed against one wall were engraved with the school name and the old council initials: BVDC – Burn Valley District Council. The blackboard had been left, fixed to the largest wall, where it would have faced the class, lit by the natural light flooding in through the windows.

This had proved too much of a temptation to the burglars.

DOMESDAY BOOK 1086
BURNHAM MARSH POP. 134
17 OCTOBER, 2014
BURNHAM MARSH POP. 0

Shaw considered the graffiti for a few moments, coming to the conclusion that the burglars might regret this particular inscription, because it potentially revealed so much: premeditation, education, erudition, and an ability to put together an effective polemic. Hardly the skill set of the average burglar. And that last line was surely a bit of propaganda – population *zero?* Could that be true? Shaw recalled that the second-home rate in north Norfolk was ten per cent, higher in some villagers. But a hundred per cent? For a start they'd seen the man with the mower outside the villa up by the seawall.

And then there was the date: October the seventeenth. The day their victim died out on Mitchell's Bank. It was getting increasingly difficult to keep these two cases apart.

If the village was empty they needed to get an overview of the number of break-ins. And they'd need forensic back-up quickly.

Shaw did a circuit of the kitchen, a boot room, the three bedrooms, a walk-in shower, and an office. He'd been to three other burglaries which they were treating as the work of the so-called Chelsea Burglars – two converted barns and an old windmill – so he had an idea of the gang's modus operandi. While they didn't treat the target properties with complete respect – drawers on the floor, pictures examined and discarded, wall safes hammered out – there was never anything wanton about the damage. They'd simply been in a hurry. He'd attended enough violated homes to know what burglars were capable of: precious ornaments smashed, food and drink half-consumed, pictures ripped out of frames, books pulled down from shelves. And worse, much worse. But the picture here was quite different. There was a measure of control, even restraint.

Back in the main room he found Valentine taking a note of the graffiti.

'Thoughts?'

'This line, about population zero – that's got to be bunk. We've seen at least two this morning. And there's a pub as well.'

THIRTEEN

The Ostrich was at the far end of the lane beyond the ruins of the church, built slightly into the sea-wall bank. It was whitewashed, with eggshell-blue window frames, and a sign showing a heraldic shield incorporating the eponymous exotic bird – a common local symbol along the coast, an echo of the Crusades. Shaw recalled a local newspaper story covering the sale of the business by Adnams, the brewers, to a village cooperative. A micro-brewery had started up in Burnham Deepdale and they took their 'Burnham Beers'. There were three picnic tables outside, and an A-board, chained to a drainpipe, advertising morning coffee, and a Monday night quiz.

Shaw thought he could remember sitting here with his father, watching the tide come in, his mother's mood hidden by a pair of reflective 1960s sunglasses. It was the view that had stuck: the narrow mouth of the creek, between Gun Hill and Scolt Head, revealing the open sea beyond. His father had produced a compass, a small brass antique, which he'd set on the table to show the arrow pointing directly through the gap to the magnetic Pole.

Valentine peered in through the bar window.

'Bar cloths over the pumps, spirit bottles on optics, so it's still in business.'

Shaw discovered a note in a glass cabinet screwed to the door:

> *Joe and Eve are sorry – The Ostrich is closed 16 Oct–7 Nov inclusive. We're off on our annual holidays. We'll be in Arles on the mobile if anyone wants us. If you phone we can't guarantee being sober! We will be bringing back a few cases of the Coulange '94. Be here for the grand reopening: 7.00 p.m., 8 Nov.*

Shaw was at the window too and saw something Valentine had missed. In the lounge bar there was a large tank of tropical fish, the air compressor producing several trails of bubbles, the water lit a lurid green. One fish – large and black with a white go-fast stripe – rose to the surface as Shaw watched and sucked in some food through a perfect O-mouth.

PC Boles appeared along the staithe with a clipboard.

'Just to let you know, sir. So far we've found three residents at home. Two came down yesterday – Saturday afternoon. One – the elderly gardener – arrived at dawn this morning from London. Apparently he can do it in two hours ten minutes from Marble Arch if he lets the Bentley out full-throttle.'

'No one here Friday night?'

'Nothing so far.'

Valentine set off to organize a thorough inventory of all the village properties, and a 'census' for the nights of the seventeenth and eighteenth of October.

Shaw's brain needed clearing so he walked down the quay towards the church. The penultimate house on the harbourside was called Overy View, a fine piece of naval architecture, with double bay windows on two floors, facing directly on to the track. Inside the first he could see the remains of a party: cans on the floor, a full ashtray, cushions scattered and the remains of a takeaway meal – silver cartons in the hearth, plates smeared with a virulent sauce. The knocker was brass, in the shape of a dolphin. As soon as he heard the sound echo inside he knew he was out of luck. Flipping up the letterbox he could see the hall. A carpet, brass rods on the stairs, a pair of socks discarded halfway up. No – not a pair. One white, one blue.

He waited thirty seconds then checked in the other bay window to find a sharp contrast to the first: a library, with a polished table, a silver pepper and salt set precisely at the centre. He knocked three times again to be sure, checked the upstairs net curtains for movement, and gave up.

The church ruins were partly lost in a nest of ivy. The nave had collapsed long ago, leaving just the south-facing wall, and a few shattered Gothic windowsills. By contrast the west end remained almost intact, although the tracery of the great west window encompassed fresh air, not stained glass. And the tower still stood, and was open underneath, so that Shaw could look up into the interior, and a square of sky. An exterior steel staircase had been put up to give access to what looked like a small electronic weather station. Wires ran up to a small anemometer mounted on the tower. Shaw climbed to the first landing, where a gate barred the way further up to the summit.

He looked down on Burnham Marsh.

He saw now that there was one house beyond the church: a large, rambling pile of stone in several styles with all its windows shuttered. Just beyond it was a small dock running in off the beach into a wooden boathouse. There was a flagpole, but no flag. The garden had once been tended but was now run to seed. Of all the houses he'd seen this looked the most lived-in, but also the most deserted. The paintwork was slightly peeling, the lawn patchy.

He twisted on the metal platform and looked back at the rest of Burnham Marsh. Had it really been a ghost village on the night of the seventeenth of October? There were a few 'lost villages' on the coast – abandoned during the plague, torn down by landowners wanting to graze sheep, or cleared to enhance the view from one of the new Georgian country houses. But this was a lost village of second homes, a twenty-first-century lost village, like thousands of others in France, and Hungary, and Italy, and Spain – abandoned by a generation, except for a few days a year when the rich descended to walk their dogs, enjoy the cool mountain air or play on the beach. Such places were rare in England. Burnham Marsh, perhaps, was the shape of things to come.

At the bottom of the steps Shaw realized he'd missed another sample of graffiti. On the surviving south wall was a series of gravestones and memorials to which someone had added in spray-can black:

BURNHAM MARSH

1000–2014

RIP

FOURTEEN

They were back on the coast road, heading for the autopsy at the Ark, when Valentine, ahead of Shaw, flashed the warning lights of the Mazda, signalled left and turned off the coast road, running inland. After a mile they came to six post-war council houses on one side: three pairs of semis, big and dull, and in the wrong kind of brick, as if a small section of suburbia had been accidentally dropped on the north Norfolk hills. A stone plaque in the façade of the middle set said they'd been built in 1957. The gardens were smart – all except one, which had an old bath in it and a collection of children's three-wheelers.

Valentine was out of the Mazda before Shaw brought the Porsche to a halt.

'Sorry, Peter. Someone you should meet. Five minutes, tops. Believe me, this can help.'

The DS set off up the path of the last semi, a cigarette already lit between his lips.

'George Bloody Valentine,' said the man who opened the door of number 6. 'Still alive. Pickled or smoked – which one is it?'

They could see an Alsatian in the hallway, muzzled and chained to the newel post. Upstairs a radio was playing Classic FM, but was quickly switched off. As Shaw went into the front room he heard a rhythmic mechanical breathing from above, as if they'd got a dragon up there, and it was curled up on the landing at the top of the stairs.

'DI Peter Shaw,' said Valentine. 'Meet Geoff Wighton – formerly DS Wighton, stationed at Wells.'

'Geoff,' said Shaw. He wondered if he'd known Jack Shaw too, but decided to let him make the connection if he had.

The front and back rooms of the house had been knocked through and turned into a gym. There was an exercise bike, a rowing machine, some weights. On the mantelpiece stood a picture of Wighton at the tiller of a clinker-built sailing boat, above it a watercolour of a tea clipper at sea. Wighton was fleshy, maybe thirteen stone, short and broad, but with plenty of muscle to leaven the fat. Shaw guessed he was in his fifties, but his complexion didn't augur well for his sixties: his cheeks were that dead shade of red, like cold roast beef.

Wighton had a towel round his neck, the ends hanging down, and he pulled one, then the other, as if slowly drying the back of his neck. Shaw noted his fists, which were heavy and knuckled, like the claw on a mechanical digger. If DS Wighton had given you a clip round the ear you'd stay clipped.

'George rang and he thinks I can help,' said Wighton, backing into the centre of the room. 'I chucked in *The Job* a few years back – now I babysit second homes. Three are down at Burnham Marsh, so it looks like I might have some disgruntled customers.' Overhead they heard something fall to the floor, but Wighton didn't react. A book perhaps, or a slipper.

Valentine asked him to outline his business.

In 2009, when he left the force, Wighton dropped a thousand business cards through letterboxes in the Burn Valley. How had he chosen them? Touring villages in his van he looked at the properties with a burglar's eyes: anything behind walls, with security systems, key boxes, manicured gardens, flagpoles, boat-houses, double garages, pretentious little plaques with names etched on slate, BMWs, or 4×4s, Bentleys. Or two cars or more, especially if one of them was the new Mini Cooper with the go-fast stripe over the roof.

If they called back, or emailed, or sent a text, he'd go round for an interview. That's when he asked them questions, not the other way round, because there were some things he didn't do, like teenager-sitting, or cooking, or taking diverted calls from the house number, or just 'keeping an eye on the place' for three bob a week. He had his own life to lead, and while the police pension was very handy, he needed to use his time efficiently.

His 'do' list was, however, extensive: he'd feed cats, walk dogs, clean out fish tanks, change bird-feeders, take deliveries, supervise tradesmen (a very popular offer – why spend your two-week summer holiday waiting for a plumber to turn up on July rates when he could do the waiting on cut-price winter tariffs?). He offered a simple *elite* package that included a daily visit, a quick check of all doors and windows, all boundaries. Lights could be left on, switched off, radios too, or even TVs – a very effective anti-burglar ploy. There were separate rates for actually staying in the property – usually one night a week, but occasionally for an extended period of up to a month.

'Then there's the call-out service. A lot of these properties have an alarm system which is linked to a call centre. They then ring the owners. My name can go first – so I get to react, check it out, then bother the owners if needs be. Most of the time it's a cat, or the wind, or a trapped bird. So that saves them a lot of hassle – and that's what they're paying me for, to take the hassle.'

Wighton walked to a wooden cupboard mounted on the wall and used a code to open a steel hinge lock. There were sets of keys hung on hooks but no house names or numbers – just letters, A–Z.

'And you've three clients in Burnham Marsh?'

'Yeah – worse luck. There's Spithead House, down past the church. They're in Japan for four months. They've just bought the place anyway, with plans to modernize, which is a shame, but there you go. I stay once a week, visit one other day. A conservatory's on the to-do list as well, and I'll be on site most days over New Year and into the spring.'

So that explained what Shaw had noted: the former owners had probably actually lived in Spithead House. Now it awaited its transformation into a second home.

'Then there's Overy View, almost next door. The Todds. Nice family. Then over the sea wall there's Wisteria Cottage – although it's got fifteen rooms, so hardly a cot. I'm on call for them, but they've just got audible alarms. I drop in once a week – sometimes more. If they're coming up they let me know and I make myself scarce. So three – none with an external security link.'

'The rest will be with other firms?' asked Shaw.

'Maybe. A lot still rely on deterrence: a big wall, iron gates, and a flashy alarm system on the outside, with boxes and lights. If the alarm actually goes off it can be very effective, because other second homeowners get jumpy and ring us – sorry, you. It's not like a city street, where there's loads of noise. Out here, a bell rings, someone jumps.'

'Not in Burnham Marsh, they don't,' said Shaw. 'Not last

Friday night, anyway. Looks like the village was empty – nobody
at all. Population zero. And it's two miles from the road, three
from Burnham Norton.'

'The alarms cut out after a fixed period, usually an hour. Were
they triggered?' asked Wighton.

'We're checking that out,' said Valentine, hoping they were.

There was something of the salesman about Wighton, thought
Shaw, and a cynical edge, which was unappealing. In a monied
world he'd found a way of cashing in forty years' worth of being
a copper. This should have been admirable, but Shaw found it,
conversely, vaguely disloyal to the service. It wasn't poacher
turned gamekeeper, but it was on the way.

'And all this happened when?' asked Wighton.

'Friday night, we think – late. One of your days in the village?'
asked Shaw.

'Yeah. I did all three Friday – but in the morning. I'd have
been back tomorrow. I stay Monday nights at Spithead House.
Check it out Friday – like I said. So sorry – not on the scene
when you needed me.'

There was a sudden snatch of speech from above, nightmarish
and garbled.

Something like irritation flitted across Wighton's face. 'Excuse
me a moment.' He climbed the stairs, but not in a hurry, and
they heard a brief conversation.

Shaw caught Valentine's eye. 'Wife?'

'Emphysema,' he said. 'She's bad, but she's been bad for
years.'

They heard Wighton's footsteps descending.

'We better be going,' said Shaw. 'But to be clear: who else
has this kind of inside knowledge, other than you, and those in
the same business?'

Wighton walked to the window and looked out over the open
fields which faced the line of semis. A tractor ploughed a furrow
on a hill, trailed by seagulls.

'Who else knows what I know? You gotta think there's two
markets out there,' he said. 'There's rented stuff – that's different.
The agencies run them. It's unpredictable – and there's not that
much in 'em anyway. Hardly a burglar's paradise, is it? Cutlery,
a TV, bed linen. The second-home market is pretty distinct

although a lot do "mates' rates" for friends. But they're going to be about, at most, twenty weekends a year and maybe three weeks in summer, one at Easter, one at Christmas–New Year. So the people who know are the people who provide services: local pubs, restaurants, takeaways, newsagents, village shops. Then the trades: boilermen, carpenters, builders – especially builders.'

'Thanks,' said Shaw, offering his hand. 'That's given us a real insight into the business.'

Wighton shrugged, patting the Alsatian out in the hall. 'Personally, I think it's all crap. When it comes to security, you can't beat a decent set of locks and a bloody great dog.'

FIFTEEN

Max Warren's office was on the fifth floor of St James' and looked out on Greyfriars Tower, part of the Franciscan priory ruins. With its infamous tilt of six degrees off the vertical it was down-at-heel Lynn's answer to Pisa. Briefly famous thanks to the BBC's *Restoration* series, the tower's principal role was now to offer a home to the town's pigeons. The birds tended to cluster on Warren's windowsill, shuffling and scratching. As Shaw sat in the secretary's office facing the nameplate reading *Chief Constable*, he reflected that Warren had done well to avoid – no doubt following protracted discussions – the withering prefix *acting*.

Warren opened his own door. 'There you are,' he said. 'I hope this isn't bad news, Peter, especially on a fucking Sunday.'

Or any news at all, thought Shaw. Warren had thirteen months left before he handed over to his successor, and if he managed to negotiate that period of time without disaster he'd be Sir Max Warren – not bad for a kid who'd left school in Shepherd's Bush without a school certificate. More to the point, it would be Lady Margaret Warren. Glittering prizes for them both, and now those trophies were within their grasp, they were quietly determined not to give them up.

Warren had no neck, plump butcher's fingers, and a chest admirably suited to the chief constable's uniform. He'd come north from the Met in the 1990s to help clean up West Norfolk after a series of PR disasters – one of which was the failure of Shaw's father, in partnership with George Valentine – to secure a conviction in a high-profile child murder case. The judge had implied that the pair might even have been tempted to plant evidence during the investigation, a suggestion that had ended Jack Shaw's career and led to Valentine's banishment to rural policing for a decade. Shaw Senior and Valentine were the problem then, and Max Warren had been the answer.

Jack Shaw, bedridden with the cancer that had finally killed

him, had once told his son that it gave him some lingering pleasure
to imagine Warren in retirement, guarding his bungalow garden
in Sheringham from raids launched by local kids with an eye on
his gnomes. It was a cruel caricature, but there was no doubt
Warren, who'd arrived tough and streetwise, had rapidly gone to
bureaucratic seed. Jack Shaw's name had ultimately been cleared
of any corruption – as had George Valentine's – but Shaw's father
had died under a cloud. Warren, by contrast, was looking forward
to his own parking space at the golf club, marked with simple
understatement: *Sir Max.*

Shaw didn't sit down. He'd made that mistake once before
and learnt his lesson.

'Take a seat, Peter. But first off, shut the sodding door.'

Warren sat like a Buddha, his perfectly ironed shirt pressed
up against the edge of the desk.

'I've got twenty minutes before I have to get a train to London.
Meeting with the Home Secretary at seven-thirty tomorrow
morning. A brief update would be delightful. I'm presuming we
have a murder inquiry on our hands.'

There was a tapping at the window as pigeons flew in, crowding
along the ledge. Shaw recalled that the collective noun for pigeons
was a 'kit', but he decided this item of trivia was unlikely to
brighten the chief constable's day.

Shaw had learnt one thing from his father: how to avoid being
intimidated by authority. He took a deep breath. 'I wanted to see
you because I don't think it's feasible to keep a lid on the second-
homes story, sir. The murder at Overy Creek is almost certainly
linked to a series of burglaries at Burnham Marsh. Not a few
houses, sir; the entire village – seventeen properties. Political
slogans have been left in several.'

Shaw had decided on this tactic in order to make it quite clear,
when the story broke in tomorrow's local paper, that he and
Valentine were innocent of the leak.

'Fucking hell,' said Warren, his neck reddening instantly. 'Tell
me. The murder's linked – you're sure?'

'No. Not sure. As I said – almost certainly linked. I'd like to
proceed with building an ID picture from a statement we have
from a witness – a woman who saw one of the burglars up close.
I'd like to interview her, see what other facial details she can

recall beyond the bald outline she's given. That would give us a good start with the media – the face, in three-D.'

Warren had started stubbing one of his black brogues against his desk so that the surface of a cup of tea he had before him filled with concentric rings.

'There has also been a development. An escalation,' Shaw added. 'The burglars left a threat. Next time, they implied, arson is on the menu. I'm sure the expression "come home to a real fire" needs no further elaboration from me, sir.'

'Oh, shite,' said Warren, standing up so quickly his chair toppled over.

He left it lying on the carpet and went to the window, pushing one side open and lunging at the pigeons.

Abandoning the birds, he turned back to Shaw. 'This is not going to happen here. Not on my watch, Peter. They're bluffing.'

'If you say so, sir.'

'Don't be fucking cute, Peter. Anyway, things are slightly out of our hands on the media front. Bob Bartlett asked to see me last night at his office, impertinent little tosser that he is. The paper's got the story, pretty much. If he wanted to he could run it tomorrow. The upshot is I've offered him the lot – pictures, interviews, the works. Entire thing done up in sodding wrapping paper like a Christmas present. It'll run a week tomorrow. That gives you a week to catch the bastards. Once we arrest someone Bartlett can run the stuff next edition – but at least we don't look like a bunch of pricks. You can have any manpower you want; forensic budget is yours to blow.'

Shaw didn't move a muscle.

'Would you like to know why I have taken this course of action, Peter?'

'Sir.'

'Bob came to me with these,' said Warren. He flipped open a manila file on his blotter, then splayed a set of black-and-white photocopies with his fat fingers. They were the scene-of-crime pictures from several of the earlier break-ins where slogans had been left on walls.

Shaw tried to look interested and shocked, but given he'd passed these same prints on to Valentine to leak to the paper in the first place he was struggling not to look smug.

'Source?' he asked.

'Good question.' Warren put a finger on the nearest black-and-white forensic picture. 'I hope and trust the Marsham Street "fingerprint" – if I can call it that – means what it appears to mean: that this is a problem for the smarmy public school bastards who comprise most of the sodding Civil Service. Either way, it is extremely urgent that we resolve this case. By urgent I mean *within days.*'

'And the rag's going to keep it, is it? Not flog it to Fleet Street?'

The thought of this story on the front page of the *Telegraph*, copies left beside members' chairs in the Carlton and the Reform, and the Commons tea rooms, prompted Warren to cover his face in his hands. Shaw got the strong impression the chief constable was making a conscious effort to regulate his breathing.

'Yes. I told Bartlett that we were close to an arrest and that any publicity would endanger the operation. I said if he went ahead tomorrow, as he planned, I would make a statement to the effect that he'd blown our chances of catching the Chelsea Burglars. And, as I said, I offered him the inside track and plenty of official quotes from me, not to mention a paragraph from the Home Secretary herself. That did it. He can smell a media award. He's an ambitious little bastard.'

'That leaves us seven days. I wanted a month. It was as good as I could get. Apparently the source is a London hack with contacts in the Home Office, works for the *Guardian*. He's prepared to hold off until a week on Tuesday – not that it's a blistering national scoop. Not yet, anyway. But if one of these jokers does light a fire, who knows? TV, nationals, radio. We'll be up to our fucking armpits with the scum.'

Shaw didn't respond. Warren's skin colour was high. Shaw was no doctor but even he could diagnose a blood pressure problem. Perhaps he wouldn't live long enough to see Buckingham Palace.

'Is George pulling his weight on this?' asked the chief constable. 'Do you need a decent DS to bolster the team?'

'There isn't a better DS on the force,' said Shaw. It was the loyal thing to say, and it was the truth, so he put some genuine feeling behind the answer. Valentine and Warren had what could only be described as a strictly professional relationship. They hated each other with a passion. Valentine had a way of looking through the chief constable which was tantamount to insubordination.

'Also,' continued Shaw, 'this is George's manor – he spent ten years out at Wells. He knows every village, every farmhouse.'

'Every pub.'

'He's pulling his weight, sir, every last ounce of it.'

Shaw smiled. The reference to weight was a sly one. Warren was sixteen stone and gaining. If anyone on the force wasn't pulling their weight it was the chief constable.

'Right. No excuses then. What happens next? Is the victim one of the burglars?'

'Too early to say. Although there is some circumstantial evidence. That's down to George, by the way. Victim had an old credit card in his shirt-front pocket. One side worn. Apparently it's standard equipment for burglars – you run it down the door jamb and it can spring a lock. One movement.'

Shaw sliced the air with his right hand as a chopper.

'I'm going to split the inquiry into two,' he said. 'It's just possible the murder is not associated with the burglaries. We have to keep an open mind. So one half of the team looks for the killer – concentrating on the victim, CCTV, suspects, the samphire trade. I think you're aware of the background on that . . .'

Warren nodded.

'If it turns out the dead man is a samphire picker then maybe he was killed by local low-life from Lynn. There's a bunch of ex-East End thugs on the patch. We know where they live. We'll pull them in and get some warrants.

'However, I think it's much more likely the murder and burglaries are linked,' Shaw continued. 'Maybe the thieves fell out – over the spoils, or over politics. Perhaps the village wasn't entirely empty that night and the victim is a resident, or someone who came upon the burglars by accident: a delivery man, a gardener, a tradesman.

'So while one half of the team concentrates on Mitchell's Bank and the victim, the other half looks for the burglars. George and I will monitor both halves of the inquiry and wait to see if they meet in the middle.'

'Don't wait too long, Peter. Your father's career ended thanks to one irritating case. I for one would be very sad to see it happen again.'

Shaw considered reaching across the chief constable's desk and grabbing his golf club tie, although odds-on it was of the irritating clip-on variety. Instead, he considered the reality of the situation. If this case hit the press unsolved it was Warren's career that might end in ignominy. Keeping it out of the media had been a poor decision. It begged the big question: why had the news blackout been ordered? There was no doubt Warren could come up with answers to that question. The fact that he had tried to sweep an embarrassing case under the carpet might be over-looked. But what if a fire was the next step? What if someone got hurt?

Shaw was perfectly happy to leave the chief constable to wrestle with such issues.

'I'd better get to work then, sir,' he said, standing, mustering his best surfer's smile. 'Give my regards to the Home Secretary.' He breezed out, leaving the door open.

SIXTEEN

The CCTV suite was in the basement of St James', an annexe to the old records room. This had been Mark Birley's lightless kingdom for the last twelve hours. Given that Birley spent most of his spare time outside, either on the training field or on the rugby pitch, this represented a kind of torture. To alleviate the physical tension he'd brought a gizmo that he could fit across the door jamb which allowed him to do pull-ups. Batches of one hundred did the trick, with the occasional one-fifty to get his heart thumping.

Early on that morning he'd sat down and rung the National Trust to request a download of the digital film from the Gun Hill webcam. The camera was live twenty-four hours a day, although the night-time footage was never checked. A copy was kept on the server at the Trust's headquarters. A team from Essex University who were trying to put a number on the grey seal population for the North Sea had open access to the footage.

Within an hour Birley had a downloaded digital version covering the three days up to and including the seventeenth of October, and for the eighteenth.

After one hundred pull-ups he sat down to view his first one-hour section. He stuck to daytime footage and viewed it at four times 'real time', stopping and starting to note boats, walkers, bird watchers, kite flyers, and pretty much anything else that moved. He created an online log.

The night-time footage required a different level of concentration. He developed a technique for watching this footage at a higher speed. The webcam's single static view encompassed four navigation lights in the channel – two green and two red. To this could be added three constant security lights which shone from separate properties on the quayside at Burnham Marsh, and the general light pollution from Burnham Overy Staithe – a combination of several lights, and occasional passing traffic on the coast road. If he sat, alert, directly in front of the CCTV main screen, he could watch the image at ten times the normal speed. Any new light would create a visual blip – an obscured light would flash.

A brief, fluttering interruption was almost certainly a bird – either in flight close to the light source, or crossing in front of the webcam lens on Gun Hill itself. Atmospheric disturbance – rain, hail, mist – was the second most likely cause. In the run-up to the night of the murder there had been several storms, including violent downpours of hail, which had obscured all lights. With the onshore storms, gusts of wind of up to fifty mph created waves which rocked the navigation lights, interrupting the light beams.

On the night of the seventeenth of October – the night the victim died – the weather was calm. The lights were largely constant. Birley sat, drinking espresso in double measures, watching the eight hours of night-time film at ten times normal speed. He watched it three times with one hundred pull-ups between each sitting. On the third run-through he'd seen one of the Burnham Marsh lights blink out. He'd missed it first time, and second time, because it wasn't actually a blink at all. It went out, stayed out for about five seconds then came back on. He isolated the footage to a few minutes either side of this single incident, creating a length of film thirty minutes long in real time. Watching this he noted that both the navigation buoys in the channel also blanked out for almost exactly the same time interval: to be precise, 5.6–5.8 seconds. The three light breaks ran serially from west to east – first the security light, then the green light, then the red light.

There was only one explanation. A boat, unseen, was moving, without lights, across the webcam picture from the village towards the open sea. The on-screen clock timed this mysterious voyage at between 2.06 a.m. and 2.18 a.m. The length of the boat and its constant speed meant that each time it interrupted the light source it did so for almost exactly the same length of time.

Birley tried to think clearly about what he'd found. If he'd identified a boat leaving Burnham Marsh then it meant that the daytime film must show it entering, *not* leaving. So he sat down and logged all the boats entering between Gun Hill and Scolt Head that turned west towards Burnham Marsh. Some of the yachts, and all the small fishing boats, had large painted registration numbers – mostly indicating that their home ports were Lynn, Cromer, Boston or Grimsby. Most left on the next available tide.

Except one, which had arrived on the morning of the seventeenth of October. At a speed of eight knots it had slipped under Gun Hill at 10.36 a.m. The cabin area was covered and so he couldn't see the man – or woman – at the wheel. And it undoubtedly had a wheel – no doubt in pine, with brass fittings, to match the rest of the boat: a classic sloop, sails furled, wooden, polished, immaculate. Whoever was at the helm knew their way around Overy Creek. The boat turned sharp to port then followed the buoyage towards Burnham Marsh, passing an inundated Mitchell's Bank fifty yards to the north. The static webcam image lost sight of the boat as it began to thread a way through the small yachts moored off the staithe.

Which raised one last possibility – the boat was *still* at Burnham Marsh. Birley had a file of shots taken from the staithe at Burnham Marsh that morning. All the vessels shown in the shallows were yachts. No sight of the sloop.

Which left one logical conclusion.

Finally, he got the best image and magnified it. There was no ugly painted registration on the side, but there was a nameplate: brass by the look of it, but even at times twenty he couldn't read the name. He tried times thirty and the screen disintegrated into a jumble of pixels.

He copied the image and attached it to an email for Peter Shaw, with copies to Valentine and Twine.

Sir,

This boat came in from the open sea on the morning of Friday, 17 October. There is no daylight record of it leaving on the webcam and it's not in the harbour now. The night-time footage shows a vessel leaving – without lights – at 2.00 a.m. on the morning of 18 October. The speed is constant, so I don't think it is possible that it stopped long enough for the body of the victim to be offloaded. It could, however, have been dumped from the moving vessel. I've found boats like it online – apparently it's a 'carvel' in shape, and I can just about make out the rig at the back – that's an auto-pilot. Prices start at £150,000 for such a vessel, and then go upwards. Bad news is there's no regis-tration and no discernible name. I've emailed the pic to the harbour masters along the coast.

Mark

PS. Final thought. Is there a boathouse at Burnham Marsh?

SEVENTEEN

The Ark, West Norfolk's forensic lab and mortuary, was in an old nonconformist chapel behind St James'. The exterior was disfigured by a large extractor pipe in aluminium which rivalled the original Victorian bell tower. Inside, the simple nave was divided by a wooden half-partition, with glass completing the wall up to the wooden rafters. Tom Hadden's kingdom – the forensic suite – consisted of half a dozen 'hot desk' bays, a small, windowless photographic lab, and a full-length ballistic tube for firing and analysing bullets. Beyond the partition lay three fully equipped mortuary bays. The wooden partition was low enough to reveal if any of the tables was occupied. Valentine's eye caught the unmistakable clay-grey of dead flesh.

There was very little of the original church architecture left within the interior except for a single stone angel, in a niche in the end wall above the mortuary tables, which held its hands to its face, weeping, as if unable – like George Valentine – to consider the bodies of the dead, laid out so coldly below.

There was a sharp tap on the partition: a diamond ring striking the glass. Dr Justina Kazimeirz, the pathologist, was beckoning them into her world. Mid-fifties, stolid, a Polish immigrant who'd arrived in the eighties and eventually applied for citizenship. At first Shaw had put her brisk rudeness down to difficulties with the language, but Kazimeirz was simply impatient with the faults of others. She'd mellowed slightly since the recent, untimely death of her husband, Dawid. In the final months of his illness she'd taken a cottage in the dunes behind the Shaws' café at Old Hunstanton and become a friend of the family. This friendship had been created, as they often are, by one casual, unplanned visit. The pathologist had left her husband sitting in the dunes on a dull winter's day and gone swimming, suited up, beginning an obsession with what the trendy magazines now called 'wild swimming'. The sleek black suit had been undermined by a swimming hat of blue with white daises on it like floral barnacles.

As she walked, heavy-legged, out of the surf Shaw had met her with a flask of hot sweet tea, and then taken the couple back to meet Lena and Fran. The swim became a ritual, the tea routine.

Now, taking Justina's hand briefly, he thought he could smell sea salt on her skin.

Valentine edged into the room and stood back six feet from the mortuary table which held the victim. There was a clock in the mortuary below the angel, the one he'd used before to divert his mind and his eyes: big enough for a railway platform, with Roman numerals and a juddering minute hand, plus a sweeping red second hand. Lots to watch, plenty of movement to distract him from the butchery.

Shaw stood beside the dead man's head. The neck wound gaped and seemed more brutal than it had when the face had been caked in the ink-black mud and dried blood. It was as if someone had taken a butcher's cleaver to the spine: a single blow, revealing dead meat and bone. It was an extraordinary wound, and one unprecedented in Shaw's ten-year career.

'Some luck, I think,' said the pathologist. 'And I haven't even drawn my knife.' She smiled sweetly at Valentine.

The corpse was naked. Shaw had never quite seen the logic for this. The cause of death was clear and the pathologist had already completed an external examination of the body, so why did the victim's dignity not stretch to a simple white sheet?

Kazimcirz lifted the left arm and twisted it slightly. Rigor had long passed; the movement of wrist and elbow was easy, if not fluid.

There was a tattoo on the bicep, high enough to be hidden by a short-sleeved shirt. A white flag striped red flew from a flagpole, the letters KSC forming the background in red.

'KS Cracovia,' she said. 'Oldest football club in Poland. Krakow's other football team. This is common of a certain class in Poland, as here.'

Valentine sniffed.

'A Pole?' asked Shaw. 'Right – well, that's awkward. We'd rather discounted the original theory behind the killing: that this was a clash between local samphire pickers and interlopers from Lynn. The gangmaster hires Poles to run the boats. So that's not good news, as I say. That takes us back a step.'

Kazimeirz shrugged. 'I wish I could not be awkward. But there it is.'

A set of knives and saws waited on a tray. She let her fingers dance over the hilts.

'Heavy smoker, also. I found, incidentally, a few stubs in his pocket. Either he saved them to roll a cigarette from the butts, or he was careful about not dropping them. The brand name is Zenit – common also in Poland, but Russian made and therefore common also in Eastern Europe.'

Kazimeirz circled the table.

'A thirty-five- to forty-five-year-old adult male. Heavy muscle development. There is significant scarring to the hands which I would say was typical of – what? Working on a farm, working on a ship, anywhere with heavy machinery out of doors, I think. The skin itself is heavily weathered.'

'A fisherman,' said Shaw bleakly. If this was one of John Jack Stepney's Polish captains he wondered what kind of reprisal would be forthcoming.

Kazimeirz didn't bite.

She parted the hair on the left side of the skull to reveal a bruise. 'This happened before the blow that killed him,' she said. 'Certainly he was alive. An incapacitating blow, certainly, but not fatal. Timing? A few minutes before he died, or a few hours? The science does not help us, I'm afraid. We can say only that it was before.'

Coming round the table she inserted a spatula in the neck wound: 'I think this is the cause of death. Obvious, yes. But also intriguing. You see, this isn't easy . . .' She held the skull with both hands and turned it so that the cleft of the cut was fully revealed. Valentine watched the second hand on its rhythmic journey past twenty-five, towards half past and onwards.

'Think of this,' she said. She picked up an umbrella which stood by her desk, took two steps towards Valentine and swung it like a weapon at his upper body.

'George does what anyone would do,' she said. 'He takes a step back, so that he would be moving *away* from the weapon when it struck. This radically reduces the force of the blow. Also, because I was stationary as I delivered the blow, his movement took him beyond the arc of the falling weapon, so that it was delivered by my extended arm – again, reducing the impact.

'Further, in this case the killer blow is, I believe, delivered from the front. We can see this from the angle of the wound. The victim must have been able to take evasive action. And yet the blow is a devastating one – slicing through the neck muscles, the bone. To deliver this blow I have to do this . . .'

She stood back and raised the umbrella until it was behind her head. 'The problem is obvious. If you do this then the victim has several seconds to retreat, or indeed, attack – coming in under the swinging arm which must also have been hampered by the weight of the murder weapon. This man did not die beneath an umbrella, of course. A shovel, perhaps.'

'Nothing else?' asked Shaw, trying to see the moment of death.

'No. A spade, I think. A flat, traditional digging spade, but perhaps half-size – a woman's model.'

'Sorry?' said Valentine. 'A woman's spade – what's that?'

'To do this with a full-sized spade would take extraordinary strength – and a strangely cooperative victim. Not impossible, but unlikely. A lot of men use half-sized spades. They are lighter, and you end up lifting a lot less weight each time you haul up earth, or mud, or peat, or whatever is being dug over. So they're very popular. Next time you pass these smallholdings . . .' she searched for the exact word, '. . . allotments, look at those working and what they use. A woman's spade. Dawid had one – even if it hurt his pride a little bit.'

Shaw was trying to see the picture the pathologist was describing. He'd worked with Kazimeirz for more than five years and he knew how she worked: it was her job to give him facts, his to speculate.

'There's one way this could work,' he said. 'The victim was tied up, restrained, unconscious?'

'Not unconscious, unless his head was held up for the blow.'

'He was standing?' asked Valentine.

'Upright. Sitting, standing, kneeling, perhaps – the angle of the blow is difficult to calculate. But maybe kneeling. If he was held, those holding were very close to the blow too. Very close.'

'But tied to something,' persisted Shaw. 'Because the body did not move in anticipation of the blow. So perhaps he died somewhere else, and then got dragged out to the sandbar, or dumped from a boat?'

Mark Birley had briefed them on the results of the webcam sweep in the CCTV suite. The team knew now that it was possible a boat was involved in the crimes of that night.

'Perhaps the first blow, to the side of the skull, knocked him out, and then when he woke up he was tied up?' said Shaw. 'That works.'

'Yes. Possibly. But there is no physical evidence of a boat. No rope threads, no paint, no grease, no oil. But yes, possibly . . .'

Which was good enough for Valentine. 'The gang could have fallen out during the burglary,' he said. 'The raid's well organized. Do they each take a house? One of them strikes lucky – jewellery, cash, something portable. They must plan on pooling the stolen goods – perhaps this guy tried to keep it all to himself. He gets found out, tries to run for it. Anyway, they catch him, and that's when he gets smacked on the skull.

'When he comes round there's a summary trial and execution, and then they dump the body out on Mitchell's Bank to make it look like something else. The scissors and the sprig or two of woody samphire are designed to make us think it's not connected to the burglary. Exit by boat.'

'So it's a coincidence he's a Pole? And he's not one of John Jack Stepney's hired men?' asked Shaw.

'Samphire's out of season – you said so yourself. He lays the men off in the winter. Why wouldn't they be thieves?'

Valentine sucked on an unlit cigarette and began tapping out a text on his mobile, walking back through the swing plastic sheet doors into the forensic lab.

Shaw let him go. There were fifteen burglaries in the file with political slogans found at the scene. None of them had been on the coast. The idea that the gang was a bunch of twenty-first-century pirates arriving by boat was, until further evidence was found, pure fantasy. However, it was a fantasy which had got George Valentine out of the room just in time.

Kazimeirz lifted a knife and pressed a gloved hand down on the victim's chest, splaying her fingers.

EIGHTEEN

Valentine parked the Mazda on the harbour a foot from the edge and stood for a moment watching kids try to catch crabs in the dusk. A cherry-red sunset marked the end of another Indian summer's day. Wells-next-the-Sea was the closest the north Norfolk coast ever got to kiss-me-quick seaside entertainment. Flashing lights from the three amusement arcades were reflected in the water. Somewhere a Victorian clown laughed in a stagey horror-show cackle. The aroma of melted sugar hung in the air from John's Rock Shop. The tide was up, nearly brim-full, a foot from flooding. A few ghostly yachts rode at anchor in the channel, while beyond them the sea marshes lurked in an early evening mist.

In the long decade of Valentine's banishment from CID at St James' he'd lived in Wells: a flat over a second-hand bookshop in the little high street. With the house on Greenland Street rented out, he tried not to visit Julie's grave more than once a week. Instead, he found he could talk to her here, sitting on the harbour wall. The Ship was his local, although he was known by name (and rank) in the town's other five pubs.

But he wasn't here to talk to Julie tonight.

Wells was a town caught between two worlds – the old Norfolk coast and the new world of the incomers. Most of the pubs had jumped one way or the other – the Nelson, up on the green, was now serving scallops and Sandringham lamb, and beer at £3.70 a pint. In the Balloon, by contrast, the landlord was moving the tables to one side to make room for the first darts match of the winter: kitchen closed, and beer at £2.50. The Ship trod a more subtle line, due to its prime position on the harbour. It was the unofficial headquarters of the town's fishing fleet, and the locals who ran the amusements and shops, but on a good evening, with a livid sunset smeared across the horizon, it drew in visitors, keen to sit and watch the bustle on the water.

Valentine was half an hour early but Jan Clay was already

there, and like any decent copper's wife she'd chosen the seat
by the side of the bay window, which had a good view of the
bar and out to the harbourside. She was in her late forties, neat,
compact, with blonde hair cut short so that it always seemed to
fall in the right place.

'Georgie,' she said, adjusting an empty wine glass.

Valentine nodded at the drink and she nodded back quickly.

At the bar he felt the familiar prickling of hair at the back of
his neck. He wondered what she saw when she looked at him,
which made him square his shoulders and extend his spine. Jan
had been his cleaning lady for nearly seven years, every Monday
and Thursday morning from ten till noon. In that time he'd seen
her here and there – to hand the key over, at the CID Christmas
Party, the going-away dos. He'd always felt profoundly uncomfortable in her presence for two reasons. Her husband, DS Peter
Clay, was a teetotal pen-pusher who wore aftershave at work;
and she knew too much about Valentine's life: the empties, the
ashtray on the window ledge, the single birthday card from his
sister, the sagging, overused wing armchair in which he sat and
read, or watched TV, or just slept off a few beers.

He'd been called back to St James' and the central CID squad
six years ago. DS Clay had died the year after. Valentine couldn't
remember the cause of death, but there'd been a card to sign in
the incident room, and he was pretty sure someone said it was
cancer. There'd been an awkward moment when he'd hesitated
over the message of condolence. 'Sorry to hear of your sad news'
seemed pathetically limp. In the end he'd just written his name
on impulse: not George Valentine, but Georgie, which he'd immediately regretted because nobody called him that now, except his
sister. But Jan had always called him Georgie, right from the
first time they'd met on his doorstep, him with the key, her with
the hoover.

She had two teenage daughters and a job at one of the harbour
front's fish and chip shops. They'd met a few months earlier
when Valentine had taken a room at the Ship to be handy for an
inquiry. It had made him really miss Julie, that first meeting,
because he suddenly realized how much he enjoyed talking to a
woman, particularly one that didn't seem in any hurry to judge
him or his life. Conversation with his colleagues – men and

women – always felt like a contest, as if there would be a score sheet at the end indicating who had won. Chatting to Jan didn't feel like a competition.

'How's the family?' he said, and suddenly thought the whole thing was a bad idea. Where did he think it would lead? How many of the locals at the bar thought she was his daughter?

'Good. Sam's got into Essex to do teacher training. It's what she's always wanted.'

'She'll be off your hands.' But the thought came to him: kids are at home, or they've gone. He and Julie had never had children so this was an opening, a window, into another world.

Jan was still talking, answering his question with meticulous care: 'Rosie's at home. She's still at the Co-op,' she added, pulling a face. 'She'll be on FaceTime or Skype now, talking to her friends. I know she's on her own up there most nights but all I can hear is other people's voices. It's another world, Georgie.'

He'd taken a seat beside her on the banquette and they drank in silence for a moment. Because they hadn't had children he felt that he'd been closer to Julie than many husbands were to their wives. It was just simple maths. There were fewer people in that first, intimate ring of human contact. So when she'd died the gap left behind was more profound.

'I probably reek of chip fat,' she said at last.

'Talking of food . . .' said Valentine.

'What time're we in?'

'Eight. So we've got an hour.' He'd booked a table at an Italian restaurant up by the church – Sergio's. It would be the first time he'd eaten out in twelve years, in the sense that there would be a table and someone else at it but him.

The prospect of sixty minutes of conversation seemed to overwhelm them both.

'Something's been worrying me,' said Jan. 'I don't know why I want to tell you this – because so few people know except Rosie and Sam, I guess, although we never talked about it and they don't mention their dad now.' She took a gulp of wine. 'I know Peter had such a clean-cut image at the station. He was very handsome as a teenager. He played tennis – that's typical, isn't it, the whites?'

She touched her wine glass. 'He drank, Georgie, at home.

Secretly. Spirits – vodka mainly, because there's no smell. At least, that's what he thought. At work too, I think. We said cancer but it was his liver. I think people knew at the end because his skin was so bad. I thought I'd say something. He didn't even try to stop. And I still don't know why he started. I just had to say it. I couldn't live like that, not again.'

NINETEEN

S haw left the Porsche in the St James' pound and walked down through the old town to the Boal Quay. The night was cool but the bricks and pavements still radiated the heat of the day. He kept kit for the lifeboat in his locker at St James' and had chosen a pair of waterproof boots and trousers for the journey ahead. The force's police launch was riding the tide, lights flooding the deck. Tom Hadden was in the stern, binoculars to his eyes, looking downriver towards the giant paper plant and the Magnox power station, tracking a flock of starlings in flight, a fingerprint against a sky in which the first stars were appearing.

Shaw stepped lightly on-board and joined the ex-Home Office scientist in the stern. Hadden handed him the glasses. 'Infrared. Great at night.' Shaw scanned the townscape of warehouses and wharves, pausing briefly to examine the old Campbell's cannery tower; a huge brick silo, once the hub of the sprawling plant, it had become the town's unofficial icon, boasting the emblematic Campbell's label on the side, as if it too was full of soup. It seemed to sum up Lynn in one single structure: ugly, striking, industrial, mysterious, with just a hint of hidden grace in the curled script of the logo.

Hadden poured himself a cup of coffee. 'I wanted to show you something you'll like – don't think it's got much to do with the inquiry.' This statement made the scientist shut his eyes tight in thought. 'Not on the face of it, anyway. But you'll love it, and we can drop you back at home at the beach. That OK?'

'Sure. George is picking me up in the morning. It's a treat, commuting by boat.'

The launch pulled away from the quay, the town to its right, a grassed sea wall to its left. The floodlit Customs House stood neat as a Georgian doll's. The dark wharves were broken only by the lights from a couple of pubs. By the time they were a mile up the Cut towards the sea Lynn had shrunk to a skyline of church spires and towers, the biggest being the great grain silo which stood over the Bentinck Dock. But there were medieval warehouse towers too, built by merchants eager to catch a first glimpse of returning cargo. Hadden lived in the Baltic Tower, a converted warehouse just back from the quay. Shaw had been inside and discovered no surprises: neat, tidy, ordered, adorned with a few wildlife shots and a single shot of a teenage girl on a ski trip.

At thirty knots they threaded their way out into the Wash, the sandbars to port and starboard glistening silver, the water black. The waxing moon seemed to track them like a spotlight. Hadden had an Admiralty chart out to plot their journey: Bull Dog Channel out into Roaring Middle, passing close enough to the lightship to hear the water slapping her sides. Then past Hunstanton, the pierhead lit, the town dotted with amber street lights. Shaw used the binoculars to find the spotlight in front of the Old Beach Café as they slipped past.

Holme lay in darkness, as did Thornham, both villages lost beyond the marshes and sea walls which protected them from the North Sea. The entrance to Overy Creek, notoriously difficult to locate at night, was somewhere in the subtle folds of the coastal sandhills. Shaw had the buoyage and lightships by heart, but it was still tricky spotting the channel. He caught a glimpse ahead of white water where waves were breaking on the submerged sandbar below Gun Hill – but before they could swing in through the gap they headed directly for the beach below Scolt Head. On a rising tide there was no danger, so they nudged forward until the bottom grated on the sand. Hadden jumped first, splashing into a foot of seawater, and Shaw followed. The crew dropped a sheet anchor and began to break out sandwiches and coffee.

Shaw felt the chill in the water through the thermal boots. The moon was to their backs, but the way ahead seemed to be lit by the fluorescence in the falling waves. Out at sea a light flickered and Shaw wondered if it had been distant lightning beyond the horizon, illuminating a skein of cloud. Emerging from the water they stood on the beach of shattered shells. Someone on the boat tuned into a radio transmission and they heard a burst of static, then silence but for the sea and wind.

At the high-water mark Shaw took stock of his precise

position. The night before he'd swum to Scolt Head Island and
traced the waterline on the landward side, until he found the
footprints, and then climbed over the line of high dunes which
formed the island's spine, descending – he now realized – to this
precise spot.

He saw the stones in a rough heap to one side, the place where
they had previously stood marked by a circular patch of blackened
sand.

Hadden stood over the spot. 'So you reckoned, what? A fire?'

'Yes. Unlikely to be the killer. Or the victim. Maybe a night
fisherman, walking out at low tide weighed down with food and
fuel, then back after high tide on the morning of the seventeenth?
They might have seen something. It's a loose end.'

Hadden shook his head. 'Stones first. As you know, this is a
sandy shore. No rock until you get to Hunstanton and the cliffs,
and they're sandstone and chalk. These are flints and granites
– all geologically different, by the way. A collection, almost.
Why drag them all the way here? You don't need them for a fire
unless it's really windy. And why do you need to mark the spot?'

'So the stones explain the deeper footprints?'

Hadden didn't answer directly. 'Now let's look at the fire.' He
slipped both shoes off and his socks, and stood in the black
circle.

'Nope. Shame – it's gone now, but when we came out the
morning after you found them you could still feel the heat in the
sand, let alone the stones. Cold now – just. But it's not a fire.
It's much more interesting than that.'

Down on his knees Hadden dug away until he'd revealed what
looked like a strange rock, the colour of deep-fried battered
calamari; browned, almost cellular, as if it might once have been
alive.

Shaw knelt beside the black circle. 'What the hell is that?'

Hadden beamed, clearly enjoying himself, teasing Shaw's curiosity. 'Well, you're not going to believe this. So let's take it in
stages, shall we? What was the defining characteristic of the
weather on the day we found the victim on Mitchell's Bank –
and indeed on the two days prior to that?'

'Electrical storms.'

'Right. Lightning. In fact, for nearly forty-eight hours the storm

was largely immobile, which meant that when lightning struck
the thunder came with it – a simultaneous phenomenon.'

'A thunderbolt.'

'Bull's eye.' He slapped his hand on the black sand. 'This is
the top of a thunderbolt.'

'No, it's not. Thunderbolts are made of sound waves and
electric particles discharging, going to earth. You can't stand on
one, any more than you can stand on a sunbeam.'

'The difference between a thunderbolt and a sunbeam is the
voltage,' said Hadden. 'A single lightning bolt can reach thirty-
five thousand degrees Fahrenheit – that's six times the surface
heat of the sun. When it strikes a mineral like sand it melts it,
forming a solid new rock. We get this.'

He patted the rock in the sand. 'If we dug this out we'd find
a long stone finger branching down into the sand, formed in the
few seconds of intense heat when the lightning bolt struck. It's
rare, but not unheard of. The gem museum at Cromer's got some.
Geologists call it fulgurite. A decent one, which would pretty
much look like Zeus' thunderbolt – would fetch you a thousand
pounds on eBay. More if you contacted museums or
collectors.'

'And it's still in there?'

'Yup. Know what I think? I think someone saw the bolt strike
from the mainland and came out to find it, bringing the stones
to mark the spot so that they could come back and dig it up.

'They haven't come back, and that's suspicious. Although I
guess you don't have to be a killer to know it isn't a great time
to be wandering around Overy Creek, given the police presence.
Perhaps they just don't want to admit they were out here the
night our man died on Mitchell's Bank.'

'So when I found the stones the heat was from the lightning
strike?'

'Yes – not a fire. Well, not a man-made one. You said the
stones were warm. So I think the marker was built the night
before we found the body – the night the victim died.'

Hadden led the way up through the sand dunes and marram
grass to the ridge.

Down below they saw the beach facing inland, across the
channel, to Burnham Marsh. To the east lay the flashing black

and white buoy, marking the spot where the victim's body had been found on the now submerged Mitchell's Bank. On the beach below they could see a series of cones in the moonlight, running into the water.

'That's the path of the footprints you found that night. Whoever came ashore – if they were wading – came off Mitchell's Bank. I think they came here, found the strike point for the lightning, built the cairn and then set off back. If the timing's right they could have seen him – dead or alive.'

Shaw turned back to look north into the sea and the night.

'Forensics? Anything?'

'Nothing – sorry.'

Hadden zipped up his dayglo jacket. 'So, are you up for it?'

'Up for what?'

'I've brought spades and four men willing to help. Let's dig up the thunderbolt.'

TWENTY

The D'Astis' house in Burnham Market overlooked the green, with its picturesque parish pump, cherry trees and Georgian lamp posts splashing golden light on the grass: a bucolic scene undermined only by the BMWs, sports cars and 4×4s parked bumper-to-bumper by visitors using the restaurants and pubs. At this time of night the windows of the Burnham Arms flickered with candlelight. From the open doors of the Beachcomber came the thin whine of a jazz clarinet – suitably discreet but unmistakably live.

Lucilla and Cornelia shared a room on the third floor. Its single sash window looked out over the rooftops and on fine clear days gave them a view of the hills. At home in London, in the townhouse on Cheyne Walk, they had separate bedrooms on different floors. Given the two girls would almost certainly go to different schools – Lucilla was frighteningly bright, whereas Cornelia was happy and easily distracted – the decision had been taken to let them share on holiday, at least. Leo had been brought up separately from his three brothers and they were all strangers now, united only by a series of trust funds.

He could hear the girls now, over his head, through the rafters and beams, and above the crackling of the fire. Embracing the heat of the coals and glowing logs, he sat forward, hands out, palms down. His body was still icy cold. The doctors had said initially that this was due to shock after the family's traumatic rescue from Mitchell's Bank. It wasn't that his skin was chilly at all – in fact, he was sweating slightly in his baggy jumper – it was that something lay inside him, like a rough boulder of ice and grit. Still haunted by what might have happened on Mitchell's Bank, he had begun to develop a mild aversion to closing his eyes, afraid of what he might imagine. One scene kept recurring: he stood outside himself, watching as he lifted a tarpaulin to identify the three children, who had been laid on the grass bank by the harbour office at Burnham Overy Staithe, their heads in a line, so that the length of their bodies was cruelly unequal, Cornelia's feet hardly reaching Paulo's waist.

Juliet, Leo's wife, had driven up to the hospital and stayed a night. She'd brought half the shop with her and the house was heavy with the scent of roses; they didn't really have the vases, and had to use glass pint pots and a bucket in the kitchen. She'd gone back to oversee a wedding contract but she'd promised to return for the weekend, and then they'd all relax, she said, as if it was exclusively a communal activity, which would have to be postponed in the interim. She'd been solicitous, in a slightly patronizing way, which implied that his guilt – what there was of it – was in equal measure with that of the children. They'd all been silly, they'd succumbed to an adventure, but it had all ended well. Leo had gone along with this depiction of events in order to protect the children. But one day he'd tell her how close they'd all come to death on Mitchell's Bank.

The scent of the flowers in the house was strangely anonymous. It made the old building smell like all their homes: Chelsea, Lucca, even the flat in Paris. Leo was struck by this unsettling irony, that they had all these houses but that they were all the same on the inside. The view out of the window might change but the brushed chrome coffee maker was identical, the artwork, the vases, the drapes, the bed linen. What was the point, thought Leo, of *travelling* at all? Especially after dark. The windows were blind eyes then: it didn't matter what was outside. Staring into the flames of the fire he could see himself moving through the world without ever quite touching the sides, failing repeatedly to make contact with any spiritual sense of place.

Which made what had happened on Mitchell's Bank oddly precious: the landscape (combined with the seascape), the *place*, had conspired to nearly rob them of their lives; but at least Leo would remember *where* it all happened. The intensity of those few minutes would be with him for the rest of his life. An idea formed now, as he looked into the flames, and as soon as he recognized its shape, he knew that the moment might change the rest of his life. Why didn't he move here, to north Norfolk, with the children, for good? They could visit the other homes but this would be *home*. The family business would be fine without him. One of his brothers, more diligent and talented than Leo, worked at the head office in Milan and would eventually take over from his father. Instead, Leo could invest in a local business here in Norfolk. An organic farm, perhaps, or a boutique hotel. He could do the financing, business planning, take a back seat. Could he get Juliet to agree? She liked the drive and could stay at the London flat in the week. She'd miss the kids, but she'd love the independence. They'd make a real home for her to come home too. He didn't want to be footloose any more.

This vision of a new life was intoxicating. It was also therapeutic. Leo saw now that what had happened on Mitchell's Bank could be a turning point, a new beginning, a chance to move on and change the shape of the world in which he lived. There was a small Catholic chapel in the village – St Henry's – and he promised himself he'd light a candle the next time he passed, to mark the decision.

He smiled in the firelight.

Only one duty remained before he could put his feet up with a glass of wine. The strange detective with the one-dimensional face and the inappropriate name – Valentine – had asked him a favour. A profoundly unromantic-looking man, reeking of nicotine, with a mildly arthritic stance, he seemed, Leo had sensed, not to care much for the children, being one of those adults you couldn't imagine on their knees with a set of Lego or a Christmas board game. Aloof, perhaps; or just afraid of entering a child's world. When he'd got Leo's statement down (and what a tedious task that was – couldn't they just take notes and then send you the statement to check?) he'd surprised him with a final request.

'We've not bothered the children, sir. They're still upset and you'll want to take them home. But later, when they're not so shaken, perhaps you could ask them to think back. You went out to Mitchell's Bank yesterday as well, you say? So that's two days – consecutively. The victim on Mitchell's Bank died the day before you found him, probably after dark. Perhaps they noticed something – or someone – out on the marshes that first day, or over at Burnham Marsh? They live in their own world, kids. But they see stuff we miss. Anything that glitters. They're like magpies.'

Leo thought he would get it over with tonight while the

children were still excited by their rescue, still proud of the shared experience. He closed his book, *The Riddle of the Sands* by Erskine Childers, the classic spy story set among the sandbanks of the Frisian Islands. Childers had written the book in his London flat on Cheyne Walk, thirty yards north of Leo's own front door. Childers had been a foreigner in his own country too, just like Leo. Once the children were asleep he'd finish the tale. But for now it was bedtime, and all its routines.

In the D'Asti family – at least the D'Asti family in its north Norfolk incarnation – this demanded a certain degree of pantomime. His wife had bought an old paraffin lamp at a local 'antique' shop in the village. Leo lit it and climbed the stairs as he did each night, remembering to switch off all the lights in the stairwell which reached up through the heart of the house. The stairs creaked theatrically. When he got to the girls' room on the third floor he knocked three times. After a short, hysterical bout of giggles he saw the bedside lights go out under the door. This was the signal for him to enter, setting the lantern down on a chest of drawers.

He sat between the beds on the floor and held both their hands.

Telling them what the strange detective had asked him, he said they should both close their eyes tight and tell him three things they could recall about the last two times they'd walked out to Mitchell's Bank. Had they seen anything? A lonely bird watcher, perhaps? A boatman rowing in the marshes?

So that they had time to think, he volunteered to go first. 'I remember a green buoy which was on the sand – that was there both times. And the wreck of a ship which pokes up near the bird hide – Paulo spotted that. And a seal. With whiskers. In the water near Burnham Overy Staithe. That was the second day – before . . .' He left it at that, because they'd know what the seal came *before*.

Cornelia, three-and-a-half, remembered losing her shoe in the mud and having to squeeze her foot back in the black gunge, a kite flying over Gun Hill but they couldn't see the person on the other end of the string, and a dead seagull. Leo recalled the kite now – how clever of her to keep the image. That had been on the day they'd found the victim. So he'd tell Valentine – but he might not be interested. Lucilla, eight, recalled the kite too – it

had been in the shape of a black hawk. She'd seen waves of
geese in a double-V, and she'd seen the moon, rising over the
village. On the first day it had appeared behind the ruined church
tower, but on the second it was already sailing high, clear of the
pine trees.

Leo said goodnight, thinking what observant girls they were.

Paulo's room was in the roof, up a short switchback wooden
stair. The bed lay in a space created by a dormer window with
glass on three sides. In winter it was bitterly cold but the boy
loved it because he was able to watch the stars with the duvet
pulled up to his chin. The children played a game in which they
had to choose between their different homes – which had the
best fire, which had the best food, which had the best view. Paulo
always said that this was his best bed, which upset Leo, because
he always thought the boy was unnaturally silent in this house,
even subdued.

He told his son what he'd told the boy's sisters. Paulo's eyes
widened in the moonlight coming in through the window. A
serious child, he considered his options. Then his hand appeared
from under the duvet to count off his three observations.

'One: a blue fishing boat passed us coming in both times. It
was one of those with the funny stand-up cabin for the helmsman.
I couldn't see the name but it said LN two-two-three on the side.
That means its home harbour is King's Lynn. I looked that up.

'Two: I saw a dead seal on the far sands. I looked at him with
my telescope.'

'And three?' asked Leo, quickly, tucking him in.

'The boat I said I'd like for Christmas.'

Leo remembered too. That had been on the day before. 'The
wooden one, coming in from the sea?' he asked. It had been
beautiful, even Leo had to admit that. Clinker-built, graceful,
with brass portholes.

'It didn't have a number like the fishing boat.'

'Oh well, I'll tell the policeman anyway,' said Leo, standing.

'But it had a name,' said Paulo. 'I used my telescope. It was
called the *Limpet*.'

TWENTY-ONE

D arkness. The mobile buzzing on the bedside table. Shaw's heartbeat already running at seventy – up from its resting rate of fifty-eight. Not the lifeboat; because he had a pager for the RNLI, and he'd set it to chime, and he'd hadn't heard the maroon go off from the coastguard hut on the cliffs. Lena stretched and lay still, a black arm across the white pillow, a single exhaled breath indicating she was only just awake, poised to slip back into sleep. She'd always needed her sleep and deeply resented late-night calls. A month earlier Shaw had been struggling with a case involving street attacks on working girls which had led to a spate of late-night text messages. Lena's patience had finally snapped and she'd made up a bed in the café. She'd only just returned, signalling a truce at least.

Shaw held the mobile screen to his good eye, then took the call.

'George.'

'Peter. The nick at Burnham Market runs a nightline. They clocked a call from Louise Wighton about an hour ago – she's the wife of Geoff, the ex-copper who now babysits second homes?'

'And . . .' Shaw was already out in the corridor, gently closing the bedroom door.

'Wighton set out late evening to check one of his properties. One of the security firm control centres phoned to say the alarm had been triggered. He hasn't come back. Big posh manor house in a hamlet up by Burnham Norton. I've got a mobile unit on its way from Wells. She says he never – ever – fails to come home on time. As of now he's eight hours late. His mobile's taking calls but he's not answering.'

'A hamlet, you said?'

'East Tines. Never heard of it, but I've found it on the OS. Postcode's 4PG NN6 if you use the GPS. I'll text it.'

Shaw dressed in the kitchen then ran the 1.4 miles to the

lifeboat house. The Porsche purred in the night as he edged it up the lane towards the coast road. The dashboard clock read 04:05. He met a fox trotting down the track towards the beach, curiously unconcerned. The dunes loomed, pale and cold in the white security lights triggered by the car's movement, revealing the new boathouse, a café, a row of converted fishermen's cottages. Outside one stood a single bottle of milk. At the top of the lane a white owl sat on a fence post, the turntable head tracking the car as it slipped past.

The journey to East Tines was 8.46 miles – according to the car's satnav, which led him along a narrow B-road bound for Burnham Norton, hugging the contour of the hills. Valentine's Mazda came into view, slewed across the carriageway, 200 yards short of the edge of the hamlet. Down in the valley Shaw could see the church at Burnham Overy Town, its square tower rising out of a skein of pre-dawn mist which tracked the river.

'Unit from Wells is on the other side . . . here,' said Valentine, shining a torch on to a map spread on the Mazda's bonnet. He indicated a small road on the far side of the hamlet.

'Back-up?'

'Sorry. I've pulled all the rank I've got and there's a traffic unit on the way from the A10 but it'll be half an hour – probably longer.'

The OS map revealed that East Tines constituted half-a-dozen buildings, two of them clearly once farms, with buildings set around yards, a single track in and out. They could see nothing against the horizon except a grain silo and a stand of pine trees. A dog barked down in the valley. A sky full of stars wheeled over their heads and Shaw succumbed to a regular illusion, that he could hear the heavens turning, as if they emitted the whisper of celestial mechanics.

'We could wait,' said Valentine. 'If he's run into the burglars he could be lying low waiting for them to move on. Or they might be doing several houses, and he's keeping his head down until he's sure they're done. We could sit tight too, wait for the back-up unit. This might be our chance to nab the lot.'

'Lying low for eight hours? If he's here, George, he can't get out. Plain and simple,' said Shaw. 'We need to get him out, and we need to do it fast.'

Shaw splayed his fingers over the image of the hamlet on the OS map: 'Radio the mobile unit, George. Tell 'em to block the road with the squad car on their side and then proceed with caution. We'll meet them in the middle.'

The map showed a short track leading out of the centre of East Tines towards the brow of the hill. Tines Manor was marked: a large house with two wings, and what looked like a walled estate garden. The remains of a medieval moat were shown as two parallel dotted lines.

Setting out along the lane their footsteps spooked something in the ditch, which scurried ahead of them and then bustled through a hedge. As Shaw's eyes switched to night vision, the hamlet began to emerge from the shadows: two houses with low roofs to the right, one showing a light over a door. The silo stood to the left. A triangular rough green opened out to reveal a bench, a rustic water pump and a pair of cat's eyes in the shadows.

A pool of torchlight flickered into view along the sandy path and a voice asked, 'DS Valentine?'

The uniformed police officer was called Richardson. Shaw knew the face because he'd won some kind of medal for clay pigeon shooting and had featured in the force's newsletter. His partner, PC Johns, had stayed with the squad car, he said, and would deal with the traffic unit if and when it arrived.

'No sign of Wighton?' asked Shaw.

'Nothing, sir. But we got a call from control. One of the residents here has phoned in to say there's an odd noise coming from Tines Hill – that's up there . . .' He pointed north, to where the pine trees broke the starry horizon. 'The big house is in the lee of the woods.'

They walked for two hundred yards and then Valentine called a halt. 'There,' he said, 'the noise.' He stood, hatchet head skewed to one side. Shaw had noticed his DS's ability to hear beyond the normal range before: not high notes, but bass. It was as if his feet could pick up faint shockwaves in the earth. Perhaps it was the slip-ons.

In the silence they heard a rhythmic, regular chiming, like a toneless bell. Shaw measured the signal: once every four seconds. The note had a vibrant quality, as if it contained several tones, all in the same flat key.

'There's no church,' said Valentine, effortlessly reading Shaw's mind. Looking back down to the village they noted two more lights at windows in the cottages round the green and a single dog bark set off a necklace of answering howls.

Tines Manor came into view, framed by two dark cedar trees, which seemed to throw protective arms around the brickwork. The walls were seven foot high and topped with crushed glass. As they approached up the lane the rhythmic thud changed in nature. There was a more resonant edge now, as if someone was playing a tubular bell. The gates stood open, a security light illuminating the façade: twelve Georgian windows, a Downing Street door, a climbing wisteria.

'It's not an alarm, is it?' asked Shaw. 'The noise. Perhaps it went off and they just thumped it with a wrench to disable it, and this is what's left.'

Valentine examined his phone. 'Signal's good. So that's another question: why hasn't he phoned home?'

Shaw took a step back and scanned the windows, shaking his head. 'What's your first name, Constable?'

'Paul, sir.'

'OK, Paul. I think we have a duty to try and find Geoff Wighton asap – and not just because he used to be a copper. So here's what you do. Circle the house, get round the back, keep your eyes open, and try not to make too much noise. If someone does a runner follow them, radio for assistance, keep your distance. Otherwise, complete the circle and meet us back here. If we're gone, we're inside. Follow us in. No heroics. Got it?'

He nodded, readjusting his cap.

As Shaw and Valentine approached the front door, they heard Richardson's boots on the gravel, then silence, as he stepped on to the lawn and disappeared into the shadows beneath one of the cedar trees.

Shaw stood on the step. The resonant drumming seemed to be radiating from the walls themselves. Placing his gloved hand on the door, he found it swung open, the polished black paint shimmering with a reflection of the stars. Inside all was dark and smelt of air freshener and wood polish.

Shaw played his torchbeam up the stairs. 'Ground floor, George. I'll take upstairs. Let's keep talking.'

Shaw didn't believe in creeping around in the dark. With one hand he flipped six light switches.

'Police!' He used his serrated voice, and the echo made a wall mirror vibrate. 'Police! CID. Make yourself known. Now.'

Upstairs he counted five bedrooms and called out, in turn, that each was empty. Valentine checked two living rooms, a boot room, and a pantry. All empty. No evidence of burglary.

Valentine was waiting for Shaw at the foot of the stairs. Around them the constant drumming had gained in volume, and the beat was slightly quicker.

'One thing you should see,' said Valentine.

The kitchen, which was still in darkness, held a massive widescreen smart TV on one wall. Someone had created a Word document and typed in an illuminated message, bold, in seventy-two point type:

WE'LL BE BACK

On the central island worktop there was an iPhone.

'Wighton's?' suggested Shaw. He picked it up in his gloved hand and the screen lit up. He brought up messages and the first was from Standard Security Systems Ltd to say that the alarm system at Tines Manor had been tripped at 8.04 p.m.: a rear window in the garden boot room.

A torchbeam played on the windows and they saw Richardson standing beyond the double glazing. Valentine switched on all the lights and the garden lit up, revealing a large, sky-blue kidney-shaped swimming pool.

The constable shook his head quickly, then moved on.

Shaw put his hand on one of the large double radiators. 'Sound's coming from these . . .'

'Loft?' suggested Valentine.

'Cellar?' countered Shaw.

There was a Yale key in the lock of the door under the stairs. As Shaw began to turn it the thudding stopped dead. The breath of a cellar greeted them as the door opened; that particular blend of damp and rot, staleness, and coal dust.

A single light bulb illuminated bare brick walls. Geoff Wighton sat on a stool by the wall drinking coffee from a plastic cup held in his right hand. In his left he held a coal scuttle with which, it seemed, he'd been rapping a pipe which emerged from a large lagged boiler.

'What took you?' he said. He looked bored, and perhaps scared, but he was hiding that well. There was blood at his hairline and a definite bruising to the temple.

'You all right?' asked Shaw.

'Oh, yeah. I might die of embarrassment, but nothing else.'

They helped him up the stairs to the kitchen.

Wighton directed Valentine to a drinks cabinet in the front room and the DS came back with three malts. Shaw added water to his but Wighton just knocked it straight down his throat and asked for a refill. Valentine went out to find PC Richardson and stand him down.

A minute later they were all back in the kitchen.

'I got a call from the insurers about eight. Alarm tripped – rear boot room. So I came in here, put my mobile down – I won't do that again – and went and checked the locks. It all looked good to me – no sign of damage, nothing. I went down to the cellar to reset the security panel. I'd got to the top of the cellar stairs, switched off the light, turned to lock the door behind me and my lights went out. Next thing I know I'm down at the bottom of the stairs, on my back.'

He tipped his head forward to reveal the wound on the top of his skull. 'It's not just the one blow, by the way – feels like they got in a second before I hit the ground. Bastards. Didn't even see a shadow.' He stood up, stretched, then sat down again quickly. 'Sorry. Bit dazed.'

'Take it easy,' said Shaw. 'Stay put. There's an ambulance on the way.'

'One thing,' said Wighton. 'I keep my eyes open. I never just turn up at a property. I park a bit away. I left the van down the far lane in a farmyard, then walked up, making observations. Textbook stuff. Down by the green there was a van parked.'

He licked his lips: 'White van – Ford. Crest on the side said Norfolk County Council. I bet it ain't there now.'

Shaw recalled the one empty bench, the water pump but no vehicles – vans or otherwise.

'If you saw that parked in the street in daylight hours what would you think?' asked Wighton. 'Drains, council tax, street lights, council house rents. It's the vehicle equivalent of standing around with a clipboard. You could go anywhere, park anywhere, and who's going to notice? Pretty much perfect anytime between early morning and nightfall. Even at night on a street. Mind you, looks bloody suspicious at four o'clock in the morning in the middle of East Tines. My guess is it's the vehicle of choice for the Chelsea Burglars.'

Wighton beamed. 'Did I mention I got the reg? Well – I can remember a bit of it. DN10. Definitely DN10.'

He tore the page out of his notebook and gave it to Shaw. 'Enjoy.'

TWENTY-TWO

A doorstep, six-thirty, and the town soaked by a sea mist. The paintwork solid black, with a Georgian skylight, and an old gas lamp, now rusted. A foot-scraper too, with a pint of milk lodged in the hole. Valentine stood under the lintel and watched the water drip methodically an inch from his nose. He'd not returned to bed after the call-out to East Tines but had instead gone to St James' and spent the last few hours in the CID room reading the case notes on the Chelsea Burglars. Two facets of the crimes stood out: their meticulous planning, and the graffiti. In his experience criminals – the rank and file – were heroically stupid. While they might prosper in the short term on rat-like cunning, reckless courage, or sheer chutzpah, they almost always did something totally brainless which allowed them to be scooped up by the police. This lot were different. One or more of them clearly possessed more than a GCSE in pilfering. And not only were they meticulous, well prepared and organized – they also felt the need to express political ideas. Or at least one of them did.

Which explained his presence on a doorstep in Adelaide Gardens: a backstreet half a mile from the town centre, with parked cars bumper-to-bumper on one side. Damp had got under the terrace façades and one or two of the narrow, four-storey houses were boarded up; almost all had multiple door buzzers, with the names of bedsit residents scrawled under the plastic. Valentine noted the nationalities implied: Polish, Chinese, Portuguese, Romanian. There was a pub on the corner – the Bathfield – which looked like a hangover in brick: lightless, slightly off the vertical and the horizontal, waiting for opening time to bring it back to life.

A figure appeared out of the mist. Slightly built, maybe five foot eight, with a large head on a thin neck and narrow shoulders. The footsteps were neat and businesslike, and he carried a leather satchel.

'DS Valentine?' The voice was authoritative without being in any way distinctive. A pair of glasses with metal rims caught the red glow of a street light which had fallen out of sync in its daylight, night-time routine.

'Hope I'm on time. I live in the North End so I walked – don't do that enough. Any of us.'

'Thanks for making it so early – it's a help.'

'No problem. I'm an early riser. Always have been.'

He'd produced a key and the door was soon open, some pale electric light spilling out on the damp pavement.

'Come in – make yourself at home, such as it is.'

There were no carpets inside, just a bare staircase, and a corridor festooned with posters: Troops Out, Defeat Thatcher, CND, and a framed one, a reprint from 1945, of a giant V on the landscape with the slogan: 'And Now – Win The Peace'.

Valentine counted three bare light bulbs as they made their way to the first floor, then the second, and along a corridor to an office.

'Clem Whyte,' he said finally, offering a small, narrow hand. 'Welcome to the citadel of freedom. Party's been here since 1903. We've always shared it with the Trades Council – they've got a chamber upstairs, very grand – well, it was, before the Great War. Not exactly an idea whose time has come, is it? Trade unionism. Hasn't seemed to stop the Germans making a modern country out of the same ideal. But there we are.'

Valentine wasn't listening to a word he said. Politics, in the formal party sense, had never been of any interest to him. Faced with a ballot box he voted Labour, but only because he felt that it was expected of him.

Whyte had to be fifty, with a little bushy moustache, and a narrow face to match the shoulders. Shaw wondered if they made adult shirts with that small a neck measurement.

'How can we help?' he said, filling a kettle at a small sink. 'I've got half an hour. Then it's time for the work they pay me for.'

Valentine walked to the window and saw that the mist had thickened and the pale sun had gone.

'Nothing exciting, I'm afraid, sir. We've got an outbreak of graffiti – house fronts, a few public buildings, bus stops. Petty,

I know – but annoying, and the last thing we need is the taxpayers on our backs.'

Whyte took the one comfy seat behind a desk and steepled his fingers.

'And the subject matter of the graffiti?'

'Broadly anti-second-homes slogans. Go home bankers – that kind of thing.'

'And you thought: I know, I'll pop round to the Labour Party.'

'I was hoping you might be able to give me a list of the current membership – purely for elimination purposes.' Valentine knew he wasn't going to get any such list. But the request gave him a reason to cross the threshold, and when Whyte turned him down he could gracefully concede the point, and then fish around for the details he was really after.

'West Norfolk Constabulary can afford an anti-graffiti CID unit these days? Last time I looked, you lot were looking for a million pounds in cuts.'

Valentine detected a mild anti-police tone, but he decided not to retaliate. Besides, he was looking forward to a cup of tea.

'It would be of help to our inquiries.'

'I'm sure it would. And I'd love to help, but it's not possible. Our membership details are confidential.'

'It's not an unreasonable inquiry, is it? I don't suppose anyone's ashamed of being a member, are they? I'm looking for a politic-ally motivated campaigner – motivated enough to commit a crime, which is what it is. I thought you might have some young bloods in the party.'

Whyte looked up from making the tea. 'We had our AGM last week, detective sergeant, complete with a visit from the junior shadow minister for agriculture. Twenty-one people. Eight of them OAPs. Socialism has never been that strong in East Anglia, and now, with UKIP, we're just clinging on. I'm not sure parties within the party are a mathematical possibility.'

'What's the party's view on second homes?'

'We're the party of aspiration. At least, that's what we're told. One day we might support a small rebate on the council tax – five per cent. The real issue is providing affordable housing in areas where local people can't get a home. Last elections we urged the council to spend more. But that's all we can do – urge.'

'But what do the members think? The local members.'

'Frankly – and I wouldn't say this in public – most of us think second homes are what Sellar and Yeatman in *1066 and All That* would have called 'a good thing'. Without tourism, and second homes, the north Norfolk economy would be dead on its rural feet. Every second home provides work for local people – tradesmen, cleaners, decorators, builders. All right – it might be nice if the Chelsea set spent a bit more in local shops, but they do spend money on high-end goods – organic meat, fish, veg, clothes, books, technology, cars. Just take cars: there's a lot of specialist garages on the coast for MGs, Bentley, Rolls, BMW, Rover – old Rovers are big business. And what is the anti-second-homes lobby really saying?'

Whyte had slipped into a rhetorical mode, as if addressing a public meeting. Valentine was fighting the urge to cut him short.

'That if rich people didn't buy them they'd all go to the locals? I don't think so. There are bigger issues. Much bigger issues, like migrant workers. UKIP's gaining ground. Immigration in this part of the country is a divisive and corrosive issue – as I am sure you are well aware. We need to help people to understand the economics, the politics, and get a real grasp on the facts. We need people to stop being afraid and angry.'

Whyte had tea bags in mugs with spoons, sugar in a bag.

'Bugger. I'll just get the milk; I left it on the step.'

Valentine reckoned he had sixty seconds. Whyte's answers had been comprehensive and to some extent persuasive. But the DS had checked the *Lynn Express* archive online at the office and found three news items covering protest events, organized by a Socialist splinter group, against second homes – or more accur-ately, in favour of a local surcharge: two dated in the summer of 2011, one in 2012. The proposal was for second homeowners to pay ten per cent on top of the standard tax. Not recent protests, it was true, but hardly the distant past either. Valentine wondered if Whyte was protecting someone, or a group, who took a harder line on the issue than their local Labour Party.

He pulled open the top drawer of the filing cabinet and found a box of Typhoo tea bags. The second drawer held membership files. The newspaper report on one of the anti-second-home protests came with a picture of the demonstrators – who, according to the caption, had declined to be named. The first file was marked on the front with the name Archibald Booth. He flipped it open but there was no ID picture required; just standard details. Picking another file at random from the H's, he double-checked. Still no ID picture.

Swearing briefly, he slid the drawer back into the cabinet.

He heard footsteps on the bare boards and a tuneless whistle, which might have been 'The Red Flag'.

They chatted over tea until Whyte suggested Valentine might like to see the Trades Hall. Cradling their mugs – Valentine's held a portrait of Nye Bevan – they climbed to the top floor.

The two drawing rooms of the original Georgian house had been knocked through to make a grand hall, framed at either end by full-length sash windows. The walls were panelled and a gold copperplate script listed the chairmen of the Lynn & District Trades Union Council. Commemorative boards marked visits by dignitaries – Atlee in 1950, Feather in 1973, Benn in 1978, Kinnock in 1983. There was a fine cherry wood table, and matching chairs, and in pride of place, on the long unbroken wall, the council mace in a glass box.

'Impressive,' said Valentine politely. He'd have made his excuses and left by now but he forced himself to be patient, only dimly acknowledging that this was because he knew Shaw would have stayed and listened. There was something dutiful about the DI's attitude to policing which was mildly contagious.

There was a noticeboard at one end of the room and an old sideboard holding three rows of cups and saucers. Posters for Unite outlined the benefits of union membership for fishermen, field workers, pickers and workers in the new offshore wind farm industry.

'That's the big issue here,' said Whyte. 'The footloose workers, migrants, the rural poor. Getting them to join a union's tough work. They won't admit it, but a lot of gangmasters refuse to take on unionized workers. So these people – a lot of local people as well as Poles and Roma, or Bulgarians or Portuguese – end up being exploited. That's an easy word to use, I know. But it means blighted lives. Damp rooms, sordid toilets, old shoes, cheap alcohol, poor food, kids with lice. It isn't pretty. That's the problem with the landscape – the golden beaches, the picture postcard villages. They hide so much.'

Whyte's voice had changed, losing its pleading note. Valentine could see his small grey eyes had hardened. It struck him for the first time that Whyte was probably one of those people you wouldn't want as an enemy. Valentine could imagine him being dogged and single-minded – even bloody-minded.

'What about samphire pickers? They got a union?' he asked.

Whyte laughed, taking off his glasses to polish the lenses. 'No chance. They're more interested in giving the taxman the slip. I don't think they'd entirely embrace the TUC motto, 'Unity Is Strength', do you? They're loners, adrift. And do you know what they're adrift in? The underclasses. Everyone talks about the big cities and the poor, but if you want to find the black economy in Britain today, sergeant, try walking round a seaside resort with your eyes open. But that's not going to make any tourist posters, is it? Golden Sands. Black Economy.'

TWENTY-THREE

An Indian summer morning on Old Hunstanton beach: a red ball sun, blue sky, a mist burning off a millpond sea. Shaw ran the mile from the Old Beach Café to the lifeboat house in four minutes forty-three seconds. On his back was a small haversack with a hard cardboard tube sticking up like an aerial. He let himself into the hovercraft bay and used the shower to change into his work clothes: white shirt, no tie, black cotton trousers, boots.

As he drove he kept glancing to the horizon on his left, trying to concentrate on the case but distracted by a conversation he'd had with Lena over coffee on the stoop. The topic, again, had been the plans to open a beach bar – or, as he called it, the 'super pub', while Lena preferred Surf Bar.

Tired, edgy, he'd been pushed into saying out loud what he felt: that he was distressed by the idea that his beloved, deserted childhood beach was going to be packed with hundreds of holidaymakers every summer's evening. Lena, who'd enjoyed a sleepless night after the early morning call, argued that they'd be lucky to get a hundred customers. It was a mile walk to the nearest road at Old Hunstanton, and there were pubs there, anyway – three of them, and a wine bar. They'd attract walkers, birdwatchers, a few surfers. It had been a mistake, she conceded, showing him pictures of similar bars in Cornwall, packed out with lager drinkers, each one with dyed blond hair. This bar would attract a very different clientele.

'They'll be people like us,' she'd said, exasperated.

Shaw kicked the Porsche into first and sped through a sleepy village. *People like us.* He'd always harboured the notion that they weren't like other people, which was why they'd ended up living away from other people. Living lives that weren't just average. They might not succeed, but it was something to aspire to.

Twenty minutes later he parked the Porsche outside the mobile incident room at Burnham Marsh. The team quickly assembled on the quayside along the grass verge: eight DCs, and George Valentine.

'I'll be brief. It's day three of the inquiry. The murder's now public. The burglaries will stay under wraps for another five days. The press office has organized a media conference at three this afternoon on the Mitchell's Bank killing: TV, radio, the works. Fortunately, we have had two major breaks overnight.'

Shaw stood with his back to the water, a flotilla of six sail boats behind him using an offshore wind to slip out to sea below Gun Hill.

'First off – and the centrepiece of the presser – we have a boat entering the village on the day of the burglaries and the murder – a boat which is no longer here. One of the D'Asti children clocked the name with his telescope: the *Limpet*. We need to find that boat today. So speed, please, and lots of communication. Harbour masters, RNLI, Coastwatch, the lot. We need to get an image of the boat and put it out for people to see.

'Our second break is not for the press. The chief constable's media blackout on the Chelsea Burglars is still in place. The good news is we have identified a vehicle which might be the one used by the thieves. The van carries the insignia of Norfolk County Council. Given that we also have the registration number, or part of it, we should be able to find the driver in short time. That's our priority this morning. Find the van *first,* then the driver. That's two different tasks. I want forensics on the van as soon as we have a location. I don't want anyone wiping the van clean because they've seen us picking up the driver. Remember: it's a gang. George and I will interview the driver if and when we have them in custody. Right. Anything I need to know? Paul?'

'Basic legwork's nearly complete,' said DC Twine. 'We've checked out Stepney's alibi, and his Polish captains', and most of the samphire collectors on the coast. Nothing's watertight – but they all look good on paper. The pickers hired by the captains are proving more elusive. There are some gaps. We're on it, but it'll take time. We have found Painter Slaughden, Stepney's local man, and he's got a cast-iron alibi for the night in question.'

Cast iron was the kind of casual cliché Shaw hated. And Twine knew it. 'I say cast iron. I mean titanium. Hip replacement at the Queen Elizabeth Hospital.

'We're reviewing all the paperwork on the previous burglaries, interviewing all the owners here at Burnham Marsh – those in the UK anyway. I've got Mark trawling missing persons, in case our victim had been reported absent somewhere else. And we've talked to everyone we can find who spends time out on the marsh – harbour master's office, HM Revenue and Customs, wildlife trust, twitchers, dog walkers – even lightning hunters. So far it's a blank.'

Shaw clapped his hands: 'OK. Coffee. Then let's get to it.'

He took the small round lid off the cardboard tube he'd brought from home and slid out a large sheet of A3 paper.

'You might as well see this. We need to get an ID for our victim, and fast. This is the best I can do at putting some life back into a dead man's face.'

DC Twine took one corner, Shaw held the other. One or two of the new DCs whistled and clapped. It wasn't just a forensic piece of artwork, it was art. The face of their victim looked out at them: the pale arresting eyes, the pumpkin head, the heavy skull bones, the deep-set, shadowy eye sockets.

'This will be released this afternoon at the presser. For now we'll call him Mitchell. I've got the budget for a thousand posters – uniformed are organizing – so get used to it. This face will haunt us until we can pin a name to it.'

The team dispersed.

Valentine got himself a mug of tea and went and sat on a wooden bench on the quay. It had one of those little metal plaques to commemorate a villager. They always made him feel uneasy, as if he was resting his legs sitting on a coffin. He lit his eighth cigarette of the day and considered – for the hundredth time – what Jan Clay had said to him the night before at Wells.

She didn't want to live like that *again*.

Was she trying to let him down gently? Or was it a call for him to clean up his lifestyle? It was a disturbing thought because he'd never thought he *had* a lifestyle. He liked the odd pint, but in thirty-five years of police work he'd never taken a surreptitious drink, let alone one from a vodka bottle.

The rest of their 'date' had been slightly chilly, as if some kind of invisible foreign border had been crossed. With Julie he'd always been confident that he knew what she was thinking, as she was thinking it, as if he'd been given real-time access to her brain. Jan bemused him, because she was able to maintain a façade, a mask. That's what twenty-five years of living with DC Peter Clay had done to her.

What next? Did he ask her out again? Did he ring? He felt like a sixteen-year-old again, watching the girls dance round their handbags.

An unexpected noise snapped him back into the present, something he hadn't heard out on the coast for years: a siren, on the distant main road. Several of the other DCs standing outside checked their mobiles. Then a second siren, and a third. Shaw was already trotting towards the Porsche.

Twine came out on the step to give them the news from the landline: 'Major incident. Burnham Market. Police and paramedics. Roadblocks on all major routes.'

TWENTY-FOUR

F ish flesh had always unsettled Shaw. Not salmon, trout, smoked mackerel or any shellfish – but white fish on the slab: cod, monkfish, halibut or a plump piece of plaice. The paleness was too reminiscent of human flesh, and the bloodlessness was unsettling when you cut down into the meat. Add to that the slippery wet texture and the whole aesthetic was on an edge – between delicious and disgusting. And that's what he felt now, standing in the fishmonger's shop, looking at the fish through the immaculately clean glass counter-front.

The scene was luridly lit by one of Tom Hadden's scene-of-crime lamps. The tarpaulin window blind was down. Outside a small, almost reverent crowd had parted to let Shaw and Valentine in through the front door. Paul Twine's final text had been direct to the point of a newspaper billboard: *Code 66 opposite Burnham Arms.*

A Code 66 was an unlawful killing. The narrow green at the heart of the town held three squad cars, an ambulance, and Hadden's SOCO van.

The corpse lay on the marble slab under the glass counter with the fish. Naked: white-blue, the black body hair streaked as if he'd swum into the shop and simply washed up on the crushed ice and sprigs of samphire and oyster shells. The face looked out through the glass, the eyes as dead as those of a large grey mullet which lay beside his neck. Some small black eels had been draped over the legs; the toes rested in a pile of sprats.

Shaw noted condensation on the curved glass of the counter and wondered if that meant the body had been warm when pushed into its see-through tomb. Or had the victim still been breathing?

'Hell of a catch,' said Valentine. 'I reckon he's six foot three, two hundred and fifty pounds? Name's Henry Davies, by the way, local fisherman, according to the bloke who found him. That's Cobley – the fishmonger – he's around somewhere.'

It was smart of his DS to gauge the victim's stature, set as it was, horizontally, against a few dead fish. Valentine was right: this man, alive, on his feet, was an everyday giant.

The killer's attempt at ironic black art, placing the victim on the cold slab, was completed by a bloodstain on the glass where the body had hit it, and been pulled back into place. The red smear reminded Shaw that this man's heart had been pumping away as busily as his own just a few hours earlier. The source of the blood was not difficult to track down. The body was twisted round to reveal a gunshot wound, where most people think the heart isn't – pretty much central, and high enough to be almost part of the lower throat. A black residue and burn mark around the neat hole revealed the gun had been fired at point-blank range.

Given the nature of the wound, there was surprisingly little blood. But there was a trail of it, which led them back down a short corridor to a goods-in entrance with roll-up doors, which in turn opened into a back lane, where they'd discovered an old Post Office van. A work area by the doors was dominated by an industrial fridge unit, stainless steel sinks and two counters. Four large oil drums stood to one side, a large fish tail just emerging from one. An area of the hardstanding concrete had already been taped off around a conspicuous bloodstain.

It was pretty clear the victim had been shot here, at the back of the shop, and then dragged to the front for display: and that's what it was, a very public pillory, as blatant as the body on Mitchell's Bank, tethered to its buoy. There was no sign of the victim's clothes. Or a murder weapon. No one local had heard a shot or seen anything unusual that morning or overnight.

Shaw retraced his steps back to the shop and knelt down at the glass counter-front. One of the victim's arms was caught under the body, the other thrown behind. Standing so that he could see inside the claw-like hand, Shaw noted that the killer, or killers, had laced a sprig of samphire between the fingers.

'Subtle,' he said.

'I thought samphire was out of season,' said Valentine.

'It keeps,' said Shaw. Lena had done some research because she wanted to offer it as a local delicacy in the café. Better fresh, but perfectly edible after six months in a deep freeze.

'Looks like tit-for-tat,' said Valentine.

'Or they want us to think it's tit-for-tat. Bit heavy handed, don't you think – even for the East End?'

The door to the shop opened and they saw that screens had been put up to block the crowd's view of the interior. A large man in a fishmonger's white overalls was ushered in. For a moment Shaw thought he was going to fall down: the blood drained from his face and he pressed his thumb and forefinger on either side of the bridge of his nose.

'Mr Cobley?' asked Shaw. 'Shall we talk out the back?'

They let him lead the way down the short corridor. Valentine, curious, poked his head into one of the oil drums. Catching movement in the tail of his eye he jerked his head back just in time to avoid a lunging fish head with needle teeth, the jaws clamping in mid-air with a dull plastic click.

'Careful,' said Cobley. 'Rock Salmon – eel to you and me. Isn't safe till you lop its head off.'

'Christ,' said Valentine. The fish reared again, revealing a snake-like body as thick as a weightlifter's arm. One of the other bins clicked with crabs.

Cobley pulled out a metal stool and sat down. 'Sorry, bit shaken. I found him but I can't get over the sight of it. He was such a big bloke. I could see it was him from the face but he just looked so . . .' he struggled for the word to match the image, '. . . insubstantial.'

'What time are we talking?' prompted Shaw.

'I usually get in at seven but Shrimp's had his own keys for years. Drops his catch early if that's how the tides run. Bream, Lemon Sole, a few crabs, lobster, eel.'

'So this is his catch – in the bins?'

Cobley nodded, a hand covering his eyes.

'Tell me about *Shrimp*,' said Shaw, emphasizing the affectionate diminutive.

Cobley needed a bit more time to pull himself together so they went outside into the yard. There was a small patch of garden, and a stone seat sequined with shells. Cobley turned down a cigarette from Valentine but said he could murder a coffee from the café next door: cappuccino with an extra shot, nutmeg not chocolate. So much, thought Shaw, for the simple old-fashioned village fishmonger.

Henry 'Shrimp' Davies, they were told, was a fisherman, born and bred in the Burn Valley. He lived in a cottage in Docking – one of the inland villages where property prices were less eye-watering than the Burnhams – although he often slept with his boat down at Brancaster Staithe: a fifteen-footer, which provided him with a decent living, as it had his father. He drank in the Railway at Docking, lived alone, ex-Merchant Navy. A dog called Penny had once been his constant companion. His age was a secret he'd never divulged, according to Cobley. Stature alone made it difficult to guess.

'I'd say the wrong side of sixty,' said the fishmonger. 'Strong as a horse, mind. But yeah – I know for a fact he supplied my father back in the early seventies. Then he went in the Merchant. They'll have the facts, I guess.'

'Girlfriends?' asked Valentine.

'Not really. Shy type – all right chatting with his mates on the dock, but otherwise he'd just clam up. One or two of the younger lads said he'd been spotted in Lynn, near the docks, in the pubs. Well – I guess that's shorthand for them all being down there. Fishing doesn't leave you a lot of time for picking up girls. They tend to take the more direct route . . .'

'Prostitutes?' asked Shaw. 'Boys or girls?'

Cobley held up both hands. 'Girls. I'm just saying you wouldn't go down there otherwise. So that's my guess. I can give you some names for the other lads. They're a bit wilder. Shrimp tagged along.'

'So, we're saying he kept himself to himself,' said Valentine, cheerfully churning out the usual cliché. Further evidence that other people led lives as dull as his was always welcome, even if there were hints here that something more interesting might lie beneath the surface. He tried to imagine the hulking Shrimp Davies slipping into one of the street corner pubs in Lynn's red light district.

'And he delivered to you – what, daily, weekly?' asked Shaw. The detective was having trouble concentrating because the smell of fish – especially fresh fish – always held a hint of iron. It was odd that cold blood seemed more pungent than hot.

'Well, you can't really deal with the sea like that, Inspector. If it's blowing they won't go out. But most days in summer he'd leave two or three of those oil drums just inside the shop. There's ice in the fridge boxes and he'd chuck a bit in to keep it all fresh. That was it. And the samphire, of course – a drumfull in season.'

Valentine carried on asking questions but Shaw returned to the shop. The pathologist, Justina Kazimeirz, lay half inside the glass counter, just one toe on the ground, reaching in to examine the victim's skin in situ. She was currently brushing his thin hair with a fine-tooth comb, edging anything lodged between the follicles into a small glass dish. Shaw's arrival did not divert her from the task.

Shaw, on his haunches, studied Davies' face. The paleness of death was not quite complete, so that there was a rustic echo in his complexion of a life spent in the elements, at sea, or on a beach, running cod on a line.

Eventually disentangling herself from the counter, Kazimeirz slipped a muslin face mask down to her chest. She wore a head-lamp and a complete forensic white suit. For a moment the heavy Polish features were animated by genuine pleasure in seeing the DI, and Shaw caught a hint of the beautiful girl she once must have been. Then, like a digital image reloading, her face emptied of feeling.

'Shaw,' she said. 'I think there is one question for which you seek an answer,' she added, a hand to her back. 'The clothes?'

She beckoned Shaw closer, so that he was on one side of the glass counter front and she was on the other, her head-light picking out the wound on the chest.

'A point-blank shot,' she said. 'Residue on the skin here . . .' She used a metal stylus to tease at the torn flesh. Shaw made himself focus on the point, reminding himself that the best chance he had of catching this man's killer was to use his body as evidence.

'At this range you'd expect fibres of the shirt, coat, whatever he was wearing, caught in the wound,' said Kazimeirz. 'But it is clean. Totally. I think at this point, when the shot is fired, he was naked.'

Outside they could hear the murmur of the crowd which had gathered beyond the scene-of-crime tapes. A single laugh was followed by a sudden hush of respect.

'Tom tells me there are bloodstains out in the back alley by a van? The back of the skull shows bruising, and two wounds. One is a glancing blow, the other smashed the skull. Certainly enough to lead to unconsciousness – even for a man of this strength.'

'So he was unconscious when the shot was fired?'

'Perhaps. I think he gets out of the van, goes about his work, the blow is delivered, he falls, the second blow knocks him out. Or – and this I prefer – this first blow is not enough. There is a scuffle, perhaps he fights back. Only then does the second blow end it. The clothes are removed. Then a single shot to finish it.'

She stood back, evaluating the body. 'But the nakedness is the key, yes?'

'Locard's Principle,' said Shaw.

Kazimeirz shrugged but it was difficult to see any other reason why the victim had been stripped of his clothes. Locard's Principle of *exchange* was the basis of forensic science. Every killer took evidence away from a crime scene, and left evidence behind. There was a swap – between killer and victim, or between killer and crime scene. Destroy the clothes and you radically reduce the chances of leaving behind trace evidence on the material. The killer, or killers, knew they had to manhandle Davies, so they took his clothes off, probably using gloves. By now those clothes would be ashes.

'They took their troubles,' said the pathologist, mildly mangling her adopted language. 'Perhaps, too, there was blood. Not just his blood. In the fight he may have wounded them. This too could have been on his clothes.'

'Professionals,' said Shaw. A turf war over samphire, with locals like Shrimp Davies taking on London-backed hoods like John Jack Stepney. Which could mean Davies was not just a victim, but a killer. He certainly had the strength to deliver the devastating blow which had cleaved the skull of the man on Mitchell's Bank. Was this his personal pay-off? And all for a slightly salty sea asparagus? No, not just samphire – next year protection money, perhaps, then slot machines, drugs, contraband. None of which helped Shaw answer the pivotal question: what was the connection – if any – between the murders and the ransacking of Burnham Marsh?

'One mistake,' said Kazimeirz, smiling. 'I think he – she – they, used a silencer on the gun.'

'Why is that a mistake?'

'It can reduce the speed of the bullet.'

She knelt again, beside the glass. 'One shot, through the heart, point blank. They hold the victim down on the floor – a hard floor, cement or brick – planning to collect the bullet, or what is left of the bullet. Two mistakes then: they use a silencer, which slows the bullet, and they underestimate this man. He has a mighty chest. The bullet hits the ribs, loses speed, hits the spine, it lodges. There is no exit wound, Shaw. This is a big mistake because we have a bullet. We will have the bullet, once I open his chest. Then, perhaps, you can find the gun.'

TWENTY-FIVE

A chalk A-board in the marble entrance hall at St James' announced that the press conference would be at two o'clock in the Gayton Suite: third floor. The thought of it seemed to suck the life out of Valentine's limbs as he came through the swing doors, so that he came to a halt, threw his head back, and looked up at the white dome above. A mural depicted Justice balancing her scales. Shaw would be upstairs now, checking his notes, talking someone from the media department through the press release.

Valentine couldn't face it. He'd be on time, but no earlier. Up on his feet since the early hours, he deserved a decent cup of tea. The fire exit door bounced open into the rear yard. An exterior entrance led down into the basement. Unlike many police headquarters – most notably New Scotland Yard – St James' was actually a police station, not just an administrative HQ. Back in the late eighties he and Jack Shaw had gone down to Old Scotland Yard on a case and entered through its police station – known officially as Canon Row. St James' version had no separate name, but it was a small world of its own, with a line of cells, front counter, and a duty officer – usually a young PC.

Valentine felt at ease because the place always smelt like a coppers' lair: industrial piping, tiled floors, and a hint of filing cabinets, disinfectant and nicotine. Despite being deep-cleaned since the smoking ban, the woodwork still breathed out the aroma of thousands of Silk Cut, Marlboro and, reaching back, Woodbine and Embassy. One of the cells was set aside as a makeshift canteen with a kettle and tea and coffee-making kit. Valentine, who'd used this informal café many times, made a mug of mahogany brown brew and idly read the day book on the counter: the record of all incidents recorded in the last twenty-four-hour period. There was a uniformed constable on the desk, a kid with glasses about five foot nine, who seemed to know Valentine because he kept smiling at him.

'It's been quiet,' the constable said. 'Two in the cells – both drunk. I'm checking every ten minutes – less.'

Valentine nodded in sympathy. They'd all like to get through their careers without a death in police cells. It didn't matter what the facts were, the slight stain of the incident was indelible. In Valentine's first year in the job he'd been assigned to cell duties for three months. Once, unable to trust a distraught drunk who'd threatened to cut his wrists, he'd sat in the cell with him all night, both of them chain-smoking.

Valentine enjoyed documents like the day book. For him they represented the bread and butter of policing. Raw, street-level, unprocessed data. When he was a young DI he'd made a point of coming down and reading it if he had a spare ten minutes. It was like picking up the shipping forecast on the car radio; the litany of petty crime seemed to offer a warm, encircling comfort, often in stark contrast to whatever case had landed on his desk in CID.

The phrase 'air pellets' caught his eye, so he read the whole entry again:

Arnold John Smith-Waterson. Arrested 8.10 a.m. on suspicion of theft outside the Convenience Store, London Road. Cell Six. Contents of overcoat pockets: catering-sized packet of Tunnock Bars, a half bottle of Tesco's whisky, eight Aztec bars, ten Aeros and five packets of Revels. Wallet: £8.00 cash. Credit card. Box of air pellets – unopened. Released 12.45 p.m.

'Smith-Waterson,' said Valentine, turning the book round so the youngster could see the entry. 'You book him in?'

'Yeah,' he said, then caught the hardening in Valentine's eyes. 'Sir. He's reporting back tonight. Sergeant Pilling's got the case notes. Goes by the name of Gutter on the street. Tramp. Shop owner rang us and said he was hoovering up sweets. It won't be the first time. Lives down on the Outfall. Well, he sleeps down there. Spends most days hanging round the churchyards with a book. Big reader, is Gutter.'

Churchyards.

Valentine nodded and left. The press conference was due to start precisely on the hour, which left him fifteen minutes. His slightly arthritic military step got him down to the riverside in under five, although his heartbeat was perceptible in his chest.

The riverside was concrete, with benches, and observation platforms which offered a view north, along the Cut to the sea. A set of steel steps led down towards the sticky mud of the estuary, but after three corkscrew turns they reached a platform, which formed the lip of a wide sewer tunnel, over which a sluggish trickle of water fell into the estuary. This was all that was left of the Millfleet River, built over by the Victorians.

The spot was known as the Outfall. A man-made cave went back fifty feet, before narrowing to a large metal pipe, blocked with a semi-circular iron grid. On the smooth dry concrete 'riverbank' stood a little shanty town of cardboard boxes and old mattresses. One tramp stood in the water, barefoot, smoking. A dog on a rope showed Valentine a wet throat and a lolling tongue.

He put his warrant card in the face of a teenager in a puffa jacket, torn to reveal the multicoloured insulation within.

'I'm looking for Gutter.'

The kid pointed further along the bank to a neat set of cardboard boxes. Arnold John Smith-Waterson was sitting on an old office chair reading a book. He was about seventy, with a pair of rimless glasses with one cracked lens. He wore expensive clothes, worn to the edge of oblivion: a tweed jacket, cords, brown leather shoes, a wool shirt, a scarf, and finally leather gloves – which, oddly, looked new. A price label for the right one flapped at his wrist.

He looked at Valentine out of the corners of his eyes.

Valentine showed him his warrant card and asked him about the air pellets and why he had them in his pockets.

Gutter set the book aside like a relic, carefully folding a corner of a blanket over the cover.

'Did you steal the gloves too?' asked Valentine.

'Spring tide this evening,' said Gutter, finally. 'They won't believe me. We'll have to move up top. Absolutely, yes.' He shook his head as if someone, unheard, was disagreeing. 'It's the word that misleads them: *spring*. They think autumn, winter, summer. Wrong, of course. You'll know . . .' Fleeting eye contact, and Valentine saw the intelligence, the fact that there was another person behind the glassy, reflective surfaces. 'It's because it *springs* . . .' Gutter made his gloved hands into two animal claws.

'Sixteen feet nine by eleven thirty-two p.m. Over your head, right now, where you're standing.'

Valentine squatted down, and got close. 'Show me where the gun is or we're going back to St James' now.'

'I don't need to steal. I've got a credit card and there's £6,435 and fifty-six pence in the account as of this morning.'

Valentine lit a cigarette. The press conference started in eight minutes but he wasn't going to move a muscle. Peter Shaw was pretty good at a lot of things, but in front of a room full of media newshounds he was even better. The last thing he needed was a tatty DS to hand round the press release.

Valentine sent him a text. *Interview ongoing. I'll be late.*

'So it's not just in spring, you see,' continued Gutter. 'That's the mistake they make. But you wouldn't make that mistake, I know that.' He tried a smile, revealing good teeth, bad gums.

'What have you got against angels?'

Gutter's mouth lolled open in shock at the question.

'Show me the gun and we'll talk. No promises. But if you don't show me the gun we're going back to St James' and you'll be staying. Indoors. Inside. It's that simple.'

In Valentine's experience the vast majority of so-called 'tramps' were simply claustrophobics, unable to deal with the strictures and regulations imposed on those who had to live under a roof.

Gutter's cardboard cot, which had once held a 'complete carry-cot system' according to the label, looked cosy. He closed the flaps as if locking his own front door, and his neighbours watched balefully as Valentine led him away, up the steel steps to the quayside above.

Gutter led the way south along the riverbank. In less than a hundred yards they came to a mud bank which they climbed. Before them lay a grassy inlet, behind the Boal Quay, which less than a decade ago was a meander in the River Nar. One high tide had cut the 'neck' of the loop in the river and left it high and dry, a few of the old forgotten boats stranded in the channel forever. One or two were just piles of old wood now, lying in the grassy dry channel. Others, appropriated by squatters, sported makeshift washing lines.

Gutter's choice had no name but BEWARE THE DOG had been spray-canned down one side in letters a foot tall. An old wooden barge, it had a derelict wheelhouse and a broken mast. Gutter didn't need to step aboard, but instead simply slipped a hand in through the shattered clinker hull where a porthole had once been. After a brief tussle with some boards the gun came out wrapped in an oilcloth. The haft held an engraved plate: *Arnold Smith-Waterson.*

Valentine took the weapon and noted that Gutter did everything with his right hand, the left held awkwardly to his chest.

'What's wrong with your hand?'

Valentine almost walked away then, because he could see the fear in the old man's eyes. Trapped, cornered, like an animal with no available means of escape. Valentine hadn't come into the police force to make vulnerable people feel scared. He bit back the sudden urge to apologize. He'd been a bully, and it wasn't an attractive self-image. He needed to rethink this relationship, and he'd start by calling the other man by his proper name.

'Arnold. Show me your hand. Then I can help.'

Gutter didn't want to tell him what was wrong with his hand, but now it was inevitable that he would, and that this would change his life forever. He began to shake, quite visibly, his shoulders vibrating.

'Show me,' said Valentine, in as kindly a voice as he had in what was admittedly a narrow repertoire.

It took a series of small tugs to dislodge the glove from the fingers.

When it was completely off he let it fall to the ground.

Three of the fingers were pale and white, the fourth, next to the thumb, was black – exactly the same spectrum of black you can observe in an over-ripe banana, from a deep yellow to a purple.

And there was a sweet smell. Valentine took a step back despite himself.

'Necrosis,' said Smith-Waterson. 'The flesh is dead,' he added, as if the hand belonged to someone else.

Valentine had seen the pictures Fiona Campbell had put up in CID. Victims of the adulterated drugs, with dead, blackened limbs.

Gutter's other hand, still gloved, fluttered in front of his lips.

'I can't tell anyone his name. The man who did this. The fallen angel.' He held the disfigured hand up in front of his face. 'But I wanted retribution.' His eyes met Valentine's and hardened. 'I need retribution. I have no peace without it. So I take it where I can. I kill angels.'

TWENTY-SIX

Jack Shaw, who had always looked down on what he called the 'gin and tiller' set, used to tell his son that you should never trust the owner of a boat that has patio doors. John Jack Stepney's *Highlife* was a flagship of what the locals disparagingly called the white ships – fibreglass gin palaces with reflective glass saloons, radar and sonar on a scale which would embarrass NASA, and – without exception – patio doors.

The little resort of Wells-next-the-Sea was buzzing with a late summer crowd, despite the fact a violent thunderstorm had blown through the town that afternoon, leaving the pavements steaming in the sunshine. A long line of trippers trekked the mile along the sea wall back to town from the beaches. Fried fat, batter and the sweet smell of candyfloss filled the air.

Shaw stood on the quay examining *Highlife*, relieved to be back outdoors after an exhausting press conference which had included a live BBC TV interview for *Look East*. The media had been given what facts they had on the murder of Shrimp Davies. Yes, the murder was possibly connected to the death on Mitchell's Bank. Yes, they were investigating reports the deaths might be linked to the lucrative samphire trade on the coast. And yes, they had a lead: the *Limpet*.

Its owner had been traced quickly through the harbour master's office at Cley. His principal residence was in Normandy. An airline pilot, he had been contacted through a third party at EasyJet. An initial telephone call had established that he was not in the country on the night of seventeenth October. The boat should have been moored in the harbour at Blakeney. It had last gone to sea in late August. A district PC at Blakeney confirmed that the boat was not in the harbour. Fishermen, the RNLI, Coastwatch and HMRC had all been put on alert to try and find the *Limpet*. Meanwhile, the owner had sent them a digital image of the boat which they were releasing immediately to the media.

That was what Shaw had told the press. But meanwhile, behind the scenes, they were working flat out to track down the vehicle spotted by Geoff Wighton at Tines Manor. DC Lau was at the county council offices trying to locate the white van, one of nearly forty in a pool used by council officers. The incomplete registration number was causing some problems, as was the fact that the register of drivers was not up to date, and relied on a slipshod system for booking vans in and out of the pound. It looked likely that they would have to wait until all the vans had been returned that evening, or at least booked out overnight by telephone call or email.

Which left them with their prime suspect, John Jack Stepney. Shaw had no doubts he'd have a decent alibi for the murder of Shrimp Davies. Stepney had gone up in the world since the days when he'd had to dole out violence in person on the street. But were the two murders really connected to the samphire trade? Or rather, were they *solely* connected to the samphire trade? Could Stepney be complicit in the burglaries too? Exactly how far-flung was his north Norfolk criminal network? Whatever the truth, Shaw needed to confront Stepney. If they could unsettle, intimidate, he might make a mistake. Shaw had ordered a twenty-four-hour surveillance unit to shadow him from dusk that evening.

In keeping with most of the white ships, *Highlife* had a quay-side bell. Valentine gave it a vicious ring. He hated bells – particularly those rung to indicate last orders. A long day had left him tired and dispirited. He'd left Arnold 'Gutter' Smith-Waterson with the custody sergeant at St James'. Fiona Campbell was organizing a transfer to the Queen Elizabeth Hospital. A formal interview would follow after he'd been treated for the necrosis in his fingers. Leaving Gutter in a cell at St James' had felt like a betrayal.

The sharp note of the bell brought Stepney's daughter on deck.

'He's in the Palace,' she said, indicating one of the three amusement arcades on the little front. She was in skimpy shorts again, and a floppy T-shirt, having apparently enjoyed a very brief sunshine holiday. There was no sign of the child who'd been bundled off in a taxi from the house in Balamory. In one hand she held a large tumbler of white wine; the glass blushed with condensation.

'Rain, did it, in the Canaries?' asked Valentine. 'Tenerife, you said,' he added, noting her bemused look.

'We've got a flat. I just go to check the water, pay the bills. It's work really.'

Shaw retrieved her name from his memory banks: 'Emilia,' he said. 'Why's your dad in the Palace?'

'Because he owns it, and it's been struck by lightning.' She seemed to think this provided the *coup de grâce* to their conversation, so she walked off down the deck, the wine glass held at an angle so far from the vertical that she lost a little with each step.

The Palace appeared to be closed, unlike the other two arcades, which emitted canned music and the strange mechanical thuds and klaxons associated with fruit machines. The façade of the amusement arcade was made up of several folding glass doors, like a 1930s cinema foyer. Inside they could see workmen entangled in wiring which hung down in a series of bundles from the ceiling, where several asbestos tiles had been removed to allow access to the service ducts.

Stepney was in the back office, through a fire door, off an alley which hugged the back wall of the building. They had to wait while he finished an ill-tempered conversation with one of the workmen who had just announced, with a note of barely disguised satisfaction, that the Palace would be unable to reopen for at least two days.

'Poor insulation,' said the electrician. 'So one bolt of lightning and bang! The lot's blown.'

Shaw wandered out into the main arcade while Stepney tried to explain that such a timetable was not acceptable. Two questions bothered Shaw: where had Stepney got the cash to buy the business, and why didn't the police know he was the owner? All gambling venues were licensed and regulated by the Gambling Commission, and notified to the police authority. If Stepney's name had come up the West Norfolk police would have at least attempted to block the application, but Stepney's police records mentioned nothing. It was, however, apparent that his involvement with the Palace was hardly clandestine. So what was going on?

Out in the main arcade there was a lingering aroma of shorted wires. Stepney appeared from his office, grinning. 'Thought you'd be down at the fishmonger's looking at the prize catch. Apparently he's six pounds fifty a pound – cheaper than the salmon. Mind you – cheap's relative. They know how to charge in Burnham Market.'

Shaw had hoped to keep the precise details of the scene of crime confidential, but at least half-a-dozen witnesses had seen the body before the police arrived, and all had shared the story with family and friends. This particular news genie was well and truly out of its bottle, so Stepney's comment betrayed no insider knowledge. A double bluff, perhaps?

Grilling Stepney over Shrimp Davies' death was a waste of time. The problem with the killing was that it was undeniably in Stepney's interests that everyone *thought* Davies had been murdered in order to establish the East Ender's grip on the samphire trade, and much else. So why do him any favours?

Quietly, methodically, they were working to build up Stepney's background file. Shaw had put a call into the Met, to C Division at Mile End, to request his full file to be sent up to Lynn. Twine would organize a formal statement tomorrow at St James' so that Stepney's movements over the last twenty-four hours could be double-checked. Overnight the team would apply for warrants for both *Highflyer* and Stepney's house – next door to the daughter's in Balamory. Might Stepney be the fence for the goods stolen from second homes? He'd certainly had the contacts. And he had the vans.

'Your daughter's holiday was short-lived,' said Shaw.

'She dropped off Michael – my grandson. There's family out on the island – brothers, an uncle. It's not a white slave trade or anything.'

'She – that's Emilia – seemed to think you owned this place.'

Shaw saw it then – like a reptile's third eyelid suddenly glimpsed, the anger flickering. 'Stupid cow. I am merely an employee. If you want the owner you'll have to talk to the lawyers. I've got a number somewhere.'

'That would help,' said Shaw. 'Do they know about your criminal record, the owners? Violence, of course. And burglary. Tell me about the break-ins. Residential, business, I forget the details.'

Stepney stiffened the muscles in his shoulders and took a step towards Shaw, expecting the DI to flinch back, but he held his position precisely, so that they ended up a few inches apart, face-to-face.

'You've got no right bringing that up. Those convictions are spent. This is harassment.'

'Ever tempted to get back in the business? Lift the odd latch. Nick some old dear's purse off the mantelpiece. Or something a bit up-market. Artwork, jewels, white goods, three-D TVs?'

Stepney worked something round in his mouth and for a moment Valentine thought he was going to spit in Shaw's face.

Then he smiled. 'Just get on with it. I haven't got all day. I'm a very busy man.' He walked to one of the machines and put a ten-pence piece in the slot. 'People are funny,' he said. 'These things are all buttons and circuits now – but they still like to pull the arm. Know what they call it?'

'Light up my day,' said Shaw.

'A legacy lever,' he said, spinning the oranges, pears and apples.

'My DS has got a few questions, Mr Stepney,' said Shaw. 'Nothing you won't be expecting.'

Valentine asked him for details of his whereabouts in the last twenty-four hours, asking him – point blank – if he was involved in the murder of Shrimp Davies. The denial had all the generous sincerity they'd come to expect. The alibi was impressive. Not only had Stepney been on the boat, he'd been on the boat during a five-hour party. Guests had included two local councillors, a town magistrate and three members of the WI.

'Just trying to build bridges with the local community,' said Stepney.

To Shaw the alibi suggested that while Stepney had not taken part in the killing he had known its date and time. This was the principal advantage of organized crime, that different parts of the organization could be mobilized to carry out dirty work on someone else's patch, largely removing the possibility that motive could be used to track back to the killer.

Shaw wandered among the slot machines. Stepney was clearly unhappy at having police on the premises so they might as well take their time. Shaw recalled a scene from the film of *The Grapes of Wrath* – which he was pretty sure was in Steinbeck's original text. The family, migrant workers fleeing the 1930s dustbowl of Oklahoma, pull up for petrol at a lonely desert garage. While the truck's taking on fuel they crowd round a table in the little café for coffee. A driver comes in and pulls the lever on a slot machine. As he does so the café owner, behind the counter, surreptitiously adds a chalk mark to a tally. He waits for one of the poor 'Okies' to try their luck with their last dime. Then he adds another chalk mark and walks casually round to make the next play. The machines are fixed to pay out on a set number of lever pulls. He collects the jackpot. Shaw wondered how modern slot machines were regulated.

Valentine, finished with his standard inquiries, had one last question for Stepney.

'What's the RTP on that bandit?' he asked, pointing at one of the one-pound slot machines.

Shaw had forgotten that Valentine had spent six months on a gambling task force back in the 1980s. They'd shaken down the arcades in Lynn and Hunstanton, and Cromer and Sheringham. Valentine had enjoyed it because he loved a bet, found it deeply satisfying to evaluate risk, and then take a chance. Oddly, he had never felt a twinge of addiction.

Stepney gave Valentine the full 100-watt glare. That was his Achilles heel, thought Shaw, and the one thing he really feared, that he'd be made a fool of, the veneer of education exposed for what it was – bluster, powered by the projection of a palpable sense of physical threat. It was clear he didn't know what RTP was – and more to the point, neither did Shaw.

'Return To Player,' said Valentine. 'You put a hundred pounds in over a session, or a hundred dollars for that matter, and the RTP tells you how much – on average – you get back. In Nevada it's seventy-five pounds, or seventy-five dollars – in New Jersey it's eighty-three dollars. It's all regulated because the machines are tested before they leave the factory, each one sealed.'

Valentine produced a one-pound coin: 'Every one of these machines has an RTP on the front. Right? So the punter knows the risks.'

Stepney was going to speak but Valentine cut in: 'The RTP's

set and tested by the maker. The regulator licenses operators. If you're not the licensee, who is?'

'I've got the paperwork. But like you say – it's all regulated, above board. Fair.'

'Unless someone tampers with the machines and alters the RTP.'

'It's north Norfolk, not Reno. The operator's a licensed supplier. She deals with the machines. I don't touch 'em.'

'*She?*' asked Shaw.

The smile fell off Stepney's face. 'Whatever.'

'Not always fair though, is it?' persisted Valentine. 'Not quite. After all, it's all very well knowing a machine pays back at ninety per cent, but what if it pays all the money back only in a jackpot – or only in mid-range prizes? That's what the customer never knows, isn't it? The strategy, the spread. If you're a proper gambler that's what you need to know. And there's only one way to find out, and that costs a fortune.'

Valentine slipped the coin into the nearest machine and spun the seven reels. A HOLD, a HOLD, then three NUDGES, and he'd won. The machine chugged out pound coins.

Stepney went and got the number for the lawyers. It was a printed card marked Norfolk Entertainments, Inc.

Shaw took the card. 'We'll be back, Mr Stepney. One of my team will be calling later today to arrange for a formal statement. Not planning any trips to Tenerife yourself, I hope?'

'What if I was?'

'I'd postpone it for now. We will need to interview you formally at St James'. Do I need to ask for your passport?'

'Now you've got me all upset, Inspector.'

'That would be a shame, Mr Stepney. Have a nice day. We'll be contacting the owner, after speaking to your lawyers. They may want a word. We'll see you again, soon.'

Valentine put in another pound, pulled the arm and walked away before the reels stopped turning.

TWENTY-SEVEN

While the body of Shrimp Davies lay on a mortuary slab at the Ark awaiting a full autopsy and the removal of the tell-tale bullet, his life had been lived here, on the coast, and Shaw and Valentine were reluctant to simply leave the hunt for his killer to forensic science. Shaw needed to know more about the man, not just because it was a necessary step in the inquiry, but because he always tried hard not to treat the dead as mere ciphers; white paint outlines at the scene of crime, the sum solely of motive and opportunity. Just for a moment he wanted to step aside and see the world as Shrimp Davies had seen it – through the eyes of a sixty-three-year-old bachelor who'd once loved a dog called Penny. Most of all he wanted to touch a life that held some virtue after an hour in the toxic company of John Jack Stepney.

There was no doubt Shrimp Davies' world was a boathouse shed on the old staithe at Brancaster; a long way from the north Norfolk coast the tourists saw, or most of the second-home set. Here, tucked away, was a shanty village of sheds, boathouses and old warehouses beside a marine fuel unit, a dock crane, some rotting boats and a muddy creek. A ridge of sand dunes topped with gorse hid it from the sailing club and a line of holiday cottages in Norfolk stone. Despite the industrial setting it had its own, sumptuous view: out along the channel to the sea, snaking through the marsh, the horizon a golden line of high dunes.

Shaw let his eyes fill up with blue sky. Was it really just a week earlier that he'd sat with Lena on the deck at the Old Ship Inn, half a mile east, sipping white wine and shuffling scallops around a giant china plate?

Valentine got a key to Davies' boathouse off the harbour master – an ex-Royal Navy veteran called Patten. He'd described Shrimp as 'a bit close' – which for north Norfolk amounted to virtually mute. Davies' father – known universally as 'William J' to distinguish him from a shoal of cousins who worked the coast – had taken the same boat out on the same tides to pick samphire from the same beds. He hadn't so much followed in his father's footsteps as stolen his shoes.

Patten was able to add one unexpected layer to the picture they were constructing of the dead man: 'You'd think he was an old codger, Shrimp. He'd ham it up for tourists – the Norfolk burr, the rustic charm – then he'd charge them twenty-five quid for a conger eel. But a couple of times I saw him out at dusk by the boathouse and you could see from the glow he had a smart phone – like he was playing with it. Once, when I heard him stumbling about around his van, I saw him use it as a torch. You find that, did you – the smart phone?'

They hadn't. But then they'd not found his clothes either. Or the gun. Or anything unexpected in his neat cottage at Docking, a dozen miles inland. A single armchair placed squarely in front of a box-like TV had reminded Valentine of his old flat in Wells. The bathroom had been a mild revelation: a power shower, a shelf of deodorants, a pile of *Geographic* magazines by the loo. Neat, ordered, uncluttered. It was difficult to avoid the yawning cliché: shipshape. All of his mates said that while he'd go home to the cottage in winter, most days he'd sleep over in the boathouse because that's where he wanted to wake up.

Valentine slipped off the padlock and the corrugated-iron door screeched on rusty hinges. The interior, smoky black, reeked of tar and old fish heads. Valentine, who hated the sea for the salty crust it left on his lips, felt his skin crawl. There were dark corners, and rotting tackle, and the word 'maggoty' slipped into his mind.

Patten, in the harbour office – his eyes out the window on the channel even when he answered a question – said he'd turned a blind eye to Davies' sleeping in the shed, even if it was against all the regulations. In the summer Davies would drink in the Jolly Sailors up in the village, then stagger back to the staithe to collapse among the old tackle.

'Up at first light, mind. Whistling on the wharf,' said Patten with obvious approval.

Once their eyes had become accustomed to the windowless shack they could make out where he slept, in a kind of nest made out of old nets, under a single brass oil lantern. There were two plastic beer holders set on the floor, cylindrical, dark brown, with a special cork to allow the ale to breathe. An ashtray – clean – and a book of nautical signals lay beside a pillow made out of the local free-sheet newspaper tied in a bundle.

A gust of wind slammed the door and they were plunged into darkness. Then they saw the holes: several on the eastern wall, so that the sun shone in narrow beams through cracks between the metal sheet panels.

'Wouldn't fancy it on a winter's night,' said Shaw.

Valentine pushed the door back open and wedged it there with a breeze block.

They stood looking at what was left of Shrimp Davies' life.

'At the risk of sounding like a long-playing record, we shouldn't disregard the obvious,' said Valentine. 'He was a fisherman. Samphire was a nice little sideline. It's only a guess, but twenty-five years in the Merchant Navy doesn't turn you into the kind of character who's going to roll over and crawl away when a thug comes round and tells you that you can't do what you've always done – what your father did before you. He had that little Post Office van. He could have driven in to Lynn after a few bevies and slashed Stepney's tyres, or got some of the young bloods to help.

'Look at it from Stepney's point of view. He gets his van fleet vandalized then the body turns up on Mitchell's Bank. If the victim was one of Stepney's pickers he'd think a war was on. He jumps to conclusions. He'd like us to think he's Jean-Paul Sartre but he's really just a crook, and we know they're not that bright. So he thinks he's losing a war and he hasn't fired a bullet yet – all he's done is stove in a few boats. You can see the reasoning. Unless he makes a statement, an unequivocal statement of intent, he's lost authority.'

'Why Shrimp Davies?'

'Sedentary, predictable, lonely old Shrimp Davies? Why'd you think?'

Shaw, running a hand along one shadowy wall, found what they might have missed. The shack did have a window – covered with a large interior shutter, which dropped down on hinges. The flood of marine light when they got it open was extraordinary, driving the shadows into the corners. It also revealed, above

Davies' bed, a wooden joist to which had been pinned a series of photographs.

Shaw understood immediately the rationale behind the arrangement of the pictures, about thirty in all, from left to right. Those to the left, at what he took to be the start of the sequence, were old black-and-whites. The first showed a woman's head, bare shoulders and no shoulder straps – she might have been naked. In fact, Shaw sensed she *was* naked, and that her body, unseen by the viewer, was in full view for the photographer. She looked Arabic, the natural beauty disfigured by too much make-up, a glossy oil in the hair. Outside, through an open window, the sunlight was brutal on what looked like a Middle Eastern street – dusty, a donkey passing pulling a cart, inky shadows below an awning.

'Port Said, Valetta, Nicosia, Aden – take your choice,' offered Shaw. A first love, he wondered, or just the first.

Valentine had started at the other end of the sequence: a vivid colour snapshot with the Boots PhotoShop logo in one corner.

'That's why he's got the iPhone,' he said. 'So he can keep his little collection going.'

This girl was probably eighteen but she could have been thirty, the blue eyes shielded by a precocious cynicism. Just the head again, but more of the shoulders and the clear skin of the chest, the first curve of her breasts. A window again behind, but no sunlight this time, just a dull yard with a standing tap, some flaking whitewash.

'North End, Lynn,' said Valentine, tapping the print. 'One of the cribs. Not that I've got any first-hand experience. She's on the game, mind – no doubts.'

'Know what I think?' said Shaw. Valentine knew him well enough not to try and interject an answer. 'I don't think he had sex with them at all. I think he'd paid his money and asked to take a picture.'

They both stood thinking about the secret life of Shrimp Davies, sprawled on his bed of nets, contemplating his conquests. It was a sad life, thought Valentine, but ultimately a gentle one.

Shaw knelt among the nets. Beneath the line of snapshots were three more prints from the iPhone pinned to a lower wooden joist.

The first was slightly out of focus and Valentine said it looked like Davies had tried to use the telephoto option on the camera. It showed a man astride a motorbike on the sea wall by the lifeboat house at Wells. Shaw guessed from the angle it had been taken from Shrimp's boat as it came in on the Run – the channel that led to the harbour. The rider had unzipped the top half of a set of leathers so that his splayed arms dangled like a spider. His torso was white, hairless and gym-shaped. The bike looked like a Harley-Davidson, with the wasp-like insect tank, in black paint. Shaw couldn't shake the thought that Shrimp had taken the picture as a warning, because the rider was looking directly at the camera.

TWENTY-EIGHT

The foundation stone for Greenwood House had been laid in the flood winter of 1947 on the edge of a bombsite on Lynn waterfront. Shaw had once seen a picture of the ceremony in the library archives when he'd been helping Lena search for images to frame and hang in the Old Beach Café. The scene was almost Victorian, the block of flats just a building site against the vast Brunel-like dockside cranes, hoists and derricks, a coaster's superstructure stark against a grey sky, and a horse tethered to a cart of bricks. Mud and slush lay thick over the ground where the seawater had only recently receded. It had been an act of faith in March 1947, this declaration that there was a future, despite the war and such random, devastating acts of God as the flood that had inundated the Fens, battered the coast and killed thousands with its freezing damp, all in the wake of a pulverizing Arctic winter. Morale, weighed down by rationing and post-war gloom, had plummeted. Shaw had studied the faces of the dignitaries in the picture and thought that they all looked to be in collective shock, their bodies stiff, skin pale, expressions blank. He could almost feel what it was like to stand there that day in a heavy damp coat, the smell of wet earth on the air, ice in the puddles underfoot.

Greenwood House stood still on the edge of the docks, nearly seventy years later, its five serried balconied floors looking out towards West Lynn on the far side of the Cut. It was dull red-brick with cream-painted concrete edges, all in a streamlined 1930s style with Crittall windows and open stairwells, impregnated with seven decades of disinfectant. A smart unvandalized sign at the ground-floor entrance proclaimed the building to be owned by the King John Trust, a local housing association. But for half a century it had simply been council housing: five floors, three stairwells and sixty-three flats, with one spare for a caretaker on site, now a locked store and boiler room.

Shaw couldn't stand on the steps without thinking about the

thousands of children who'd run up and down them since 1947.
The children of the Welfare State. He wondered what the eponymous Arthur Greenwood, leader of the parliamentary Labour
Party during the war, would have made of this memorial. He
tapped a metal toecap against the brickwork.

'That's the van,' said Valentine, reading a registration number
off his mobile phone. 'The only one in the vehicle pool with
those four characters – DN10.'

A white Ford stood on the acre of wide concrete in front of
the flats. The scene looked Soviet, a workers' palace designed
with space for a car for all, each marked out by bureaucratic
white lines; except it didn't look like anyone else could afford
a vehicle.

The van would have been as anonymous as any white van
except for the Norfolk County Council logo on the side.

'Lau says this bloke should be inspecting flat fifty-four,' said
Valentine. 'That's what he put on the vehicle request form, along
with fifteen other appointments over two days. He's nothing if
not meticulous.'

They climbed to the top floor and circled the building using
the balcony. It gave them views across Lynn town centre, to the
small, stately bell tower of Customs House and over the shining
water to the chimney pots of West Lynn, the little ferry inscribing
a white wake as it ran shoppers to a wooden jetty.

Shaw went round the last corner first and saw a man locking
a front door: shirt, tie, a suit under a good quality outdoor jacket.
There was something in the way he failed to react to his footsteps
which made Shaw think they might have found their man.

'Mr Whyte?'

'How can I help?' He had a large head, much too big for a
slight frame, possibly five-eight, or less, and very narrow shoulders. His eyes were lost behind a pair of metal-rimmed glasses
which caught the light.

Valentine appeared next and Whyte's face fell.

'Sergeant,' he said.

'Mr Whyte. Of course – I'd forgotten the name. Labour Party
business? Or council?'

'Bit of both.'

Valentine quickly brought Shaw up to date on how he knew

Clem Whyte: district chairman of the party and one of the council's three assistant chief housing officers. That's what he said
out loud but he'd briefed Shaw on his meeting with Clem Whyte
on the day he'd visited Adelaide Gardens. He'd said then he
thought Whyte knew more than he was prepared to divulge to
CID about the anti-second-homes protestors.

Shaw told Whyte why they were there: a white van, registration DN10, with the council logo, had been spotted in the vicinity
of a series of burglaries. They'd tracked the vehicle to Norfolk
County Council. The head of the motor pool said the van in
question was pretty much permanently out for the use of the
housing department. Whyte had signed for it on an almost continuous basis for the last eight months. Perhaps Mr Whyte could
explain his movements? Why, for example, was the van in the
hamlet of East Tines at four o'clock in the morning two nights
ago?

Whyte blinked behind his glasses.

'That van,' said Shaw, pointing over the parapet. The next flat
along the level had its kitchen window open and they heard a
brief interlude of conversation in an exotic language.

'Sorry, yes, perfectly good question,' said Whyte. 'I get around
a bit, it's true. I leave it out in the field sometimes if I'm working
with other units. No point wasting council money if we're all
going back to the same site next morning. But East Tines – I
don't think so.'

They heard footsteps in the stairwell and a woman appeared
hauling two Tesco bags.

'Clem,' she said, by way of welcome. 'Lift's out again.
Did you know? You like the stairs, you always did, but they'll
kill me.'

She walked on, turning the sharp corner, climbing up.

'First name terms with all the residents, Mr Whyte?'

'No. A lot. I was brought up here, Inspector. We moved here
in 'eighty-nine – me, my mum and my grandfather. Flat sixty-
eight, sixth floor. Stairs never bothered me.' He worked at the
tie round his throat, giving himself some air. 'We were homeless,
so I've always been grateful. I wasn't then – grateful, I mean,
'cos Granddad was so upset. We got evicted from our house, the
one I was born in. Don't you just love a landlord . . .'

When the light wasn't clashing with the lenses Shaw could see small eyes, possibly grey, constantly looking away, down at the van.

'So, two nights ago, where were you at four in the morning?' asked Shaw.

'At home in bed. To be honest, that's where I've been at four in the morning every night for the last ten years. 'Cept for holidays. Devon usually. This year we're going mad. Cornwall.'

Whyte took a half step away from the front door of the flat he'd been leaving. It was a tiny miscalculation, because Shaw and Valentine were blocking his exit to the stairwell, and so it looked like what it was: a conscious effort to move them all away, down the stairs.

Shaw peered in through the window. 'What would the rent on this be?' He could see a sink with a single plate, a decent fridge, an old gas cooker scrubbed clean. On the kitchen table was a small doll in a rich red medieval-style coat, studded with cheap sequins.

'Basic is a hundred and three pounds a week. But you know, most of those high enough on the list to get a property may well be able to claim benefits to cover part of that, or all of it.'

'So what's the Labour Party policy on second homes?' asked Shaw.

'I explained all that to your sergeant.'

'He's not my sergeant, sir. He's a community resource, aren't you, George?'

Valentine was prowling up and down the balcony.

'I should get on,' said Whyte.

Shaw and Valentine didn't move.

'Why are you visiting this particular flat, Mr Whyte? The departmental secretary thought you'd booked the day off.'

'It's empty. I've got someone on the list – out at Burnham Norton, actually, an elderly woman in a tied cottage. She's been asked to leave. Told to leave. I needed to check this place out: wheelchair access, handrails. I do work on my lieu days – it makes life easier. We can't afford a complete makeover, but there's a few pound in the contingency fund. I think we can take her. It's good news.'

Shaw thought about the red doll on the kitchen table. It didn't look like the flat was empty to him.

'I'd like to see inside, sir,' said Shaw. 'I can apply for a warrant but I'd have to insist you remain here during the interim – an hour, maybe two. It would be easier . . .'

Whyte had a heavy-duty belt around his narrow waist off which hung a set of keys. Shaw thought how much that must be like a badge of office. It was almost Shakespearean – the gatekeeper, the locksmith.

They let him go first and Valentine stayed by the door, which Shaw took as a signal that his DS thought their suspect might decide to run for the van. There was no doubt Whyte found entering the flat profoundly unsettling. He kept coughing as if about to give a speech.

Something had died in the flat. Not this week, or this month, but a lifetime ago. A mouse perhaps, or a rat, under the floor or in the walls or roof.

'It doesn't look empty to me,' said Shaw.

'I know. Last tenant did a runner. Five hundred pounds in arrears.'

Shaw opened the fridge and it was full of provisions – both vegetable drawers crammed with carrots and beets and parsnips. There was a whole shelf of smoked and pickled meats.

'Name, please?'

'Stefan Bedrich,' said Whyte. 'He lived alone.'

The double bed had a sleeping bag on it, and there were plastic razors next to the bathroom sink. Neat, tidy, minimal.

'Odd, isn't it – when there's such a lot of pressure on cheap housing, that you found a flat for this man?' Shaw was in the corridor. He pointed out the bedroom doors. 'One double, one single, a box. Just one man. How does that work?'

'The Home Office has the details,' said Whyte. 'There was a family coming, but they were held up for some reason in Poland. That's why he got the larger flat. We'd have had to move him into a family flat eventually. It saved time.'

It was such a weak excuse the last few words were almost inaudible.

The lounge told the real story. The walls were extraordinary, the original wallpaper almost completely obscured by artwork. Most of the pictures were A4-sized and showed evidence of having been folded. Abstract studies mostly, but there were a few

landscapes and portraits. All were characterized by vibrant, startling colour. The effect reminded Shaw of stained glass but more
chaotic, unrestrained by lead or stone. There was one large
window in the room, without curtains, and the late summer light
ignited the pictures.

Whyte teased at one piece of paper, trying to loosen it from
the Blu-Tack which fixed it to the wall.

'We did warn him about this. The rules are clear: all pictures
should be hung from the rail.' He lifted a corner of a larger work
– A3 size – to reveal the original picture rail underneath.

Shaw walked up to the wall opposite the fireplace until there
was nothing in his field of vision except the colours. Each of the
pictures was signed with the same elegant scrawl: *Liddy*.

On the chimney breast was a Polish flag. On the mantelpiece
a framed picture of a young man hugging his sweetheart. Shaw
wondered if the pretty young woman was Liddy. He didn't have
to wonder about the man because he'd seen him before, his face
streaked with black sand, the flesh soaked as if it had been too
long in a warm bath, the eyes mirror-like, fish-dead. He'd been
looking up into the sky, his back soaked with salt water, his left
foot attached to a weight, snagged in the mud of Mitchell's Bank.

TWENTY-NINE

S haw turned the Porsche down the narrow alleyway into the St James' police pound and parked next to the Mazda. Valentine had gone ahead of him with Clem Whyte in tow. Shaw hurried inside and found himself in the middle of a chaotic media photo-shoot. Acting DS Fiona Campbell was dressed for the part in a light blue suit, white blouse, and the kind of make-up she usually avoided. She'd been persuaded to stand in the middle of the car park holding up what looked like a plastic test tube and a brightly coloured card. Flashbulbs ignited like fireworks as she ignored shouted commands to smile. The press – two TV crews and four newspaper photographers – were edging closer, trying to get the photogenic Campbell in the same shot as the test tube, with Greyfriars Tower as a backdrop.

Campbell had emailed Shaw overnight with the details of her next move in the hunt for the source of lethal adulterated cocaine being sold on the streets of Lynn. The inquiry so far had drawn an almost total blank. Those dealers they had identified had refused to divulge the principal supplier. Arnold Smith-Waterson, aka Gutter, was unable to give them any coherent testimony. He was still undergoing medical treatment for necrosis, but an initial psychiatric report indicated in addition a raft of mental health issues related to drug abuse. They would attempt one more formal interview, then he would be handed over to the force's psychiatric assessment unit. Meanwhile, the drug had started to appear back on the streets. The pure white cocaine was still bulkier thanks to the addition of Levamisole. Seizures so far showed that eighty-two per cent of the local supply contained Levamisole.

In desperation Campbell had gone to the chief constable and persuaded him to bankroll a high-profile media launch. She'd bought 1,000 drug test kits from a US charity to distribute on the street. Each one contained a survey card, to be returned to the police, plus a simple litmus test designed to reveal the presence of the adulterant. Each kit cost four pounds. At least three teen-agers had been hospitalized in the last three days suffering from a variety of infections linked to poor immune systems; a significant side effect of a low white blood cell count. One had necrosis of the toes. While the test tube kits might not help them catch the supplier, the police could at least be seen to be limiting the lethal effects of his product.

Shaw nodded at Campbell, then ran up the stairs to CID, where he met Valentine coming out of Interview Room Three.

'I've organized tea. He keeps saying he can explain. What do you think?'

'Let him stew. We need to brief the team.'

The sense of excited focus in the CID room was tangible. Valentine had spoken to Birley and told him they'd made an arrest on a specimen charge of burglary and he needed to assemble the team and alert Twine at Burnham Marsh. There were a dozen DCs waiting for news, all armed with coffee or unlit cigarettes. Nothing put buoyancy under a copper's career like a successful murder inquiry. They could all look forward to a significant 'bounce' if this one ended with a conviction. All they had to do was remember that it wasn't in the bag – yet.

'OK,' said Shaw, edging his boots as wide as his shoulders, taking command. 'Let's untangle a few knots.'

He accepted a takeaway Costa Coffee cup.

'We've got our suspect, Clem Whyte, in the interview room. He's clearly now the centre of the inquiry. So far he hasn't said a word. I propose leaving him to stew for a few hours, then packing him off downstairs to the cells overnight. George and I will tackle him at nine-thirty a.m. tomorrow – with his lawyer present.

'Why is he our suspect? What do we know? He's a political activist, a full-time housing officer, and he knew Stefan Bedrich, our victim. His van was seen outside Tines Manor on the night the Chelsea Burglars raided the house. It is pretty clear he is lying about several things. I don't propose to get involved in sorting that out until we have more facts.'

He sipped his coffee with a fluid movement of arm and wrist.

'We do have the outline at least of something that makes sense. Whyte's our slogan writer. Bedrich is, perhaps, a thief. Let's say they're both members of the Chelsea Burglars. There's a falling out on the night – we don't why but it's not difficult to see where tensions might arise – and as a result Bedrich ends up dead. They use the boat to dump the body out on Mitchell's Bank. When the body is found Stepney thinks he's under attack. Why? For now let's assume Bedrich is one of his samphire pickers. First, his van fleet gets vandalized. Now one of his men is dead. He hits back, and Shrimp Davies is the victim. Which would leave us right where we are now. Two dead.

'What we need to do today is very simple. Whyte says he wants to talk but we need to prepare for the worst: that he'll clam up and not open his mouth until the lawyer's got to him, and then not at all. A conviction – for burglary, and possibly murder – will rely on forensic evidence and other testimony from witnesses, accomplices, family and friends. We need to build this case as if Whyte was dead. Tom will get the team into the flat, the van, and Whyte's home. You'll have to stand off until the science is over – then get in there and use your eyes. We also need to crawl all over Bedrich's past: family, ties, cash, passport, the lot.'

He took another swig of the coffee, inviting questions.

'The gang sounds improbable – a Polish migrant worker and a Labour Party do-gooder. How did that happen?' asked DC Lau, unzipping a leather jacket with its own go-fast stripes.

'Hypothesis has to be that Whyte organized the burglaries and left the slogans as part of a campaign against second home ownership,' said Shaw. 'He provided transport. I think he set it all up. Somehow he recruited burglars – if Bedrich is typical, he went to the migrant communities, in search of the desperate. He's a housing officer so it's not like he couldn't get to these people. They're his customers.

'But you're right, Jackie, it doesn't quite add up. If you really wanted to leave slogans to be seen, why burgle the houses – why not daub them on outside walls? OK, it delivers a threat. Maybe the next step was arson. If it's a meticulous campaign, and that's what we would expect from the way in which the burglaries were planned, then perhaps it was always going to be incremental. In the end we couldn't have ignored it forever, and – as I pointed out to the powers that be – the downside of hushing it up was always that when it did break – does break – it has a lot more impact. I think there's something we don't know – let's hope whatever it is isn't a game-changer.'

'And Bedrich's death?' asked Lau.

'Not premeditated, certainly – in the sense that it was unplanned on the night. Did the burglars fall out with Whyte? Was there a fight? Once Bedrich was dead did Whyte come up with Plan B – to dump the body and make it look like a spat between samphire pickers and London thugs? He spends a lot of his time on the coast, mostly with the locals, so there's no way he didn't know what was going on out on the marshes. It had to be top of anyone's list of gossip topics. All he needed was a boat. Which reminds me – any news on the *Limpet*? The posters are great, by the way.'

Mark Birley waved a sheet of paper. 'It's been seen up and down the coast this summer. But as of now there's nobody has any idea where it is. One oddity. Coastguard at Wells said he does a tour with the RNLI out to the wind farms once a week, checking out security. Said he was out there last month when he was pretty sure he saw the *Limpet* at dusk alongside a trawler. He didn't get the fishing vessel's name but he's pretty sure the registration was OZ.'

'For?'

'Oostzaan. It's a small Dutch port.'

Which didn't fit into any of their scenarios. Why would a trawler leave a small port on the far side of the Channel and navigate the North Sea, only to meet a coastal sloop at dusk among the ghostly turning wind farms of the north Norfolk coast?

'OK. That adds something else we don't understand. It makes finding the *Limpet* our number one priority. Let's see if we can line up *Crimewatch*, the BBC national news – anything we can. We have to find that boat.'

THIRTY

Holme Beach, on a late evening in October, made the deserted stretch of sand in front of the Shaws' café at Old Hunstanton look like St Tropez. Two miles of stunning coastline, untroubled by a tea hut or a waste-paper bin or red flag. Just untroubled. Shaw had been walking for forty-five minutes and he didn't appear to be getting anywhere: the vast vista of open sand just seemed to open up, again and again, as if he was walking into some endless seaside desert.

Shaw needed the sea air. He'd spent seven straight hours at his desk at St James' as the team struggled to build a framework of compelling evidence ahead of interviewing Clem Whyte. It had been the longest day yet in the inquiry: an endless litany of computer checks, phone calls, briefings and statements. At seven he'd sent the team home, confident they'd made significant progress. Leading by example, he'd shut down his computer and headed for the Porsche. Valentine had taken the rest down to the Red House for what he described as a 'full debrief'.

What had they learnt in seven hours?

Stefan Bedrich was a twenty-six-year-old former sheet-metal worker from the Gdansk shipyards. An apprentice at sixteen, he had joined the OPZZ trade union and become embroiled in left-wing politics. In 2008 he had met Lidia Dmoch, an artist from the steel city of Katowice. They were married in 2009 and a daughter was born in 2012. There was no work in the Polish shipyards and Stefan, desperate to provide for his new family, had come to the UK at the beginning of 2013 on a short-term contract to work at a shipbuilder's in Boston, Lincolnshire.

In April he'd discovered that he – and the rest of the 150-strong workforce – had been made redundant over the loss of a major order to Russian competitors. The Boston Job Centre had recommended that he move to Lynn and attempt to secure a job in the Alexandra Dock. Unsuccessful, Bedrich had begun a series of part-time seasonal jobs – including, that summer, nine weeks aboard a small fishing boat out of Lynn picking samphire on the coast as part of John Jack Stepney's burgeoning business empire.

Then fate ripped Stefan Bedrich's life apart. In July Dmoch was killed in a road traffic accident in Gdansk outside the couple's one-room flat. DC Twine had got Interpol to locate and translate a brief transcript from the court proceedings held within twenty-four hours of the accident. Dmoch, aged twenty, had been waiting for a bus in a torrential downpour. Her daughter was sleeping in a pushchair under a hood. A bus – route number 56a – had mounted the pavement and killed her instantly. The pushchair, carried 150 yards under the bumper of the bus, was crushed, but the child recovered unharmed. Charged with driving while under the influence of alcohol, the driver was sentenced to eighteen months in prison. Temporary custody of the child – Kasia – was awarded to Dmoch's parents, resident in Katowice. Stefan was informed of the accident by a priest from the Polish Club in Lynn, following a telephone call from the consul in Peterborough. His wife's funeral had already taken place.

Flying home he'd made one attempt to take Kasia from his in-laws' house in Katowice, but he'd been stopped by local police. In order to regain custody of his own child he'd have to present a court with evidence of income, residency, and details of a suitable house or flat. Poland offered no opportunities, so he'd returned to Lynn and his temporary job of samphire picking. The Polish 'captain' who was Bedrich's direct employer had told detectives earlier in the inquiry that the Pole had not been seen since the end of the picking season, but that Bedrich, he'd said, had talked of returning to Gdansk. He was one of the six pickers still on the team's wanted list. Interpol had been asked to track him down via his in-laws.

Valentine had visited Clem Whyte's wife, Diane, to inform her of her husband's arrest and to search the family home. The request to enter the house was refused. A warrant would be obtained overnight. Warrants would also be requested for John Jack Stepney's home on Balamory and for *Highlife*. Two teams would make simultaneous visits at seven the next morning.

The excitement of the chase, the sense of closing in on the killer of Stefan Bedrich, was palpable. Ahead Shaw glimpsed his goal: a single set of brick chimneys rising from the pines on Holme Point. The tension in Shaw's muscles was unbearable, the need to expend energy irresistible, so he broke into a jog, then a run, and pounded northwards towards his destination.

THIRTY-ONE

Holme beach had been famous once, if only briefly. In 1998 a teacher called John Lorimer found a Bronze Age axe head in the mud on the water's edge. Archaeologists descended, and in their turn discovered Sea Henge, a wooden circle of split-oak surrounding an upended tree trunk, the whole ghostly geometry emerging from the sand at low water. Tree-ring analysis revealed that the wood had been felled in the spring of 2049 BC, a fact Shaw found impossible to believe in its bizarre precision. Hundreds came to see the 'Stonehenge of the Sea' – then others came to cart it off to a museum in Lynn, so the neo-Pagans arrived to try and stop them, ensuring worldwide TV coverage. Then everyone went away. Forever.

Shaw strained his good eye to look ahead. A sand devil – a spiral of dust caught in a miniature tornado – danced in the mid-distance. Reaching the five-bar gate on the lane that led inland to the village, Shaw continued north. Ahead now, just half a mile away, lay the high sandy pinewood hills of Holme Point – the blunt, subtle curve where the coast began its long, slow-motion turn to the east, breasting the North Sea, leaving the great sandy waste of the Wash in its wake.

Within fifteen minutes he was in the shadow of the first pines, picking up a path which led up the slope. The sand was deep, damp, cloying underfoot. The evening felt suddenly late, as if darkness might fall in minutes. The first sandy ridge was marked by a small clearing where a bench had been set to look out to sea. A metal plaque said the seat stood in memory of *Victoria Murano – GLASSMAKER*.

Shaw paused, his good eye scanning the water's edge, until it reached a series of raised razor-like ridges – the cockle-beds where Sea Henge had been exposed by the waves. He'd come that final day with Lena and watched from the dunes as the bulldozer carried the great oak trunk away, the Druids howling, clawing at the wheels. It had been an oddly affecting moment

for both of them. Shaw said he felt that some of the spirit of the
place had been permanently diminished, the mystery stripped
away. He couldn't help thinking that their plans for the café
might do the same to his beach, as if they too planned some
form of desecration.

The house came into view, the chimney pots showing first,
as Shaw climbed over the upper ridge, then the whole building
came into sight, a strangely inappropriate suburban villa of the
1920s, with a glass conservatory on three sides. An air of mild
dilapidation added to the sense of abandonment, except for what
looked like a brand-new burglar alarm on the north-facing, sea-
facing wall.

Sonia Murano, the diocesan restoration expert, was working
under the glass of the conservatory on the east side, using what
was left of the light from the west. Absorbed, she didn't seem
to hear Shaw's approaching footsteps, although all the windows
and doors were open. He stood for a moment in the doorframe,
knowing that now, however subtly he signalled his presence,
she'd be startled.

'Ms Murano?' he said.

She took a sudden step back and one hand went to her heart,
although she didn't make a noise.

'Yes. Oh, hello. It's you,' she said, smiling.

Shaw revised his estimate of her age down from thirty-five to
thirty. The smile was warm, almost a full beam, but Shaw was
convinced that she had used it to disguise the fact that she wasn't
pleased to see him. Perhaps she guarded her privacy, but Shaw
felt the wariness signalled something closer to anxiety, or even
fear.

'I didn't expect . . .' She curled a hand in Shaw's direction.
'I thought they'd send a constable. Or DS Valentine. It's not that
important. Sorry.'

She stood her ground and it was clear she wasn't going to
invite Shaw into the actual house.

'It's no problem. DS Valentine asked me to pop in. I live down
the beach – at the Old Beach Café. It's a pleasant walk.'

'Of course, of course,' she said, although Shaw was pretty
certain he'd never seen her in the café or the shop.

'It's just it's all become rather urgent,' he said. 'The man

who we think damaged the glass is ill – a result of adulterated
cocaine. He's also mentally fragile, a fairly acute case. I think
if we could find out *why* he was doing this we'd know more
about the drug dealers – the supplier. It is quite possible someone
else will die as a result of taking this stuff. So we thought we'd
move quickly. DS Valentine said you'd found something of
interest in the glass?'

He was still poised on the threshold.

'Of course. Stupid of me.' Her shoulders fell, defeated.
'Come in.'

She went to get her notebook. Shaw was left to consider the
view from the conservatory windows: a hundred yards of close-
cropped grass, dotted with rabbit droppings, then the edge of the
trees. No sight of the sea, or the beach. It seemed like a crime
to him, to build so close to the water's edge, but on the wrong
side of the ridge. It was as if the house sat, sheltering, with its
back to the waves.

Murano came back with a large sketch book and opened it
out, carefully clearing a space by moving aside several pieces of
stained glass, each wrapped in tissue.

'Great house,' said Shaw. 'What's that?'

Through the sash window in the wall he could see into a
further workshop, set around a large metal range below a wide
brick-built chimney breast.

'Glass kiln. The house was built and designed by a potter back
in the 1920s – one of the Davenports. They're famous. That's
why the chimney's so big, because they had kilns in the house.
They built it here, over the ridge, out of the wind, so that the
chimney would draw. My parents bought the house from them.
Mum was a glassmaker.'

'Yes, Murano. The Venetian island famous for glass. Not a
coincidence?'

'Hardly. Not her name at all, she was from the Burnhams, a
Simons, a local girl. My father was – sorry, is – an Italian glassmaker. His real family name is Benedicti, but he's always had a
good eye for business, so he changed it to Murano. They met at
a trade fair in Bologna. Dad's got a shop in Mayfair. Sorry –
that's a very long answer to a simple question. Anyway, when
my parents got married they bought the house. I grew up here.

Mum died last year. I've still got a shop in Burnham Market –
very exclusive.' She laughed again, but it still lacked genuine
abandon. 'There's a flat there too – so I'm rarely here unless I'm
working. It's got too many memories – happy ones, unhappy
ones.'

'Right,' said Shaw, nodding, but bemused by the subtext. He
wondered if she always talked so much or if she had something
to hide.

'It's extravagant, isn't it? I don't really agree with second
homes.'

'This hardly counts,' offered Shaw.

'No. That's what I think really. It's a factory, that's how I look
at it.

'Now,' she said, opening the sketchbook. 'This is the angel
that was damaged at St Andrew's in May.'

Flicking the page, she touched a finger to the next image: 'And
this the last from All Saints.' The sketchbook was loose-leafed
so she was able to spread the pictures out – six in all. The quality
of the drawing was very fine, producing a three-dimensional
effect despite the flat, jigsaw structure of the leaded glass.

'You can see my point, I think. The medieval windows of
Lynn have many, many angels – flying, praying, imploring,
worshipping, annunciating, if that's the right word. The ones this
man has tried to destroy, however, are all the same. Precisely the
same. The face is presented side-on, with only one eye visible,
and the wings are folded and held high above the shoulders –
that's very distinctive, you see, in medieval representations, that
buckled wing ridge, like some kind of heavenly backpack.'

She seemed suddenly unsure of her own observations. 'I'm
sorry, it is probably just of interest to me and of no help at all
to the police. It's such a small thing – a detail. But I thought I
should say. It felt like my duty to say.'

'Can I take one of the sketches?' said Shaw. 'I'll pass them
on to DS Valentine – he's taken a personal interest in the case,
as you know.'

She gave him the angel from St Andrew's. 'Have Gabriel,' she
said.

'How can you tell it's him?'

'Him? There's a lot of evidence that Gabriel was seen as a

woman, or androgynous, and you can see that in this face,
can't you? It's beautiful but sexless. The angel's delivering a
parchment, and that was Gabriel's job really, to be God's
messenger. So Gabriel it is – although, to be frank, most
so-called professional judgment is really just guesswork.'

'Welcome to my world,' said Shaw, and they both laughed.

'They're not all Gabriels?'

'No. But they are all reminiscent of a famous medieval angel
in the great west window at Winchester – the winged messenger.
It was one of my mother's favourite pieces. She hung the image
in the hall . . .'

She actually bit her lip. It was so maladroit as to be charming.
What did this woman have to hide?

'I'd love to see it,' said Shaw, folding the sketch carefully into
his satchel. 'Could we?'

The house smelt of wood, and something Italian seeping out
from the kitchen – possibly a ragù sauce. The interior workshop,
which contained the kiln, was like a corner of a museum of
folklore, with its arcane tools, odd mechanical devices and a
workbench studded with wooden vices. The kiln was cold, the
door open, the interior carbon-black.

The entire ground floor of the house appeared to be carpetless,
but the boards were broad and had once been polished. This one
facet of the interior – the wide original boards – made the place
feel opulent and homely, whereas the bare boards in so many
houses were narrow and mean, and made them feel raw and
unloved. As far as Shaw could tell there was no sign of any form
of modern heating in the house. He'd always found it an oddity
of artists and crafts people, that they seemed to glory in working
in an ambient temperature.

The picture of the winged messenger of Winchester, in a gilt
frame, was in the hallway, which was, in fact, a large room,
reaching up two floors into the gabled roof space. A 1920s nod
to a medieval hall. Set against one wall, about fifteen feet high,
and opposite the winged messenger, was what looked like a
Gothic window *minus* most of the glass. Shaw walked straight
to it after glancing at the rather spare, cold angel of Winchester.

'What's this?' He touched the 'stone' and found it was wood,
very pale, the colour of oak.

'An heirloom. My mother had it made – it's an exact replica of the west window of the church at Burnham Marsh, ruined now, of course. It was called the window of John the Baptist – that was the main illustration – Salome, and all that. They took the glass out in the eighties when the sea threatened to destroy what was left of the building. Even then it was in bad shape, and a lot was missing. Mum had been brought up in the village and that window was very special to her. It was what made her a glassmaker. It was her inspiration. I suppose it made me one too. It was exceptionally vivid and fine. When they took it down she offered to restore it. The plan was to put it back if they ever managed to save the church. Which they might do, by the way. There's a plan, but no money yet, of course. The thing is the window was made of local glass. Do you know Leziate – the village?'

'Near Lynn?'

'Yes. That's where they got the sand; it's the best in Britain. Fine silica – that's our raw ingredient, you see. There was a picture of the original in the workshop here when I was a child. Mum dreamt of restoring it and putting it back in the church. A lifetime's work. As you can see, she didn't get far.'

Shaw reckoned that less than a tenth of the glass space was filled. There was a spandrel showing a crown of thorns, a saint in one horizontal panel, a starburst in a roundel.

'And now . . .' she said, consulting an elegant watch.

'Of course. Thank you. I'll make sure the team knows we're not after just any old angel. Only the winged messenger will do.'

THIRTY-TWO

S haw went to the CID room to collect Valentine for their appointment with Clem Whyte, but his chair was empty, a cold cup of canteen tea left on the blotter. The wall behind now held half-a-dozen A3 colour prints of the stained-glass windows damaged in the airgun attacks. They reminded Shaw of Stefan Bedrich's flat in Greenwood House, where the living-room walls displayed that extraordinary riot of artwork, each page of which had no doubt been created by his wife for her migrant husband, trying to eke out a living for his family in a foreign and unwelcoming land. The style had been subverted Soviet, almost cartoonish, with the added vibrancy of the primary colours which left the rest of the flat's rooms grey and drab, except for the scarlet Polish doll on the kitchen table.

He found Valentine outside, smoking on the fire escape plat-form, five storeys above the street. The wind hummed gently through the steel steps. Another fine day threatened, although the Met Office was forecasting storms by evening and an electric finale to the Indian summer. Valentine had been up early, armed with a warrant, to pay Mrs Diane Whyte an unexpected visit at home.

'Progress,' he said before Shaw could speak, his thin hair blown into a vertical quiff like a wisp of smoke. 'On the outside you'd think they were a model couple, the Whytes; they live in a nice semi off the Castle Rising road.'

Shaw knew the spot, a Monkey-puzzle-tree estate of slightly worn thirties villas.

'She's a nurse at a care home. She needs the car because it's off the A10 down at West Winch. Two grown-up kids, both living away, both married. Nothing in the house. Well, nothing you wouldn't expect. The garage, on the other hand, was packed with white goods: TVs, DVD players, sound boxes – all top of the range, none of it new. Plus a few pictures, mostly picked for the frames is my guess – but nice stuff, mostly originals.'

'Stolen goods?'

'Yeah. Mark's already matched a few items with the inventories we've got on file. But I reckon the lot's lifted.'

'What does the wife say?'

'That he told her it was all stuff being recycled from council flats – well, housing associations, whatever they're called these days. And charitable donations. That was her line, that it was all stuff donated to brighten up the lives of council tenants.'

He let some cigarette smoke seep out of the gaps between his teeth.

'I think she knew what he was up to. I told her she was talking nonsense, that forty-two-inch smart screen TVs aren't standard council issue. She said if I didn't believe her we could take a look for ourselves, because he'd been overseeing a refurbishment at Chaucer House – another old block like Greenwood, but on the riverbank by the cemetery?'

Shaw nodded.

'There's a warden on the ground floor and he gave us the keys – Whyte had organized work on two flats, empty, newly decorated, and she's right, they're full of the same stuff, state-of-the-art TVs, a couple of nice watercolours on the wall. Posh rugs. One had a digital radio, for God's sake. Warden said Whyte told him it was all recycled as part of a council initiative to try and get tenants to look after the place better by "investing in their environment" – his words.'

'Serial numbers?'

'Yup. No problem – I've got Paul organizing a view tomorrow for a few of the owners. But it's all over, Peter. This is the stuff all right.'

'A modern-day Robin Hood then . . .' said Shaw.

'Robin Bastard, more like it. I reckon this lot's his share. It's still stolen goods, Peter, whatever the intention. And the rest of the gang must have fenced their shares. So that'll be cash.'

'Whyte's council van?'

'Birley says they've got a preliminary match with the tyre marks left at the Old Manor, Burnham Marsh. We'll know by close of play today. Plus the council's given us the log for when Whyte had the vehicle out. Matches the burglaries almost to a tee. I'd like to hear him talk his way out of it now, Peter.'

In the distance Shaw's eye tracked a trawler coming down the Cut towards the docks. He could just make out marker flags flying from the crab and lobster pots on the deck. The prospect of a long interview with their suspect in a windowless room made him feel suddenly claustrophobic.

Valentine launched his cigarette butt into a long descent into St James' Street. 'One thing: in his front room, over the fireplace, there was this oil painting: row of cottages, a bit of rough thatch, and a lane leading off down towards marshes, and the sea. Peasants outside – you know the deal, smocks and that. I recognized it – well, I bet the houses don't look like that now, but I know the place, because you could see the sea wall and it's definitely Wells – got to be. According to the wife, Whyte was brought up in one of the cottages in the picture. Idyllic, she said. That was his grandfather's place, but then the old man couldn't pay the rent and the whole family got the heave-ho. Can't bear to go back, apparently. Wife says that's his big problem – he harbours grudges. Can't forgive, can't forget.'

THIRTY-THREE

They'd put Clem Whyte in the 'tough cop' interview room down in the basement: tiled, no windows, with a uniformed PC standing by the door. The interview suites upstairs were modern and bright, painted in pastel colours. This was fifties austerity policing; a match for the cells down the corridor. Valentine brought a cup of coffee for the prisoner down from the canteen with three sachets of sugar, a little plastic tub of fake milk and a useless brittle plastic stirrer.

Whyte didn't even let them sit down before he made his opening statement: 'I'll tell you about what I did, and what Stefan did, but that's it. I'm not naming any other names. I'm sorry to be unhelpful. I think there's an important principle at stake.'

Shaw wasn't surprised by this tactic. He'd only met Whyte once, and they'd probably only swapped a few hundred words in total, but he'd discerned a certain preachy morality. Criminals who claimed they acted in the interests of others were, he found, the most devious. The absence of a sense of guilt also made them particularly dangerous, and arrogant. Whyte's manifesto of intent made it slightly more likely, in Shaw's judgment, that it was he who had killed Stefan Bedrich. Or that he knew who had.

The duty solicitor, a young man called Sawyer who was often on call at St James', sat beside his client and seemed mildly shocked by Whyte's announcement. He whispered in Whyte's ear, but the prisoner just shook his head.

Valentine switched on the recorder and voiced the appropriate preamble. Shaw helped himself to a mint from a small dish on the table. He held it on his tongue while he considered *his* tactics.

'DS Valentine will outline the facts as we see them,' said Shaw, pushing his chair back so that the metal legs screeched on the concrete floor.

The DS intoned a list of the evidence accumulated so far against Whyte on a specimen charge of burglary under the Theft Act 1968: the stolen goods, the vehicle sightings, the possible

tyre mark match at Burnham Marsh. Valentine casually added
that the maximum sentence for the offence, when committed in
a dwelling, was fourteen years.

'No cut-rate for second homes, I'm afraid,' he added.

'Really, Detective Sergeant. Is that necessary?' Sawyer made
an ostentatious note.

Outside in the corridor they heard a cell open down the corridor,
a single foot scuffing the floor, before a door slammed shut.

'Let's put that aside,' said Shaw. 'At least for this, our first
interview. The important question is this: how did Stefan Bedrich
die? And why? Did you kill him, Mr Whyte?'

One shake of the head. Nothing more.

Shaw produced a passport shot of Bedrich taken from documents found in the flat at Greenwood House, and set it on the
table upside down so that Whyte could get a clear view.

Whyte's small grey eyes blinked behind his spectacles. That
narrow, tortoise-like neck seemed to telescope, allowing his head
to move forward, closer to the picture.

'How did Stefan Bedrich die?' asked Shaw.

'I don't know,' said Whyte. 'When we got to the village that
night we went our separate ways. I had a plan – marked on an
OS map – and we'd divvied the place up. I'd been pretty sure
the place was deserted, but you can't be certain. I knew the pub
was closed, that's what made me look at it in the first place. So
we each took a quarter of the village, but approached the properties as if they might be inhabited.'

'How many of you?'

'Four. But as I say – no names.'

The solicitor tried for a second whisper but Whyte waved him
away.

'Why did you think the village might be empty?'

'I didn't. I knew every house was a second home and it was
the third week of October on a Thursday night. And as I said,
the pub was closed. We always worked on the assumption
someone might be at home. If the place was a ghost town, all
the better.'

Valentine handed Shaw a file. He opened it to reveal a closely
typed list of addresses.

'We found this in a desk at your house. Your wife unlocked

it for us. It's the council's own list of properties claiming relief on their council tax as second homes. Must have made choosing a target a little easier.'

Whyte's head shifted on his narrow neck as if his collar was too tight.

'My client has the right to remain silent,' said the solicitor.

'It's about right and wrong,' said Whyte, ignoring Sawyer, who gently set down his biro and leant back in his seat. 'And about degrees of right and wrong. I don't think it's right for people to have two homes when so many people have none. I think it's wrong that people can't grow up in their own homes. We're a rich society, but we have very little concern for the lives of others.'

'Great, now speeches,' said Valentine. 'Can this get any better?'

Shaw leant forward. 'Talk us through exactly what you did from the moment you arrived at Burnham Marsh on the night of the seventeenth of October. I presume you were the transport – so four in the van, yes?'

Whyte licked his lips and Shaw guessed he'd been relishing the prospect of a dispute on the ethics of the situation, a conversation he was not going to get.

'Yes, by the war memorial. I parked the van there. I cut the lights and we briefly double-checked that we all knew what we were doing.'

'Where did Stefan go?'

'The quayside down to the old church. I had the quayside and the road out of the village; the others went over the sea wall and did the houses on the old marsh.'

'Time?'

'One o'clock. We had to be back at the van by two. Everyone came back but Stefan.'

'What next?'

'We had a plan for that. We waited one hour. If there was any sign he'd been caught we'd just have driven off. Sixty minutes, then – only then – we called his mobile. No answer, although it rang. We gave him fifteen more minutes and rang again, same status. So we left.'

'You just drove away? You expect us to believe that?'

Whyte stirred his coffee.

'I don't think any of this adds up,' said Shaw. 'You and Stefan Bedrich don't add up. Tell me how this started.'

Whyte looked at the clock on the wall then shook his head.

The morgue shots of Bedrich, which Shaw had picked up from Dr Kazimeirz, were graphic, showing the deep wound which had almost severed his neck. He put three down on the interview table.

'God,' said Whyte. 'I . . .' He held the bridge of his nose, his eyes tightly shut.

'Sorry, did you think it would be pretty?' asked Valentine. 'At Peace. Gone Before. That kind of thing?'

'Gentlemen . . .'

Shaw ignored the solicitor. 'Maybe you should have gone and looked for him, Clem. If not for his sake then maybe for hers?'

An A4 shot, this one in colour, fuzzy from magnification, showing a child with black curls and green eyes.

'That's Kasia, the daughter, Clem. The name's derived from the Polish for "pure". She's not going to remember him at all now, is she?'

Shaw rearranged the pictures of the butchered father and the laughing daughter.

Whyte let his eyes slide over both images. He added creamer to the coffee and began to study the strange, galaxy-like swirl of the white in the black.

'You clearly don't think we deserve the truth. How about her?' asked Shaw.

He looked up into Whyte's impassive face. 'What really worries me about this is the assortment of motives. We know why you're in it: political slogans. Plus a pleasant little sideline in top-of-the-range fittings and décor for council tenants. That must have been very satisfying. And presumably arson was next. But I still don't see how this started.'

Whyte couldn't stop his hand edging across the table, an extended index finger sliding the girl's picture over that of her father's mutilated skull.

Then he pushed both pictures away, as if making a final decision.

'Stefan's case file came to my notice,' he said. 'The Greenwood House flats are sought after, there's a waiting list.

Stefan's . . .' He searched for the right word. 'Stefan's *plight* was acute. The death of his wife was a tragedy. He desperately wanted his child back. He didn't want to live in Poland. He'd taken night classes in car mechanics in Boston and qualified. The plan was to set up on his own – a garage, I guess, a repair shop. He had nothing.

'I interviewed him at the council offices. He explained that if he could set up on his own, get six months of company accounts under his belt, he'd be in a position to apply for custody. The problem was cash. He needed fifteen thousand pounds seed corn to start the business. The bank laughed in his face. I asked him why they'd turned him down for credit and he admitted he had a previous conviction for burglary up in Lincolnshire.

'My normal practice is to visit applicants. So I did. He had a room in the North End, a Rackman landlord, one toilet for sixteen rooms. I'd had time to think. The issue of second homes is very close to my heart. I wanted to do something radical, decisive. Something personal. I wanted to show these people – the Chelsea set – that they weren't welcome. I wanted the media to focus on the homeless, the people driven out of the villages in which they'd been born and brought up. I said I'd recommend Stefan for the flat if he'd consider a joint enterprise.'

'Burgling second homes?'

'Yes. The key was getting in and out, and for that I needed professionals. Stefan was my key. He had friends, not just in Boston, but Lynn too. They'd turned over a few suburban semis. But the cash flow was hardly worth the risk. I said they'd get more out of one second home than fifty semis.'

'What did you think when the media didn't get the story?' asked Shaw.

Whyte shrugged. 'I thought you lot were sitting on it. Fine. I wasn't going to stop and it was going to come out eventually – with all the more force if suppressed for so long. I was prepared to be patient. I was close to resorting to fire – very close. Then, maybe, a letter claiming responsibility. There were risks. I wanted to move forward gradually. Steadily.'

'So you're in this to fight the good fight for the homeless,' said Shaw. 'He's in it to bank the cash so he can get his daughter back. Saints, the pair of you. But the other two are just thieves.

That's a volatile mixture of motives. Is that what happened – a fight? Did you all fall out over who got what? That's the danger with the four of you splitting up the stuff – that needs a certain level of trust. Did you trust them? Did you trust Stefan?'

'Yes. I did, until that night. Now I don't know.'

'What did you think happened?'

'I said that I don't know. We feared he'd stumbled on a resident and been caught. Or an accident. Trapped in a cellar, perhaps, or injured getting in through a window. Or – yes, maybe he'd found something he didn't want to share and he'd done a runner. But we'd all agreed, if someone didn't make it back within an hour of the deadline we'd split. No arguments.'

'And you expect us to believe that?' asked Shaw.

'It's the truth.'

'Isn't it much more likely that when Bedrich didn't return you sent someone to find him? Or did you go yourself? After all, there was no guarantee that if Bedrich was trapped, or the subject of a citizen's arrest, that he wouldn't name names once he was in police custody. That's the deal I'd have made. A clean passport back to Poland in return for names, details, a statement.'

Whyte bent the little plastic stirrer close to breaking point, then set it aside.

Shaw folded his notebook. 'We have further questions, Mr Whyte. We'll be back. Several things are still unclear, and we have forensic results to evaluate. But one thing *is* clear to me. I don't think you've told us the truth. And certainly not the whole truth.'

THIRTY-FOUR

An ambulance from the Queen Elizabeth Hospital had delivered Arnold Gutter Smith-Waterson back to St James' with a nurse in attendance. Campbell had chosen the 'good cop' interview suite on the fifth floor, with a view out over Greyfriars Tower, and a distant glimpse of white water in the Wash. Valentine was the eponymous good cop. Smith-Waterson had asked for 'the policeman with the raincoat' to be present at the interview. He hadn't asked for a lawyer.

As Valentine entered the prisoner was talking and clearly back on his favourite topic: 'People get the neap tide wrong too,' he was saying, looking down at the sheet of blank paper in front of DS Campbell, as if she was going to take a note. 'It comes with the first and third quarters of the moon – so it's the smallest of the high tides.'

When he saw Valentine the flicker of recognition was unmistakable. There was something childlike about the man, for all the grey hair and the stiff, arthritic knees and elbows, as if the years of cocaine abuse had expunged his adult life, leaving behind this innocent juvenile. The prisoner's mutilated hand was in a white glove, resting on the table. Valentine couldn't stop himself sampling the stale air in the room. Was it there, the sweet edge of decay? All he could detect was an acrid aroma of antiseptic cream.

'DS Valentine has entered the room,' said Campbell into the digital tape deck microphone mounted on the wall. As opposed, thought Valentine, to *acting* DS Campbell. One day, he knew, she'd pass him in the career fast lane, but he felt unperturbed by the thought. Fiona Campbell was a born copper. Her father had served as a DI at Norwich for twenty-five years, so she knew that promotion wasn't just about a string of glittering exam results. The only thing that really annoyed him about Fiona was her height – six foot one in cork shoes. She often stood slightly hunched, as if trying not to stand out in the crowd. Valentine usually took on a fatherly note and told her to stand up straight.

He pulled up a chair and nodded a welcome. From the canteen he'd brought the prisoner a piece of cake on a plastic plate with a plastic serrated knife.

'The spring tide . . .' began Gutter, but stopped when he saw Campbell had produced a small cellophane packet containing a fine white powder.

'Arnold,' she said, and even Valentine had to admit she'd packed enough natural authority into that one word to chill the room. The old man licked his lips, as if the packet held sweets.

'I know about your problems, Arnold. How difficult life is.' She flipped open a folder of printed sheets. 'Doctor Jackson has written me a report. I know that your memory isn't very reliable. There are several mental health issues which you've done very well to try and overcome. I know you find it very hard to concentrate. But I want you to try for a moment because it is possible that you can save the lives of several people here today, right now, in this room. Do you understand?'

Gutter moved a twist of grey hair from his face and tucked it behind one ear. 'Yes,' he said, the voice, for once, sounding like that of a stable adult, shorn of the usual wheedling note.

'This is cocaine and we know from the blood tests that you've been taking this drug for several years. Possibly decades. This isn't about that. I don't want to send you to gaol for taking illegal Class A drugs. Although I could, Arnold. I want you to understand that. That would mean a cell, of course, indoors, for several months, if not years. Do you see that?'

Gutter nodded once and then started humming. Valentine thought he recognized a few notes, a florid phrase, reminding him of something English from the Last Night of the Proms. He pushed the plate with the piece of cake a bit nearer to Smith-Waterson's good hand.

'We know that someone is selling cocaine like this in Lynn. Dealers on the street are offering it just a little bit cheaper than the normal market rate. So it's very difficult to say no, I can understand that too. But the problem is there's a really good reason why you should say no, why everyone should say no. It's not pure cocaine, Arnold. It's been adulterated, mixed up with something much cheaper. This cheap chemical is called Levamisole. It's a drug too – but a very useful one. Doctors prescribe it for people with cancer, specific types of the disease that you might find in the brain or the neck.'

Campbell straightened her spine an extra half-inch. She seemed to tower over her prisoner now, looking down at the drugs: innocently white in their bag, like icing sugar.

'There isn't much I can teach *you* about Levamisole, is there, Arnold?'

He shook his head. She'd emailed Valentine a précis of the Met file on Arnold Smith-Waterson, formerly a senior anaesthetist at St Thomas's Hospital, London, who had been struck off in 1998 after a patient brought a complaint of malpractice. The woman had regained consciousness during a routine operation to remove a benign cyst in her breast. Smith-Waterson was initially admitted to an alcohol abuse clinic. In 1999 police at Kensington banned him from coming within a mile of the home of his ex-wife, who had remarried. Campbell had deemed three further facts significant: in the 1980s the Smith-Watersons had owned a second home at Wells-next-the-Sea; in 2000 Arnold had been arrested for possession of cocaine at home on the north Norfolk coast (fined £1,000 and given a three-year suspended sentence); and the former anaesthetist had an NHS pension worth £46,000 per annum, paid monthly, despite the disciplinary case which had ended his career.

'You've probably worked out why you have necrosis, haven't you, Arnold?'

Smith-Waterson swallowed a lot of air in a rush as if a memory of something shocking had filled his brain.

'Levamisole suppresses white blood cells,' he said. 'Dampens the immune system. Leads to neutropenia, agranulocytosis and vasculitis.'

He covered his mouth as if he'd revealed a great secret.

Campbell spread three photographs on the table for him to see. Valentine let his eyes slide over the nearest, which showed a young woman, naked from the waist up, with one breast the same colour as Gutter's finger. He fought hard for a few seconds to disguise the air *he* had to suck in, the shock of the image making him momentarily dizzy.

Smith-Waterson began to claw at the pictures with the gloved hand.

'Someone is going to die, Arnold, unless we catch the person who is peddling these drugs. Someone *has* died – a young man, just twenty years old. Do you understand what I'm saying – what I've said? I need a name. Or a place. Or a mobile number. Give me something, Arnold. We need to find the source of this and stop it right now before someone else dies.'

He started to cry, head down, shoulders shaking. Valentine wasn't particularly attuned to the emotions of others. Julie had always complained that she had to remind him to feel sympathy, or even empathy, as if there was a button he had to press. She, on the other hand, had seemed to have an open channel, always receiving, expertly holding the necessary wavelength. But even he could see that Smith-Waterson's tears were the result of a deeply felt distress; a kind of despair, the roots of which lay somewhere in those lost years of addiction.

Campbell rapped a fist on the desk top and her prisoner jumped.

'Arnold. Did you get your drugs from dealers? We think numerous dealers sold the adulterated supply. We have arrested several of them, but none of them remember selling drugs to you. Did you go direct to the source – the supplier? Is he – or she – here in Lynn? Or did you have to go somewhere else – Peterborough, perhaps, or Boston? How does the supply get into the country, Arnold?'

His head came up, the mouth hanging open. 'I can't remember anything. I just know the angels are to blame.'

Campbell edged a packet of paper tissues across the table and he took one, carefully, and dabbed at his eyes.

'I know I'm letting everyone down, like I did before, at the hospital. So I know, in the end, that I'm the one who is really to blame. But it won't last forever – the supply. It's limited.'

Campbell and Valentine exchanged glances.

'What do you mean, Arnold? Limited? How is it limited, and how do you know it's limited?'

'When I think about this I can't face living. So I close it all down. I'm going to do that now. I'm going to close it all down.'

'Arnold, wait,' said Valentine, placing a hand on the glove.

'Tell me about the angels, Arnold. Just tell *me*. No one else needs to know. I'll keep you safe, I promise. Look at me, Arnold.'

Gutter hung his head. 'The neap tide for Lynn today is at four fifty-six p.m,' he said, sighing. 'I've learnt all the depths, heights and times. It's useful information in my life. It's the kind of thing you have to know. It's a matter of life and death.'

He shook his head. 'Tomorrow's high tide will be at five-fifteen p.m. . . .'

THIRTY-FIVE

Burnham Marsh had come back to life. Several owners had returned to check out their properties and make insurance claims. A few pretended to tend gardens while watching their neighbours and the police. A teenager at Overy View, down near the church, was tying up waste bags and putting them out. A woman, exuberant hair tied up in a headscarf, was washing the windows of the pub, although it still looked closed. A carpenter's van was parked by the war memorial.

DC Twine, at the mobile incident room, was organizing a second thorough examination of the eight properties Clem Whyte claimed had been allocated to Stefan Bedrich on the night of the burglary. This area of the village – less than 500 yards square, was the new focus of the investigation. Bedrich may have been murdered by Whyte, or another member of the gang. If not, he almost certainly met his killer in one of these houses – or nearby.

Tom Hadden's SOCO unit had almost finished an overall risk assessment of the scene of crime, which encompassed thirty-three separate properties, plus outbuildings and garages. An annual budget of £1.2 million would not stretch to a full forensic examination of an entire village. But they'd evaluated every building. And every room. The trawl for evidence had so far netted encouraging results. They had two partial fingerprints, one from a broken window pane at Marsh Cottage, plus a nearby bloodstain on a tablecloth. Neither were a match for Bedrich or Whyte. They'd also recovered a plastic water bottle found in the public waste bin on the sea wall. Wrapped around the bottle was the standard Highland Spring label and a set of fingerprints from a left hand. The council emptied the bins on a Thursday afternoon. There were three in Burnham Marsh. All were completely empty – except for the litre bottle of still water. Had one of the burglars taken a minute's break, removed a glove to open the bottle then finished it before throwing it into a bin he presumed was full of litter? Other than the prints they had a few cotton fibres on a hawthorn at the rear of one of the fifties semis, and the tyre marks at Old Manor. Now they planned a fingertip search of the eight key properties – once Shaw and Valentine had made a preliminary check.

Shaw found Hadden outside the incident room with Twine, gathered round a picnic table they'd requisitioned from the pub. Hadden's deputy, Dr Elizabeth Price, was just debriefing them on the position at Burnham Market where she was in charge of the examination of the fishmonger's where Shrimp Davies had been shot dead. The news was not as encouraging: other than the bullet, retrieved at autopsy by Dr Kazimeirz, the scene was a blank. 'Which of itself is interesting,' said Dr Price, smiling at Shaw's arrival. 'An exceptionally professional killing. Floor hosed down, gloves used throughout, locks cleaned, van virtually polished. The one mistake was the bullet. A small mercy.'

Shaw liked Price. She was sixty years old and looked as if her real career was her hobby, teaching piano, specifically Bach to promising teenagers. He wondered how many of her students watching her long, delicate fingers playing over the keys knew what she really did for a living.

'What's the odds on the bullet not exiting?'

'One in a thousand – ten thousand. A fluke. But one the killer will be cursing,' she said.

They had one positive development in the Shrimp Davies inquiry. Lynn uniformed branch had tracked down three of his drinking partners in the Retreat, one of his dockside haunts. Two of them were in possession of cannabis. A round of fingerprints revealed that one of the two, a trawler hand off the Fisherfleet, had left the same prints inside John Jack Stepney's garage on the night his fleet of vehicles was vandalized.

'So that throws some light on how this all got out of hand,' said Shaw. 'Stepney punches a hole through half-a-dozen boat hulls at Morston Creek. Shrimp Davies tells his mates what's afoot and one – or more – of them, no doubt well oiled on beer, set out for Stepney's warehouse to teach the London bastards a lesson. My guess is Davies, or his mates, did a bit of bragging later in the pub. Two days later Davies is dead.'

Valentine emerged from the incident room lighting what looked suspiciously like a celebration cigarette.

'Lucky break,' he said. He spread an AA map of East Anglia on the table and stabbed a finger on the A10 ten miles north of Ely, at a point marked as Brandon Creek.

'Know this spot? Road goes over a river – there's a pub, and a sign saying welcome to Norfolk, and a lay-by for HGVs, but nothing else. Other than the pub and some houseboats there's bugger all for miles either way. Last night a haulage driver was parked up for a kip and got caught short so he wandered down the road and used the ditch. This is four a.m., nothing about. It's a fen ditch, so it's ten foot deep and six foot wide. There's something in the ditch. He's got a torch and he has a closer look and finds it's a motorcycle. Harley-Davidson. Black fuel tank.'

Valentine exchanged a glance with Shaw, then took a deep breath. 'Ten foot along the ditch is a pair of motorcycle boots sticking out of the long grass. It's the rider, and he's alive. Just.'

He checked his notes. 'Paramedics got him out. He had a very slight pulse and he was having trouble breathing. They cut his leathers off to try and get his lungs working. He's in Addenbrooke's at Cambridge on life support. Doctors reckon he had a heart attack on the road. Major problem is hypothermia. They estimate he'd been in the ditch for at least twenty-four hours. Driving licence gave his name as Leslie James Hales, aged thirty-one. His family's been informed.

'Once they got to the hospital his brother made an immediate request for the return of his leathers. They had them at Ely, at the Ambulance Station. One of the medics is a biker who thought it might have been nice if he'd taken as keen an interest in the patient as his gear. So he took a look at the suit – it's a one-piece Wolf Kangaroo, apparently – new at six hundred and ninety-nine pounds. But not much good cut in half by a paramedic. There's a pocket in the small of the back. Inside was a Beretta TomCat .32 – titanium, with silencer. Plus a wallet containing five thousand pounds in fifty-pound notes. Cambridgeshire traffic are running it all up to the Ark now.'

'Same calibre as the bullet that killed Shrimp Davies,' said Hadden. 'And underpowered enough to risk the bullet lodging in the victim's ribs. What was the wallet made of, George? If it's plastic I want it – even paper. Whatever. His prints aren't a problem, but it'd be nice to know who gave him the wad.'

'OK. The gods have smiled,' said Shaw. 'Let's make the most of it. And call Cambridgeshire, Paul. I want someone by the bed.'

Shaw and Valentine walked away, armed with the map of the village, a spring even in the DS's step. On a grass verge by the ruin of the church there was a dilapidated sign. For the first time Shaw took in the name of the church: John the Baptist. He tried to recall the Bible story. All he could remember was a woman called Salome dancing for a king, and then the prophet's head on a plate. The image of Stefan Bedrich's nearly severed head flashed again before his good eye: a black and white image, mercifully free of the blood.

'OK, eight houses. Let's take a look then Tom can get stuck in. Where shall we start?'

A couple of white yachts strained at anchor chains. The sea pounded the beach beyond Scolt Head. The teenager at Overy View, the nearest house, had tied up another set of black bin bags and was now hoovering – they could hear the whine through the open bay windows.

Valentine said it half a second before Shaw opened his own mouth. 'When was the last time you saw a teenager clearing up?'

THIRTY-SIX

There was no answer to the door of Overy View because the hoover was making such a racket. Shaw peered through the bay window and told Valentine what he'd seen that first Saturday morning, the evidence of a party, the takeaway cartons thrown in the fireplace. They found the teenager at the rear of the property throwing a sports bag into the boot of a Mini Cooper. Designer jeans, white T-shirt, expensive Day-Glo trainers and a tan that looked Italian. The car registration number included 63 – indicating it was released in the second half of 2013. The paintwork was splashed with mud and hadn't been through a car wash in months, if ever. An erratic digital beat was emanating from the sound system, the bass loud enough for Shaw to pick up the rhythm through his boots.

Shaw flashed a warrant card. 'DI Peter Shaw.'

'Seb – Seb Todd.' His teeth were so good he could have been American. Or Canadian. And the muscles under the T-shirt had been invested in too – Shaw guessed an hour a day on weights at least. But he wasn't muscle-bound. The workouts had been aesthetic.

'Just a word if it's OK – could we step back inside?'

'Sure,' he said, but checked his watch, a primary-coloured diver's timepiece worn on the reverse of the wrist.

Todd took a smart phone from his jeans pocket and set it on a butcher's block.

'In a hurry?' asked Valentine.

'I need to get back to uni. Durham. It's a drive.'

'Right – what, two hundred and fifty miles? Why'd you come back?'

'Just to tidy up.' The kid wasn't stupid so he knew he'd fallen for a sucker's punch as soon as he'd answered Valentine's question. He blushed, a vivid rose at the throat, spreading more slowly to the cheeks.

Valentine told him the facts: there'd been a party, he'd left the place a mess, and now he was back.

'Why?'

The subtle blush intensified into a deep red flush. Shaw made a mental note of the condition: idiopathic craniofacial erythema. There were few curses more deadly to the teenager than uncontrollable blushing. Historically, doctors had diagnosed mental health issues as underlying the condition. The latest research suggested that an overactive sympathetic nervous system was at the root of the disorder. None of that was any consolation to Sebastian Todd.

'Look, Seb, I know you were here earlier this week. I had a look round the house the morning after the burglary and there were a few things scattered about – and the fridge was open. Looked like a party.'

Todd was nodding. 'Right. Thought I'd better clear up – Dad's coming down at the weekend because of the break-ins, and the body out on Mitchell's Bank. Mum's freaked out, she says she won't come back. I told him they didn't touch the place. But he wants to see for himself.' He shrugged, indicating the general mistrust of fathers in sons.

'So you left in a hurry?'

'They don't visit often. I just thought I'd get it all shipshape next time I came down, a couple of weeks down the line.'

'What night was the party?'

He touched his smart phone so it lit up. Shaw noted this emerging habit in those around him; Lena, even Fran, were guilty. Ask them a tricky question and they'd check their phone to buy time to work out a decent answer.

'Wednesday,' he said, but there had been a one-second hesitation.

'Sure?'

'Yeah.' No blushing this time and something in the blue-grey eyes that suggested a more steely personality under the Oxbridge-reject veneer.

'Not much of a party on your own,' said Shaw. 'Friends?'

'Yeah – just a mate.'

'Sex?' asked Valentine, knowing the question would confuse. Panic in the blue-grey eyes. 'Oh, yeah – right. My flatmate, Pete.'

'Pete who?'

'Pete Schindler.'

'Got a picture of Pete on your phone?' asked Shaw. 'We could eliminate him from our inquiries.'

Todd scrolled up and down then pushed the phone across the butcher's board so they could see the picture. Pete was dark, stubbled, a black T-shirt, a diamond earring. He had a hand up against the glare of the sun so that they could see a leather bracelet with studs and a tattoo on his arm: Celtic symbols, intertwined.

'Looks a bit old for an undergraduate,' offered Shaw.

'Look – what is this?' asked Todd.

'It's a series of questions,' said Valentine. 'What's so hard about that one?'

Todd's Adam's apple bobbed. 'He's post-grad, teaches in the department.'

'Your dad mind you bringing friends back here?' asked Valentine.

He was sweating now, a little crystal circlet of beads on his forehead.

Valentine didn't like acting like a bully but he had a job to do. 'Good friend, is he – this Pete? What's in it for him – the trip and everything? Couple of cans and a chicken biryani? Good friends – how good is that?'

Seb looked like a rabbit in headlights.

Shaw held up a hand. 'Look. Your private life's your own, Seb, OK? But I want you to be absolutely sure you've got the right day here. You stayed over Wednesday night – and left when?'

'Thursday, early. Pete had to be back for a staff meeting.'

Overy View was one of Wighton's houses. The ex-copper had said he'd checked them all late on Thursday at about four o'clock. If the remains of the party were evident at that point Seb Todd was telling the truth. If not, the possibilities were much more interesting.

What if Seb and Pete were enjoying a private party on *Thursday* night when Stefan Bedrich tried to break in? Had violence broken out? Shaw was supremely uninterested in young Todd's sex life but the youngster was clearly less than at ease with answering questions about it. What precisely might have happened if Bedrich had burst in on the two friends? Had they thought Bedrich was a lone thief?

'Seb,' said Shaw. 'One last time. Wednesday or Thursday?'

'Wednesday.'

'Right. We're going to need a statement to that effect. And then we're going to have to check it out. I think uni's going to have to wait a day. OK?'

THIRTY-SEVEN

An ambulance stood in the graveyard of All Saints, its driver reading the *Lynn Express* at the wheel. Shaw knew its destination: Holbrook Hall Secure Psychiatric Unit on the bleak southern shore of the Wash. Taking a prisoner there one evening a year earlier Shaw had waited by the car until the man had been taken inside. A Georgian façade, eighteen windows, all barred, all reflecting the grey waters of the sea. As the door opened he'd glimpsed a male nurse, a staircase, white walls. Holbrook was about to become home for Arnold John Smith-Waterson, aka Gutter, who had made two desperate attempts to kill himself during his transfer back to the hospital, when he'd been left alone in the rear of the ambulance: one with a length of oxygen pipe, the second with a plastic serrated knife.

Acting DS Campbell had been advised that once transferred he would no longer be available for interview with regard to adulterated drug supplies. Given permission to question the sixty-three-year-old one last time, she'd asked Shaw to sit in, and he'd chosen the venue. He wanted to confront Smith-Waterson with the victim of his crime: the shattered angel in the east window.

Shaw stood in the shadow of the church and checked his phone. Valentine had volunteered to double-check Seb Todd's version of events at Burnham Marsh with his former colleague, ex-DS Geoff Wighton. Meanwhile, Paul Twine was checking out Todd's flatmate, Peter Schindler, through Durham CID.

A text from Valentine read: *Wighton not at home. Not answering mob. Neighbour says wife admitted to pulmonary unit, Luton. Will monitor.*

Shaw entered the church and was overwhelmed by the sense of the sea *indoors*. The white walls, the clean, cold smell of the stone, the small carved wooden ship over the pulpit. He could see why Valentine cherished the place, and not just for the sanctuary of his wife's grave in the shadow of the east window.

All Saints had retained its pews, fine benches in oak, carved

with fishes and birds, and whales, and boats. In the side aisle at
the front sat Smith-Waterson next to a male nurse in uniform.
Behind the altar, scaffolding obscured the damaged east window.
Ladders led up to a platform near the apex, where Shaw was
surprised to see Sonia Murano, the glass expert, trying to repair
the damaged face of the angel. At the foot of the ladder stood a
man, looking up, a full head of silver hair catching the light.

DS Campbell was in the front pew, half kneeling, so that she
could turn and look her prisoner full in the face. As Shaw
approached he could just hear her speaking, holding the man's
undamaged hand, speaking so softly the church's excellent acous-
tics could only just pick up her voice.

'I know you can hear me, Arnold,' she said. 'I know you can
understand. There's lots of things in your head now – I know
that. But there's room for this too. This last time. We need to
know where you got the adulterated cocaine, Arnold. If you don't
tell us it will take us much longer to find the source and other
people may suffer, like you suffered.'

She put his hand down but she hadn't given up. 'It's been
painful, hasn't it? Not telling us, bottling it up. Why not let it
out?'

The old man nodded once and the nurse slid an arm round his
shoulders.

'I know that you want to tell us but something's stopping you.
That must mean you're afraid to tell us. Someone's threatened
you. That's right, isn't it?'

The old man's head didn't move but the nurse peered into his
face and Shaw heard a sob.

'I'm sorry, Arnold,' said Campbell. 'I know you're afraid. But
Jon here is going to look after you now – there's a big house on
the coast, and you'll have your own room. There's views of the
sea. Lots of fresh air. Miles of open space. You'll be so safe I
think that very quickly you'll regret not telling me what I want
to know. If you like you can ask Jon – or one of the other nurses
– to let me know if you want to talk. Will you remember that?'

Shaw sat in the front pew. Smith-Waterson had his eyes shut,
pressed so tightly the minute muscles in the eyelids quivered
with the effort.

'Arnold,' said Shaw.

The eyes came open. They were a watery blue and seemed to shine with guarded intelligence, and even a slightly hooded curiosity.

'They're repairing the angel,' said Shaw, pointing up at the scaffolding.

The detective unfolded a piece of paper and let it fall on Smith-Waterson's lap. It was Sonia Murano's sketch of Gabriel, from one of the other damaged churches.

'It's always a certain kind of angel, isn't it, Arnold? The high, folded wings, the single eye, the message in the hand. Why those angels, Arnold?'

Smith-Waterson was looking up at Murano working and the effort began to make his skull shake. Above they could hear her tapping the lead, the slight screech of the glass being edged into place.

'Arnold, they're repairing the angel now,' persisted Shaw. 'So soon it will be as if you hadn't taken your rifle and shattered the glass. You hate them, don't you? Does it make you sad to see the angel back? The source of the drugs is back too, you know that. Even if the supply has dried up, he'll be back. Other people will end up like you – with blackened, dead skin. You don't want that to happen, Arnold. I know you don't.'

The man with the silver hair climbed the ladder into the scaffolding and delivered some tools to Murano, before carefully returning to earth.

'Who should we be looking for?' asked Shaw, drawing close. 'Do they look like angels? They don't have wings, do they? That can't be right. Is he a good person perhaps – or someone who looks like a good person? Is that it?'

He shook his head.

'Thank you, Arnold, for answering that question. You see, you can help us without speaking. That way you don't even have to make a single sound. You don't have to actually tell me anything. You just have to say if I'm right or wrong.'

Shaw looked up at the window.

'Is it a priest, Arnold? Or someone who works in the church? Or a messenger – a postman, perhaps? Or someone in authority – a social worker or a charity worker?'

He shook his head several times.

'I can't,' he said.

'People will die,' said Shaw, unable to stop his voice hardening.

The old man pressed his eyes closed with his fingertips.

The sun broke through the cloud and lit up the window so that they were all splashed with light.

'Look at the colours, Arnold,' said Shaw.

But he wouldn't open his eyes.

THIRTY-EIGHT

S haw kept his seat in the front pew until he heard the ambulance pulling away. He wondered if Smith-Waterson had
cast a last glance back at All Saints, and its angel window.
Sonia Murano was still aloft, a silhouette against the glass. The
elderly man with the silver hair sat at a hardboard workbench,
a wallpaperer's table, polishing shards of glass. A radio played
something soothing, a Gregorian chant, the volume of which was
now turned up so that the sound filled the great white space of
the body of the church. DS Campbell asked if Shaw wanted a
lift back to St James' but he said he'd sit awhile. That small part
of him that was conventionally religious had suggested an idea:
that if he watched the angel being installed again in its rightful
place the mystery of Arnold Smith-Waterson's obsession might
be revealed.

When he heard the church door bang shut he stood, and letting
his boots clip the stone floor, he advanced on the east window
until the man looked up from his work. Tanned, blue rectangular
spectacles and an expensive tailored white shirt, open-necked.
He inspected Shaw's warrant card with a cursory glance, as if
irritated by the intrusion.

'DI Peter Shaw.'

When he said nothing Shaw offered his hand.

'One moment, please.' He held up a hand as a stop signal,
sorting glass with the other, then making a note as if he'd forget
some vital piece of information if he didn't commit it to paper
immediately.

Shaw stood and waited. On the wall a plaque had been put
up marking the restoration. It included a brief summary of the
history of medieval church glass. Shaw noted one paragraph:

> *Modern technology has established that glass is an extremely
> complex substance. Before 1500, and right back to Roman
> times and beyond, glass was a material made by fire from*

a mixture of sand and plant ash. In the Mediterranean area
and further East, the ash used was that of maritime plants
of various kinds, notably those of the salicornia *family. These*
are rich in soda, and this alkali tends to give a more lustrous
and quick-working 'metal', the best properties of which may
be seen in perfected Venetian 'crystal' of the fifteenth to
seventeenth centuries.

Medieval Glass-Making in England
R.J. Charleston

Shaw noted that one line: 'a material made by fire'. It made glass sound magical, unearthly.

At last the handshake was completed: 'Pietro Murano, *Inspector.*' Shaw concluded that he either had a low opinion of British detectives, or the police in general. So this was the father. The way his daughter had talked of him had led Shaw to conclude he was hardly a part of her life. Of his potted life story he recalled only a Mayfair shop and a messy divorce.

'Father.' The voice floated down from above and they looked up to see Sonia Murano's face, framed in a trapdoor in the wooden platform on which she worked.

'The yellow, Father.'

'Excuse me, Inspector.'

He collected a shard of the yellow glass, marked – Shaw noted – with the eye of the angel. Carefully stowing it in a small leather satchel, he climbed the ladder.

Shaw heard a murmured conversation above, against the back-drop of the plainsong. Standing here, within the pool of coloured light, he realized how hot it must be up close to the glass itself. He could just see Murano's head, the short fair hair, the pale face, but only in profile, as if she too were one of the angels, with its single eye.

Murano Senior returned. 'I must say this,' he said, cleaning his hands on a rag soaked in white spirit, the fumes heady and pungent. '*We* must say this. The church is closed for repairs. There is a notice on the door – agreed with the diocese. My daughter does not wish to work in public. She wishes only for her privacy. And yet you bring this man here; this vagrant, this madman, who uses a gun to destroy the glass. This is most insensitive.

'The woman officer asked us – but already, it was too late. The man was here, with his nurse. What could we say? She is upset, Inspector. She asks if you have questions of her again. If so – respectfully – she asks please for you to send an email to the shop. That is all. She does not wish to speak. I am sorry.'

He held his arms wide over the glass.

'And now back to work.'

Shaw turned on his heels and walked the length of the nave, turning smartly to the north, towards the door in the porch. Abruptly, without warning, he stopped dead and looked to the east window. Sonia Murano had her back to the coloured glass, a silhouette, watching him leave.

THIRTY-NINE

There would be a last thunderstorm to mark the death of the Indian summer. Then, perhaps, winter would be with them, without an intervening autumn. As Shaw walked along the beach from Old Hunstanton towards the café a single flash of lightning caught his eye to the west; a dull pulse of lambent electricity, and then the almost imperceptible rumble of thunder.

Walking: usually he ran, a small rucksack high on his shoulders. Tonight he carried a long wooden box, expertly made in Tom Hadden's laboratory at the Ark by one of the junior assistants. It had two hemp rope handles, and was about the size of a street bollard, and something like the weight. Stopping, the sweat springing from his hairline, he switched hands and hoisted it once again across his back.

As he plodded along the sand Shaw reviewed the latest developments in the Mitchell's Bank case. Tom Hadden had called from the Ark to tell him that the prints lifted from the water bottle found in the public bin at Burnham Marsh were a match for Michael Connor, a small-time Lynn thief. Connor's wife, Grace, a nurse at the Queen Elizabeth, said he'd left home twenty-four hours earlier, in the family's Mondeo, to visit family in Fermoy, County Cork. She didn't know which ferry route he'd taken. The Border Agency, using CCTV footage, located the vehicle on the Cairnryan–Larne service. This one fact told Shaw all he needed to know; the choice of this circuitous route – via Scotland to Northern Ireland – suggested a man who didn't want to be followed. The police in Belfast, and the Gardai south of the border, were on alert for the vehicle.

Arresting Connor could break the case wide open. A small-time thief, facing a conspiracy to murder charge, would have every incentive to tell CID exactly what had happened at Burnham Marsh the night Stefan Bedrich died. Connor might even be persuaded to divulge the identity of the fourth burglar. Meanwhile, they planned to re-interview Whyte following a brief appearance at Lynn Magistrates Court, where he was due to be remanded in custody in the morning. The one loose end was young Seb Todd. Geoff Wighton's wife Louise was in a stable condition in hospital but they had been unable to get the ex-copper to a phone to check the teenager's account. There was little, if any, evidence that the youngster was involved in Bedrich's death; but it was a tiresome loose end nonetheless.

Shaw lifted his eyes to the distant café, resting the box for the last time, preparing to enter his other world. Lena was pacing on the sand, not her usual zigzag amble with a cup of coffee, but a measured, measuring step. Engrossed, jotting entries in a fabric-covered notebook, she didn't look up until Shaw was a few feet away.

He let the box down gently. 'Present,' he announced. 'You'll never guess.'

Fran ran out from the café with the dog at her heels.

Lena looked mildly annoyed, as if interrupted in a vital task. This was always a difficult moment: the homecoming. She often felt that Shaw simply crashed back into their lives, disrupting plans, demanding attention. There were moments when she wondered how he would react if she turned up with Fran in the CID room.

Shaw sensed the tension. 'What's with the notebook?' he asked, leaving Fran and the dog to examine the mysterious box.

Lena pushed her hair away from her wide forehead and made herself smile. 'What's in the box?'

'Why don't we look inside?' asked Shaw, and then sent Fran to get a toolbox from the shop.

'I was pacing out the area where we could put tables,' said Lena, when they were alone. 'A decent picnic table's a hundred and twenty pounds. We could start with twenty – two lines of ten – a rope swung between metal poles, just to make the point, that if you want to sit down it would be nice to buy a drink. No heaters. But maybe blankets? Something colourful, picnic patterns, just left on the seats.'

Shaw whistled. 'How many of those will be left after a Bank Holiday Monday?'

Lena looked quickly out to sea, and Shaw guessed she'd broken eye contact to hide a flash of irritation.

'None. Because I won't put them out on a bank holiday. End of season, early season, just to give people the idea that maybe they could sit outside. It works, Peter. I've checked it out, collected the data.'

'How many people per table?'

'Four, six. We don't have to go for picnic tables. You don't see many of the over-sixties using them, do you? Have to swing your leg round, inveigle yourself into the seat. It's tricky. Maybe round tables – metal – with metal seats. Then you could take eight.'

'A hundred and sixty people.'

'Yes. On ten days in a year? Less? Most nights it'll still be just you and me.' She spread her arms wide. The beach was deserted. 'Best Indian summer for years. Perfect sunset at the only east coast resort with a west-facing beach, and I can see three people, Peter – excluding us. Man with a dog a mile away towards Holme, and a couple to the south, and they're walking *away* from us. I'll have to pay your lot for crowd control officers at this rate.'

Shaw forced himself to say what he felt: 'When I'm here I like that it's a lonely place. I think people come here *because* it's a lonely place. I can see the irony – that if they all come, they'll destroy what brought them here in the first place. It's just how I remember it. Just me, Dad, Mum, the sea. Sorry. It's important.'

Fran dragged the toolbox the last ten feet, leaving a trail in the sand.

Shaw prised the lid off the box with three sharp blows of hammer to chisel and then he and Fran took out the handfuls of shredded paper. He slipped his hands under something long and heavy and raised it up over his head, so that they could both see it clearly against the evening sky.

'What's *that*?' asked Fran.

Lena had her hands on her hips, squinting, trying hard not to commit to joy or puzzlement.

'It's a thunderbolt,' said Shaw, with the full surfer's smile. 'Well – that's how I like to see it. It's fulgurite – a natural mineral.

When a lightning bolt hits sand it turns the loose grains into this solid stone. But you know – what does it look like? It looks like Thor's thunderbolt, and in a way it is.'

About five foot long, it had a blunt end – marking the surface impact of the lightning – and then tapered to a point, but not smoothly, but with lots of smaller points, as if it were an icicle of heat. The surface was a strange desert-brown, slightly bubbled, with lots of small spikes.

Fran said it looked like it was made of sand.

'It is – sort of,' said Shaw.

'No, Dad, sand full of water, like that trick you can do when you pick up a handful from a rock pool and then let it drip down on to hard sand and it forms a fairytale castle.'

They spent an hour trying to decide where they could put it in the café, and eventually decided on getting a glass cabinet built so that it could be mounted above the bar. Shaw fired up the barbecue with driftwood Fran had collected and they grilled sausages, the fat spitting. Lena, slightly bored with the summer barbecue routine, fetched some calamari from the fridge. Out at sea clouds were building, so that the sunset was brief.

Shaw's phone rang with a rare, sudden, five-bar signal.

'George.'

'Hi. Wighton's still in the hospital with his missus. She's coming home overnight so he couldn't talk. Just a text – said he'd be at a house in Anmer first thing if we wanted a word. The Vineyard. By the bowling green. Seven o'clock.'

'Great. I'll do it. Anything else?'

'Maybe. The motorcyclist's still in intensive care. It ain't looking good. But Tom says there's a print on the plastic wallet containing the five thousand quid they found on him.'

'We couldn't be that lucky. Not Stepney's?'

'We could. He's lifting them now, then he can check with the database. But think about it, Peter. Without the intervention of a heart attack we'd have got nowhere near this joker. He's a profes-sional. The bike was stolen in Greenwich three days ago. Plates changed. The scene of crime in the fish shop at Burnham is spotless. Job done, he goes and gets his money off Stepney. Why should Stepney worry about his prints on the dosh?'

'I'll be at St James' by nine,' said Shaw.

He cut the line and went back to the barbecue.

It was dark by ten, and Fran had homework, so that left them alone on the beach, lying on the sand, leaning on a rolled-up windbreak. Heat radiated still from the sand, and he threw a few bits of coal on the driftwood fire.

'You like shopping,' said Shaw. 'Ever been in Murano's? It's some kind of posh glassware place in Burnham Market.'

Lena pulled a face. She hated shopping, as Shaw knew, and most of all she loathed Burnham Market, with its relentlessly upmarket exclusivity and the way it seemed to reflect the mono-culture of the white monied classes. She'd have swapped it anytime for half an hour browsing along Ridley Road Market in Hackney.

'I've looked in the window. Glass. Bowls, jewellery, orna-ments.' This last word was one of their shared hatreds. The café, and the shop, but most of all the cottage itself, were free of anything which might count as a knick-knack.

'Very cold, isn't it, glass? Give me wood any day. At least it weathers, changes with time. Glass is repellent, really, the way the surface of it never changes, and then one day – *smash*! If it doesn't bend it'll break. I like to see time pass.'

Shaw sipped his wine and watched the tide beginning to edge up the deserted beach.

FORTY

Valentine, studying the map of Brancaster Marsh, experienced a wave of nausea. His near sight was fading, which was straining his eyes, but it was more the texture of the convoluted channels, creeks and ditches which crowded the chart that induced a sense of disorientation. He held it at arm's length as if that might help. The intricate maze-like pattern reminded him of a cross-section of a human brain, one of Justina Kazimeirz's forensic samples, perhaps, laid casually in its aluminum tray, a micron thick, cut by one of the pathologist's gleaming circular saws.

Valentine was the only human being in sight and he didn't like it one bit. The town was his landscape, the crowded pavements, the crawling cars, the short-cut alleyways. Here, with a view of the sea barred by the coastal dunes, the only thing that moved was the sky. It was full of birds, some flying north, others flying south, the meeting of these two vast migrations a great swirl over his head, as if some god had stirred the sky. The noise of the birds was overwhelming. They were barking; Valentine knew that wasn't the right word, but that's what it sounded like to him. Barking.

The DS's Mazda blocked a narrow track leading away from a house, the lone sign of human habitation on the marsh: four-square, naval architecture, with stout brick chimney stacks and a golden weathervane in the shape of a ship under sail. All the windows were open and since he'd turned the Mazda's engine off – and the migrating birds had moved on – he could hear a series of domestic sounds from within: a hoover, a spin-dryer in its final cycle, drainpipes in flood. From the two upper windows duvets hung out in the warm air. A brewing thunderstorm expected overnight still threatened, although there had been a light rain at dawn, and so the tarmac steamed gently in the sun.

He tried to look and act like himself, but was aware that a stray hand kept rearranging his thinning hair, and that he strained

to stand up straight, trying to minimize the effect of the stoop
that allowed his head to hang forward on his neck. Aftershave,
applied by the handful, was making his eyes water. A teenager
once again, he thought, in the loos at the Roxy, preparing to
launch himself on to the dance floor.

After ten minutes his resolve fled and he lit a cigarette.

He'd no sooner smelt the gust of sulphur on the air from the
match when the front door opened and Jan Clay skipped down
the path: not quite a girlish playground step, but certainly joyful,
excited. The sight of her made his spirits soar.

'Found the house then?' They both considered the building,
and Valentine noticed the name for the first time, etched in brick
over the door: MARSH VILLA.

'Can I have one?' she said, nodding at the cigarette he'd tried
to cup in the back of his hand.

'You don't smoke,' said Valentine.

'You'd be surprised what you don't know about me, Georgie.
It's not a habit. But I enjoy one.'

She let the sun's heat play on her skin as she took in the
nicotine. 'You didn't phone.'

'Oh. Sorry.' Now he was confused. They'd had an Italian meal.
She said she didn't want to spend the rest of her life with a
copper who had a drink problem. Had he missed something?

'I'd like to go out again if you want. I enjoy . . .' She opened
her eyes and looked at him. 'This.' She shrugged and they both
laughed. 'It's just that you can't judge a marriage from the outside,
can you? I didn't want you to think it had been idyllic. Peter
didn't drink because he had a problem. It *was* the problem. And
he despised the job. Coppering. Which was cynical of him, and
depressing. You love it, don't you?'

Valentine looked away, out over the marsh, ashamed to think
he'd never admitted that, even to himself.

She looked at his black slip-ons. 'Didn't I say boots in the
text?' she asked.

'These will have to do.' They were already caked in mud.

Setting off down a narrow path beside the muddy channel she
led the way inland. Once they were off the flood bank they were
too low to be able to see ahead; as if they'd fallen into a sunken
maze. They passed a rotting set of landings with three moored

boats, one a wreck, the other two bristling with sonar. Then over
a narrow bridge made out of railway sleepers to another channel,
with a line of small boats beached in mid-stream. The tide was
out so the vessels here were just lying in the glistening black
mud. Two minutes along the path and they crossed a stretch of
marsh reeds to a third channel.

'How the hell do you know the way?' asked Valentine, failing
to disguise the strain moderate exercise put on his lungs. His
turn-ups were full of grass.

'I've done for the woman who owns that house for five years.
One morning a week. I've got another one over in the village
and this saves me twenty minutes' plodding on the road. Then
I can pick up the bus. I never did drive. Peter did that. Which
looking back on it was unforgivable of him, considering he was
permanently half-cut – if not worse.'

There was one boat here in the third channel, clinker built,
with brass portholes.

Jan stopped, hands in pockets. 'Like I say, I like coppers,
police stations. It's weird, isn't it? How you can be at home
somewhere. When Peter died they said I could come past if I
wanted, have a cuppa. So I take them some chips, just for a break
when I've got a shift at the Mariners. I saw the poster up with
that boat you're after. I reckon this is her. Can't be many with
that name on this coast.'

Valentine had no idea if it was the right boat. He called up
the poster image from his mobile phone.

'Bloody hell, Jan.'

The cockpit was covered in a green tarpaulin which you could
unbutton. Inside the wheel and controls gleamed.

'She's beautiful,' said Jan, walking to the prow to read the
name: *The Limpet*. 'Someone loves it. It's been hosed down.
Polished. It's spotless.'

Valentine thought about that. A boat, lying in a muddy creek,
crabs clawing at the timbers, but sparkling in the sunlight.

'I better get our forensic boys out.'

'What d'ya reckon, Georgie? How does the *Limpet* fit in?'

'Maybe the killer used it to dump Bedrich's corpse on
Mitchell's Bank. We don't know where he died. Maybe he died
on-board – in the cockpit, or below. Blood, mud, fingerprints.

But she looks too clean to me.' He bent down and looked through one of the cabin windows. It looked like a London club in there, with dark wood panels, books, an elegant cushioned bench, a polished stove. 'Once he'd snared Bedrich's body to the buoy perhaps he just kept going. Get rid of the evidence, take the boat somewhere lonely, and get it clean. Anyways, I owe you.' He filled his lungs: 'What you doing tonight?'

Jan smiled and walked away along the grassy towpath trailing a hand, as if she wanted to take Valentine for another walk. But she wanted him to look back at the boat. The *Limpet* lay at an angle, leaning into the bank. They could see the hull clearly, and the dark blue stripe that marked the Plimsoll line, below which the hull had been painted a brilliant white.

'The hull's spotless too. Not a mark,' she said. 'It's been cleaned like you said, but not yesterday, or the day before. High tide was four hours ago. Sea water always leaves a film of salt, a little mud, some scurf. There's nothing. Your man – if it is a man – has been here in the last three hours. Maybe less.'

Valentine was on the mobile. 'You should be on the force,' he said, swearing at the faltering signal.

'I'm glad you said that, Georgie. I was going to break it gently when the time was right.' She took a breath, before looking him directly in the eyes. 'I've applied to join the police training scheme. Mature entrant. I tick boxes. There's a medical, a few tests, but I've been led to believe – that's the phrase they use – *led to believe* that my application will be successful. Are you going to be all right with that, DS Valentine?'

FORTY-ONE

S haw edged the Porsche to the junction by the village green at Anmer. He'd already spotted three squad cars, the vanguard of the security force which would have to patrol the area once Prince William and his wife and son were living at Anmer Hall. One was parked on the edge of the churchyard to the rear of the house, as conspicuous in its blue and white livery as an ice-cream van among the weathered tombstones. Another stood at the gates to the estate, the third by the little bowling green spread out in front of the village hall.

Shaw felt sympathy for the locals. At least his stretch of deserted Norfolk was only invaded in good weather. This area of north Norfolk, inland from Sandringham and the coastal resorts, had once been remote; a high plateau of wide, whale-backed hills and hamlets. Now it was on the map, and life would move to a different rhythm. Anmer had no inn, but he wondered how long it would take for some entrepreneur to open a gastro pub, with distant views of the royal estate. The new royal residents would also put a few more thousand pounds on the price of a local house, not that they'd ever been that cheap. Save for a row of tied cottages on the back road, most of the buildings were solid landed gentry, surrounded by artfully gone-to-seed English gardens.

Anmer Hall itself, glimpsed beyond the churchyard trees, boasted an eighteenth-century red brick façade, with a high tiled roof. Scaffolding masked the whole range of house, barns and conservatories. Renovations were under way, royal nurseries being wallpapered. Some of the locals had broken ranks to voice criticism of the building work – particularly the new red roof tiles – labelling the result a 'giant Barrett home'.

Unkind, thought Shaw. With time the new works would blend into the Georgian ensemble. Drifting through the village, he tried to read the names of the houses, wondering if anyone in north Norfolk actually had an address made up of numbers and postcode. The Vineyard appeared, glimpsed beyond a Norfolk-stone wall. The Porsche crunched over the gravel as he swung through the open gates, and he thought that nothing *sounded* like money more than that grating of tyres over half an acre of pale Cotswold Buff. A van was parked to the side of the house, just visible beyond a garage.

Geoff Wighton came out to meet him. He was smiling but Shaw thought he looked unwell, those red roast-beef cheeks a little less livid, edging towards purple.

'Inspector. I've made a pot of coffee.'

The interior had been decorated in perfect taste. Coir carpeting throughout, except on the wooden stairs, and a parquet-floored nineteenth-century kitchen, complete with Aga.

'This stuff's amazing,' said Wighton. A modern oven and fridge were mounted in the wall and twinkled with digital read-outs. 'All this – and the heating system – can be accessed remotely on your phone. They've got a cable link. So they can jump in the Jag in the mews off the King's Road, or more likely the Angel, and switch the heating on a hundred miles away. Do me out of a job.'

'But it hasn't.'

'No. Tropical fish need feeding, checking. And they're worried about thieves. I know they've not made the press yet but there's plenty of incomer-anxiety about burglars. It's the number one topic of gossip over the scallops and Chablis.'

The fridge made a small electronic beep as Wighton opened it to find milk. It reminded Shaw of the noises he'd heard upstairs at Wighton's house, the sound of the medical equipment which helped keep his wife alive. What did this ex-copper really think of people who could afford to get someone to feed their angelfish?

He pushed a coffee mug towards Shaw. 'No. You're right. I've got a job for life. I'm basically a servant, right? But there's none of the tricky social stigma that you get with actually having a servant. I'm unseen. A helpful spirit. A watchful eye.'

Something stirred in Shaw's memory banks. A sudden electric spark flared then died. If he'd been alone he might have been able to pinpoint the notion, the shadowy shape of a brilliant flash of intuition.

But the moment had gone, so he asked Wighton about his wife.

'Louise?' Wighton's eyes flooded and Shaw realized it was a brutal question in a way. He hadn't once mentioned her, even when they were in the same house, and now Shaw had forced him to evaluate her condition to a virtual stranger.

'Sorry.'

Wighton held up a hand: 'No. No. It's fine. She's alive – that's the blessing. And at home, which is where she wants to be. But it's a struggle. Every breath. Sometimes, when I see people smoking – especially teenagers – I have to go. I can't watch. I want to take it out of their lips and crush it.' He laughed. 'You can't buy air, doesn't matter how rich you are.'

Shaw produced his notebook. 'Look. It was just a small thing. But one of your properties in Burnham Marsh was Overy View, the one with double bay windows down on the quay.'

'Yup. Jonathan Todd's house.'

'You said you checked the houses out on Thursday, around four o'clock. What kind of condition did you find the place in? It would have been a week since your last visit. Had anyone been in the house?'

'Shouldn't have been. The Todds let me know when they're due. He's a dental surgeon – at Guys – nice people. There's a son comes down too, but again, I get a call. They're better than most. Least they don't treat me like staff.'

Shaw sipped his coffee, black and acrid, and tried not to sound adversarial. 'So it *should* have been as you left it. But the question is, was it?'

'This is important? I can't see why, the burglaries were Thursday night.'

'Mr Wighton. I'm the investigating officer. You are a witness. Can you answer this question?'

Wighton's mobile buzzed and he checked a text.

'More work,' he said, tossing the mobile on to a soft chair.

He clapped his hands, rubbing them together in a display of brisk efficiency.

'Look. Business is good, Inspector. Crazy, really. Wills and Kate don't do it any harm. North Norfolk's never been so trendy. New money's moving in, old money's moving out. Fact is, I don't always check every property. If I know the owners aren't about and there's nothing pressing I just give it a glance and get on.'

'You're saying you didn't check Overy View that day?'

He nodded, wiping a hand across plump lips.

'Any others missed out?'

'No. I was on the way down to Spithead House and they've got cats, and a sodding gerbil. It takes me half an hour to muck it out – it's only two inches long. I just cut a corner.'

'Risk assessment's not very smart though, is it? Your business is based on trust. Reliability. Honesty. You slip up, you're out of a job, right?'

'It's a wake-up call. It won't happen again. I need to take the plunge, pay someone to help. But I need another copper. That's my Unique Selling Point, my USP: I'm a professional. The paperwork's the thing, and the tax forms. One employee and suddenly I'm running News International.'

Shaw finished his coffee and told Wighton what he thought of an ex-copper who had taken the decision to mislead a murder inquiry. Then he told him he'd have to consider his next move, but that it might involve informing the Todds that they weren't getting everything they paid for from their house-sitter.

Which still left Shaw with the problem of Sebastian Todd and Overy View.

Back out in the Porsche he sat for a moment waiting to see if his mobile could pick up a signal.

Five minutes later Wighton's white van crunched past on the gravel. Side-on Shaw could clearly see the logo for his business. There was a mobile telephone number, a website. Discreet, classy even, in an elegant script. Then the design: an angel, a portfolio under one arm, the wings folded, but held high above the shoulders.

And the one big word, ANGELS, with the tag line underneath:

The second-home guardian security service.

FORTY-TWO

S haw followed Wighton's white van, leaving a quarter of a mile of clear road between them. Why was he following the ex-copper? He'd let several images form simultaneously in his mind: Smith-Waterson's blackened skin, medieval glass angels, empty seaside second homes, Wighton at Burnham Marsh, the boathouse at Spithead House. Two miles short of Wighton's terrace house Shaw pulled off the road. The lay-by was on the crest of a hill from which he could just see the sea to the north. In the silence he heard his mobile text box filling up as it suddenly found a strong signal.

The first was from Valentine: Limpet *found. Cleaned top to bottom today. SOCO on way.*

Another image to add to the list: the seagoing boat.

He rang DC Twine in the incident room at Burnham Marsh and told him to get hold of the owners of the *Limpet* in Cley and ask them if they employed former DS Geoff Wighton as a security man. Top priority. Then he rang DS Fiona Campbell.

'Sir.'

'Fiona. At your desk?'

'Sir.'

'Great. We had a file online for Smith-Waterson. Do I recall an arrest in Wells in 2000 for possession of a Class-A drug? If I do, can you read me off the prosecuting officer's name?'

He heard the finger-taps on the computer keyboard, the buzz of the CID room in the background.

'DS G. Wighton.'

'Great. Thought so. I'll keep you posted.'

He slid the Porsche back out into the traffic and driving on, past Wighton's house, glimpsed the van parked outside. A mile down the road he took the Porsche through a farm gate and left it on the edge of a field of wheat stubble, then walked back up the lane. Two hundred yards short of the house he saw Wighton come out, lock the door, then load a suitcase in the back of the van. Then he drove off at sixty, black exhaust trailing. Shaw rang Twine to give him the details on the Bedford and instructions to have it tailed along the coast road.

'Sir. I got the owner of the *Limpet* – he's at the house for the weekend. Wighton's been looking after the property for eighteen months. No complaints. Excellent service.'

'OK. Get traffic on this van. Tell 'em to maintain contact but not to approach the driver. Keep me up to date.'

Shaw ran to the house. On his first visit he'd missed the intercom by the front doorbell. A small sign read: *Please press button and speak.* He said he was DI Peter Shaw and he had a few questions for Louise Wighton.

No answer.

He stood back and looked up at the front-bedroom window. Net curtains, condensation, a faint glimmer of electric light. He pressed the intercom again. Three times.

The front door had what Lena liked to call a Kentucky-Fried Fanlight: a window set in the door, instead of above, as favoured by the fast-food chain. Fanlights were popular with the Georgians because they wanted the light, but they needed strong doors to keep out thieves. Putting the window in the door was a big mistake, especially for a security consultant. Shaw put a lump of York stone from the garden rockery through it, reached inside, and sprung the lock. That set an alarm off on the side of the house. By that time he was at the top of the stairs. He could hear the dog behind one of the bedroom doors.

He spoke her name clearly and confidently. 'Mrs Wighton? Louise Wighton. This is DI Peter Shaw.'

Between the wails of the alarm there was complete silence except for the distant barking of the dog: the mechanical breathing, the sound of a dragon sleeping on its treasure, had gone.

Pushing open the front bedroom door he found a room dominated by a king-sized bed covered by an oxygen tent. Mounted on the wall was an electric ventilator and a small control panel, but none of the lights showed either red or green, and the tent had partly deflated, so that the upper part clung to the face of the woman beneath.

Shaw unzipped the plastic sheeting and pushed his head within the tent. The air smelt of liniment and antiseptic. Louise Wighton's face was very pale, her lips a green-blue, her eyes closed. Shaw thought she looked as if she'd been pushed down into the bed itself, as though gravity had pulled her into the mattress. In her left hand she held an oxygen mask. Held? Perhaps not: it lay in her hand, the fingers of which were open and splayed.

Shaw touched her flesh. Warm still, but she wasn't breathing, and when he felt her jugular there was no pulse.

The bars on his phone were gone so he ran downstairs and used the landline to ring 999.

Then he ran back up the stairs, tore the oxygen tent back, applying his weight through both hands to her chest. The ribcage creaked, but he made himself exert maximum pressure, because even if the heart had stopped her blood still held some oxygen, and if he could force it round her body she might revive. The principal danger – if he could get her breathing – was brain damage: so even a few seconds of partly oxygenated blood could make a life-changing difference.

For eighteen minutes he applied a rhythmic pressure to the beat of 'Nellie The Elephant'. The room around him seemed to still hold the woman's consciousness within it – far more so, indeed, than her actual body. When he heard the siren he left her and went to the window to watch the yellow and green ambulance park neatly in the drive. Turning back he realized that any sense of her presence within the room had fled.

FORTY-THREE

Wighton's van was not picked up by West Norfolk traffic on any of the major roads. Two hours after leaving Holme it was spotted travelling at seventy-three mph on the fast lane of the M11. A squad car noted the number and tracked it for half a mile. Forward units monitored its route to Junction 26 for Stansted Airport. DC Twine rang the British Airports Authority police liaison office and they located a G.H. Wighton booked on a flight for Pisa with EasyJet. The van was parked in Q65 Long Stay, and was on a trailer heading back to West Norfolk's forensic laboratory before Wighton had got to passport control. When asked by a Border Agency official to accompany him to an interview room he dropped his suitcase and ran for the fire exit. He was apprehended thirty-five minutes later on the apron of the runway by two airport security officers. He told one he had an acute fear of flying and had panicked. The officer replied that he could relax now, as he wasn't flying anywhere.

By the time Valentine's Mazda parked beside Shaw's Porsche at the Burnham Marsh incident room, Wighton was travelling north in the back of an unmarked CID car in the company of two officers of the Essex Constabulary. Silent for the majority of the journey, he did ask twice if they had any news on the condition of his wife – and was told that West Norfolk officers would be on hand to brief him on his arrival at Burnham Marsh mobile incident room. For the last twenty minutes of the journey, over the north Norfolk hills, he appeared to be asleep.

Twilight was falling on the old quayside. The Ostrich was open, the owners having flown back from France after being advised the property had been burgled. A floodlight played on the picnic tables set out front, where a group of smokers had gathered on the patch of grass which ran down to the water's edge. The sound of laughter, a sudden throaty burst of good humour, seemed more than anything to finally lift the spell that had once held the village in a trance, like a model in a paper-weight, transfixed in glass. Life had truly returned now: Valentine could smell the distinctive whiff of barbecue gas on the air, and somewhere Radio Four played Big Ben striking the hour.

Twine appeared from the mobile incident room with a computer print-out of Geoff Wighton's website. The home page featured the angel logo.

Valentine went to speak but Shaw raised a hand: 'George. We just missed it. I missed it, you missed it. It's just bad luck. We need to move on. Priority is the first interview and letting Tom have free range down at Spithead House. I presume the boathouse is empty?'

'We checked it out on the first sweep – but we weren't looking for a boat then, so who knows what we missed,' said Twine. 'There was no sign of any forced entry so we moved on.'

'You think it's drugs, Peter?' asked Valentine. 'That he was in the village that night, running it ashore, and Bedrich just blundered in on him?'

'Who knows, George. Call me old-fashioned, but let's collect some evidence and then speculate. And that's the good news. Think about it. He had time to clean up the *Limpet*. But there's no way he would have risked coming back here while we were on site. It'll be as he left it. That's our chance.'

They walked down past the Ostrich to Spithead House. Three stories high, almost a townhouse, with one large Georgian window converted on the second floor into an oriel, an elegant box-shaped balcony. To one side a narrow inlet of deep water had been dug when the house was built to give access to a wooden boathouse. Inside, the walls shimmered with the reflected light from the dock, which was empty, the water oddly clear and luminous, as if lit from within by an invisible neon bar. Looking down into the green depths Shaw could just see shells on the bottom, and a shoal of small black fish in synchronized motion.

The boathouse was roughly the shape of the living quarters of Noah's Ark. Once inside they could see that the roof above their heads was flat. Shaw threw his head back to examine it. 'Trapdoor,' he said, pointing at a brass handle.

Hadden brought them a pair of white SOCO suits. Twine arrived with ladders and a clipboard.

As they struggled to get a ladder into place on the narrow

wooden walkway beneath the trapdoor, Twine filled Shaw in on the latest from the owner of the *Limpet*.

'Wighton did the usual up at Cley. Checked the house, fed the cat. But there was one added extra. Lott's a pilot. He's short of time, but he's not short of money. He took Wighton on because he's got his own master's licence for a boat. So when Lott came back he could take the *Limpet* out on a jolly and not worry about getting back home. He'd leave it in Boston, or Lowestoft, or Grimsby, or wherever, and Wighton would sail her home. So he knew the ropes.'

The trapdoor popped easily enough, once Shaw got his shoulder under it, and then it fell back on brass hinges. Squeezing through was extraordinarily difficult, so that Shaw had to lead with one hand, one arm, then the shoulder and head, before letting the other shoulder follow.

The space revealed was lit by an oculus window in the seaward end of the room. Shaw hadn't noticed this from outside and realized that it wasn't visible from the wharf, only from the sea. At the opposite end to the window was a door with a davit built into the wood beside it, ready to swing out and haul up goods into the loft. Beside the door was a rack of tools, boathooks, saws, wooden mallets, and a shelf of pots, sticky with paint, or glue, or pitch.

'Sorry, George,' shouted Shaw. 'You should see this too.'

Valentine was thin enough for the trapdoor, but the stiffness of his joints made the exercise excruciating. At one point he brushed aside Shaw's offer of a helping hand. When he did finally get through, he straightened up with a hand to his back, trying to brush dust off his raincoat, his breathing audible.

Shaw checked out the contents of the room. There was a mug on a long central table, which was collapsible, with a plastic surface. It had been cleaned, because in the sideways light from the oculus window they could see the wipe marks of a cloth. There was one folding chair, and a portable electric heater, a cable running to a plug on the floor beside a socket.

Shaw went back to the trapdoor and looked down at DC Twine. 'The owners here at Spithead House – do they have a boat?'

'Yes. They've got another house in the Brighton Marina and their boat's there – a white ship, patio doors, gin bottles, the lot. There's pictures in the house.'

At the far end of the room was a pile of plastic sacks, each carrying a blue script and a logo: ERGAMISOL. *Oostende Ziekenhuis.* Each one had been stamped with a circular red disc and the word FARMACIE. There were various codes and licence numbers. One bag had been opened but resealed with a clothing peg. Shaw used a gloved hand to reopen the bag and a naked wet finger to taste the contents.

He winced. 'Salt. *A* salt. My guess is Ergamisol is a trade name for Levamisole, the stuff the dealer used to adulterate the cocaine supply. How many bags, George? A guess.'

'Two hundred – more.'

They stood in silence imagining the scene. The long plastic tabletop used for mixing quantities of cocaine with imported Levamisole.

They heard footsteps on the ladder and Twine's head appeared through the trapdoor, then his upper body, so that he was neatly wedged in position. 'Sir. Squad car's here with Wighton.'

'Take him into the house, Paul. We'll be ten minutes.'

Twine retreated, but it took him a second to work his arms back through the narrow trapdoor.

Shaw saw the moment then – the vivid, terrifying second in which Bedrich must have died. Wighton, working silently in the loft, would have heard him enter the boathouse, perhaps checking it out before trying the house itself.

Footsteps then on the ladder. No light would have shown through the boards or round the trapdoor, so Wighton could have moved swiftly to plunge the room into darkness, because the socket was by the chair.

Did Bedrich speak? 'Anyone there?' Just to be sure.

Then, in the dark, the sound of the trapdoor flipping back, the struggle as Bedrich forced his body upwards into the space, trying to bring his trailing arm through with a torch.

Wighton would have waited for the moment. Two steps to the tool rack, a spade selected, then as the light came round he'd have swung it through the beam at the intruder's neck. How quickly had he calculated that murder was his only way out? There was no innocent explanation for what he was doing in the loft. Who did he think was climbing the stairs? The owners – disaster. Thieves – worse. Or dealers from Lynn, determined to cut out the middle man? Did he say anything in those fleeting, final seconds?

Wighton was a powerful man. Shaw thought of the weights and rowing machine in his front room. Striking from above he had his victim at his mercy, trapped, wedged in the narrow trap-door. The spade would have swung through the torchbeam like an executioner's axe, the single blow almost severing the head from the body. Did he fall back, slump forward? Shaw imagined the blood dripping down into the water below.

FORTY-FOUR

Handcuffed, Wighton had been marched to Spithead House, and sat down at the kitchen table. Stone floor, open range, Belfast sink, utility shelves and cupboards, the plasterwork peeling slightly – this one house, at least, had slipped the bonds of modernization and gentrification which had overwhelmed Burnham Marsh. Shaw recalled that the new owners had notified Wighton that they were planning to rip it all out and install a new kitchen. Shaw wondered where the old owners had gone. The graveyard? A care home? A block of modern flats glimpsed from a Tube train? They'd left behind a welcome echo of the past. There was even an old black-and-white framed picture of the church, the roof intact, taken inside looking seawards towards the altar, the light blazing through the window with its central image: Salome dancing for Herodias, St John's severed head on a gold platter.

Wighton's mouth hung open and he was breathing heavily. They could smell him too, that distinctive odour of fear, a combination of sweat and nervous electricity. A mug of tea stood, untouched, on the worktop in front of him, the steam rising.

Shaw opened a mullioned window into the garden. There was a peacock outside, a female, pale and red-eyed, perched on a shed. A rumble of thunder made the old china on the shelves rattle.

Valentine had brought one of the bags of Dutch drugs with him and placed it on the table in front of Wighton. Outside, through the window, they could see the St James' forensic van, its back down, white-suited officers extracting gear.

'They won't tell me about Louise,' said Wighton. 'I asked in the squad car – and now, the constable, he knows but he wouldn't say. I have a right to know.'

This was either an elaborate double bluff or Shaw was looking at a genuine psychopath.

'I'm sorry to have to tell you that your wife is dead, Mr Wighton.'

He looked to one side, towards the back door, and for a moment it looked as if he was considering a second attempt at escape. Instead, he covered his face with both hands, then ran them back through his hair.

'She was alive when I left and the respirator was working,' he said, his voice thicker, less distinct. It was an odd response, and certainly made it clear that during his few last moments in the house he had gone upstairs. What had been said? What had he done? Hadden's deputy, Dr Elizabeth Pryce, had a forensic team in the room now, and the pathologist was on her way.

'The switch to the respirator was surely beyond her reach, Mr Wighton?'

'I want a solicitor. It's my right,' he said, quite calmly, although his facial muscles were displaying several contrary emotions: fear, distress and a clear edge of anger.

'Did she ask you to turn it off when you told her you were leaving?' asked Shaw. 'Or did you leave her with a lie? As opposed to the truth: I'm driving to Stansted Airport and getting a flight to Italy.'

'She would have been fine. She knew that. She has nurses,' said Wighton. 'They come every few hours. I pay for that. It costs a fortune, a fortune I have to earn, so that she's never alone for very long, or in pain.'

Shaw felt they'd moved on very quickly from any sense of grief.

'You don't seem particularly upset at your wife's death, Mr Wighton. Is that a fair summary of your feelings at this point?'

Wighton shrugged. 'I've spent a decade looking after Louise; she's spent a decade wanting to die. It's a release for both of us. I didn't kill her. If that had been a way out I'd have taken it years ago.'

'What's wrong with the local health authority?' asked Valentine. 'Respite care is excellent. You didn't have to pay.'

Shaw had a vague memory of Julie Valentine's death. He'd been a child but he could recall the whispers at home, the forbidden C-word, visits to a cold, damp terrace house in the North End.

'Louise wanted to die at home. She insisted on that. Her problem was she wasn't dying. And she'd couldn't give up the fags. I'd wheel her out sometimes, after dark, always after dark. If she was down – really down – she'd smoke in the room and then the nurses would smell it. So there wasn't a lot of sympathy. Emphysema can last for years, a lifetime really. With the respirator, and the oxygen, she could have struggled on for another ten years. She wouldn't go into hospital. She wouldn't go into care. She wanted me to die with her, really. The words were never said – but she wanted me there, at the bedside. All those years when I was in the job, or out messing about on boats, she said the boredom drove her to the fags. So it was my fault anyway. The dying are cruel people. Much worse than the living.'

Shaw had no doubt that was the truth.

'The NHS nurses would come round, of course they did. Louise always said they were second-rate. She was a snob too, Louise. I had the money, I had the clients, and the police pension, so I could fucking well pay for the best.'

The Anglo-Saxon word seemed to release something in Wighton, and despite the fact that his composure did not falter, Shaw could see his colour draining away.

'So I paid. Then she started getting magazines – from Exit and Dignitas. It was clear to her, she claimed, that I didn't want to care for her – not really. So why didn't she just die? I had to organize it, and she never asked about the cost. It's seven thousand pounds, by the way, for Dignitas. They use helium, so you've got to laugh.'

He raised a hand from under the table to wipe his lips and it shook violently.

'But that's not the real cost. You've got to get there. There isn't an airline that would let her near a commercial flight so we're talking a private jet. It's not as much as you'd think; fifteen thousand, a little more. I'd have to take a nurse because you couldn't have her dying en route. I don't have that kind of money. And I thought when she's gone I want a life, so I'm not borrowing it off some shark.'

Twine came in with tea in paper cups.

'Last summer the pilot who owns the *Limpet*, Bob Lott, took her over the Channel. Big adventure, that, you'd think he'd found the North West Passage. I had to go over and fetch the boat back. Money was good. She was laid up in Dunkirk, the old town. I know a few people there from when I was at Wells: harbour police, customs, state-wide CID. They said there was a big problem with cocaine going out in commercial vessels to the UK – East Coast ports mainly – and they couldn't stop it. Fact was they'd given up trying. I thought, if they're not bothered I'll cash in. I requested the files and promised I'd have a look at it from our end. It wasn't difficult to find a way in to the network. I'd done some drugs work back in the nineties, so I had the contacts. But you can't make a fortune like that, not as fast as I wanted it.'

Outside they heard the peacock screech.

'I thought I'd cut it.'

He drank his tea, the hand much steadier now.

'How did you know Arnold Smith-Waterson?'

'Gutter? I used to run a boat for him out of Wells when he had a house up here – back in the nineties. Nice people, him and the wife. After the divorce I did him for possession, cocaine that time. But he wasn't finicky. I knew he'd been a doctor, and I knew he was on the streets. I tracked him down and made him an offer. If he'd tell me what to get and do the mixing I'd do the rest. He got a free supply. I'd run into town in the van and give him his fix. Once a day, out by the Boal Quay. Personal service.

'But he fucked up. Too much Levamisole. Irony was he thought he was getting a pure supply. Never knew he was poisoning himself until it was too late. Most of it had gone out on the streets by the time we knew it was dangerous. I used street dealers in Lynn. I told Gutter that if he said a word I'd get him locked up for life. A cell. Like a lot of them, he can't stand the thought of it – being caged. I paced him out a standard cell. Three by two. That freaked him out.'

Shaw thought of Smith-Waterson, sitting now in a neon-lit room, looking out of a window at the manicured grounds of the secure unit. His silence was explicable now, not the product of fear at all, but guilt. He'd mixed the adulterated supply, his own mutilated hand was evidence of the consequences. The sheer terror of being incarcerated had stopped him doing the only thing that would have saved his sanity: confessing and leading the police to Wighton.

'But you were still cutting it,' said Valentine. 'We've found the evidence in the boathouse.'

'Once you know how it's simple. Like cooking. I had to shift what was left.'

'Until Stefan Bedrich stumbled on the boathouse that night,' said Shaw. 'Talk me through that. No doubt that was *his* fault.'

Wighton looked at his hands. 'Your boy – Twine – he said I had a lawyer on the way.'

'Won't be long,' said Shaw. 'But so you know, we found the *Limpet*, and we've got it on CCTV heading out to sea that night. And we've got SOCO in the boathouse loft. What chance is there that there *isn't* a bloodstain?'

Shaw thought he saw the moment when the truth, in the sense of the shape of his life from this moment forwards, actually became a reality for Wighton. He would never again enter a room, or leave a room, without permission. Wighton's tradesman-like exterior hid a certain subtle intelligence. Did he see the irony then – that he'd done all this to escape the tyranny of that upstairs room and the oxygen tent, only to spend the years that were left to him in a cell?

'I didn't kill him. The Pole.'

'I find that hard to believe,' said Shaw.

'I hit him,' he said, the confessional moment marked by an intake of breath. 'I hit him hard with a piece of four-by-two, so there'll be blood all right, and he fell down the ladder into the dock. I fished him out with a hook. Breathing – I got him breathing – but he wouldn't come round, so I wrapped him up in tarpaulin and put him in the cockpit of the *Limpet*. I tied a lead weight to his leg with rope and tape. Then I went up into the loft and started clearing up.

'I was going to throw him overboard, I don't mind admitting *that*. When I came down with the stash he had gone. Like gone, Houdini or something, just gone, with the tarpaulin still there. I ran out on the beach and I could see his footprints in the mud. Concussion, I reckon, 'cos it's totally mad, setting out at night over those sands. I thought he'll die out there. I better run too. So I cleaned up what I could and waited for the tide.'

'You didn't see the other burglars?' asked Shaw.

Wighton calculated for a moment. 'Sure. I went up into the

village and clocked them in the van. That's when I got the reg number. When I thought you were getting close to me, after you circulated a description of the *Limpet*, I staged the burglary up at Tines Manor. That way I could put you on to them. That night, the night the Pole died, they waited about an hour and then drove off. I was safe then, but I still had to catch the tide. So I did.'

'Know what I think?' asked Shaw.

They could hear a car purring outside. Wighton's lawyer had arrived.

'I think Stefan Bedrich died in the boathouse loft. Forensics will be key, but I'm confident we'll find what we need. It was a bloodbath, and you can't clean up after a bloodbath. Yes, you took the *Limpet* out into Overy Creek, but I think you had him on-board – roped up to the lead weight, with his pockets stuffed with samphire. Then you threw him overboard. *Then* you set out to sea. That's the story the evidence is going to tell, and it's the story that'll convince a jury you killed Stefan Bedrich.'

FORTY-FIVE

The Old Beach Café had a set of extra-large meteorological instruments mounted on the wooden balcony edge: a thermometer, barometer, a wind gauge linked to an anemometer on the roof, a sunshine recorder. Shaw had never seen the pointer on the barometer so low, wedged firmly beyond STORM. Blue-black clouds dominated the sky, with ragged windows of blue beyond. The air was so still the beach felt like a giant room in which all the windows had been closed. The anemometer was static, its little ice-cream-cup vanes set to the points of the compass. The thermometer read 22°C (72°F), and although the sun was falling rapidly towards the horizon, as Shaw watched the digital readout flipped to 23°C.

Lena was inside serving an elderly couple tea and soda bread. His wife's exaggerated good humour in talking to her last two customers of the day told him the long summer season had worn her down. Fran, bored with the adult world, played out on the water's edge, her spidery form reflected in a mirror-like sea. Shaw was attempting what they liked to call the 'full relax' – a large glass of white wine, his feet up on the wooden verandah. He'd brought a spare glass with him in the hope that Lena would join him, but he suspected she would just clear up, get the working day done, and then start on supper.

Geoff Wighton had been charged with a specimen drugs offence and taken to St James'. They'd interview him in the morning, or possibly the next day. A full assessment of the forensics was unlikely to be complete before the weekend. Privately, Hadden had told the CID team that he'd managed to extract a full blood sample from the wood around the trapdoor. The hunt for the murder weapon would include a second fingertip search of the marshy edge of Overy Creek. Initial results from Wighton's house were equivocal: a full autopsy was planned for the next day at the Ark. The *Limpet* was under tow back to Boal Quay, where it would be taken out of the water for a dry-dock examination.

Shaw had enjoyed a brief conversation with the chief constable in which he'd suggested they break the media blackout on the Chelsea Burglars asap, given that they could now name two suspects under arrest: Whyte and Connor (apprehended in a B&B outside Warren Point, Northern Ireland, by a sharp-eyed police constable who spotted the Mondeo's licence plates), and had one suspect in the morgue: Stefan Bedrich. Reporting restrictions would radically reduce the media's ability to ramp up the second-homes story, given that charges were about to be laid. Shaw could deflect questions about Bedrich's killer by asserting that an arrest in the murder inquiry was imminent. Warren had agreed; no doubt overjoyed that he could now tell his wife that their dual elevation to the status of Lord and Lady was back on track.

Shaw sipped his wine. For the rest of the day he was prepared to leave his mind blank, to let his eyes drink in the light. A sense of well-being seemed to blossom, filling the wide-open space around him.

The only problem was that line of footprints across the mud, leading towards Mitchell's Bank. If Stefan Bedrich hadn't made them, who had?

His phone rang and the screen said simply: CC.

'Sir.' He fought the urge to stand up.

'Peter. Private call. Look, this is entirely in the form of a heads-up. My office has received a complaint of police harassment. You're in the frame, although George gets an honorary mention. Needless to say, we take this kind of thing seriously.'

Shaw didn't say a word.

'Yes,' said Warren, as if answering a question that hadn't been asked. 'Name of Murano – Pietro Murano. He came in to St James' and saw Bill Troutman.'

Troutman was one of Warren's two assistant chief constables, a former DCI who'd once worked with Shaw's father. He was widely referred to throughout St James' as 'Uncle Bill'.

'As I say, we'll have to deal with this by the book, but Bill said he was a total prick. In fact he took time out to check him out on records and he is known to us. Two incidents of domestic violence back in the early eighties. Dealt with by family division, but still, you get the picture. Apparently he thumped his wife about. She thumped back. As I say, it never made the courts but it looks like a messy domestic.

'Anyway, he says you've been harassing his daughter. Doctor's report says she is currently unwell – nerves, anxiety attacks. She's already done her duty, he says, by making a full statement. He wants you to keep away. Unless there's an overwhelming operational need, I can't help thinking that's a good idea.'

Shaw sipped his wine. 'OK.'

'Good. You're a fucking good copper, Peter. Don't let bastards like this grind you down. Anyway – paperwork starts Monday. Least you know.'

'I appreciate the call.'

That was it. So much for the 'full relax'. The complaint was an irritation at best, unless Murano intended to fabricate details about the interview Shaw had conducted at Holme House. Her father's reaction was wildly disproportionate. Was it *his* reaction, or his daughter's? Why was the Murano family so touchy?

He took a swig of wine and then realized what he'd missed. Keen to get the chief constable off the line, he'd let that one, throwaway remark slip past:

She's already done her duty, he says, by making a full statement.

What statement?

He rang Paul Twine at the incident room and asked him to access the CID database and enter the name Sonia Murano.

Ten seconds. Fifteen seconds.

'Here it is,' said Twine. 'Oh, yeah. She was the witness in the Chelsea Burglars case – the one who caught sight of one of the gang. Only a glimpse. What did she say? Here: jet-black thick hair, beard, moustache, sideburns. Ruddy outdoor skin. Heavily muscled arms. Blue waterproof jacket, trainers, jeans. Not much to go on. Address was Holme House. Sir?'

'Hi. Right. I missed that. OK, Paul, can you send me the statement?'

'She was interviewed at Wells' nick. There's a transcript. I can send that?'

'Please.'

Shaw let his arms hang limply, feeling blood rush to his heart, leaving his skin cold. He'd missed something here, at the heart of the case, and the thought of exploring it, uncovering its ramifications, made him feel physically sick.

Most of all he felt a righteous anger. But for the chief constable's embargo on using the media, he would have read Murano's original statement. Then he would have interviewed her to try and extract more detail for a forensic ID picture. At Quantico, at the FBI school, he'd been taught the techniques required to tease from a witness those fragmentary crucial images that made a face *live*. Memory didn't come and go in completed, framed images. It was like a ball of string. If you could latch on to a loose thread you could shepherd a witness backwards in time, to the moment when the image was real. All that would have been possible if he'd been allowed to build his forensic portrait.

The brutal fact was that he was blaming Warren for his own failings. He *should* have read the original statement.

By the time Shaw was sitting at his desk in the cottage the email and attachment from Twine had reached his inbox. He feathered the slats on the blind so that a little of the evening light fell across his desk, but the laptop screen glowed in shadow.

Statement of Sonia Maria Murano. Recorded by tape Ref 568/12/10. Case officer DC Mark Birley. Transcript by secretarial pool R5.

Can you describe to me the events of the night of the seventeenth of July this year?

'I was alone in the house, Holme House.'

Is that unusual?

'No. It's unusual at night. I was working and hadn't noticed the time passing. The house is really a workshop – and it's where I grew up – but I live in a flat over my shop in Burnham Market. My father's still alive but he now lives in London. If he comes to visit he stays at Holme. My mother died in 2004. She lived there in the final years of her illness, after the divorce. I never sleep there – it's quite . . . er, isolated, spooky really. But the glass oven's there so I'm happy to work all day if I have to, alone.'

Go on.

'It was past nine, the light just suddenly went. The trees block the sunset anyway. It's a very shadowy house. I heard a vehicle on the road and we're the only place anyone could be visiting – unless they want to walk on the beach, and then they're supposed to leave their car down at Holme and walk. I went to the scullery window to see if they were going to park and then walk. If they do that I've got a little notice I can put on their windscreen – nothing threatening, just please don't park here, it's a private house.

'I saw four men getting out of a white van.'

Was your car there?

'No. I'd left it down at Holme and walked that morning because it's so beautiful. I enjoy it. And it gives me time to think about the work. I was designing and I had lots of colours in my head so I decided I wanted the fresh air. So no car. They must have thought the place was deserted because they were talking loudly, and they had rucksacks, and crowbars and torches. Once the car lights went that was all I could see, the torchbeams.

'There's a security light on the back of the house and that was on, so I think they missed the fact that the conservatory light was on too, where I was working.

'I didn't panic. I checked my phone but there was no signal – there hardly ever is. I did think about going out the back into the woods. If they'd seen me I didn't think I could outrun them. I'm strong, but they looked young, fit – at least, three of them did. There was an older one, much smaller. I heard a few snatches of what they were saying and I got the definite impression they'd been drinking.

'I heard the sound of wood splintering and thought I should try and keep out of the way. There was a cupboard under the stairs where I used to hide when I was a child. The door is a wooden panel and it blends in with the rest, the handle's flush with the wood. So I got in there.

'They were in the house about twenty minutes. I could hear them upstairs, the furniture being moved around. They must have been disappointed because most of the house has been moth-balled since Mum died. Then I heard crying. It had all gone very quiet and I thought they'd gone at first, but then I heard this sobbing – very close.

'It's very difficult to listen to another human being in distress and not respond.'

Tape stopped to allow witness to drink water.

'I opened the cupboard door an inch and saw a man kneeling in the hallway in front of the window – our window. I should explain. It was a life's work, for my mother, to restore this window. Medieval glass, from St John's at Burnham Marsh. When she was a child the church was still in use and it was this window that inspired her, she was a great glassmaker. After the storms in the eighties a lot of the glass was lost, and then vandals smashed more. She wanted to rebuild it – mostly with glass she'd fired herself. The diocese has a plan to restore the window to its original glory.

'That's the words they always use, isn't it? *Original glory.* After she died I carried on. I was very close to finishing, after twenty years of craftsmanship, the work of mother and child. It *was* extraordinary. More than that, it provided a link back to her, and back to my childhood, which was very happy until my parents split up. A link back to how it had once been.'

Witness requests brief break in interview.

'The man kneeling in front of the window was the only one I saw clearly at all. As an image, in my head, the overwhelming feature is how black his hair was – it's a cliché to say jet-black, but this was very close, almost a blue-black, like pencil lead. A stubble beard and moustache, and here . . .'

Can you describe it for the tape?

'Sorry. Sideburns. Black sideburns – but stubble again. He was wearing a sweatshirt top with the sleeves cut away so that you could see his muscles. I didn't see his eyes – I'm sorry I didn't because I might have understood then why he did what he did.'

And clothes?

'A waterproof zip-up jacket – blue, I think, and jeans and trainers.'

Please, carry on.

'He was sobbing, as I said. And I could hear the others – out the front, shouting for him to hurry up. He got to his feet, took a crowbar out of his rucksack and attacked the window. It's the right word.'

Would you like to stop?

'No. I want this over. He *flew* at it – a frenzy. The window's about fifteen feet tall so there were some bits of glass he couldn't reach but he destroyed most of it. It rained down – glass falling, so that it covered the floor. The noise was infernal, just unbearable. The shattering. I couldn't watch for a moment and then when I did look again I saw he was being dragged away by the others.

'I saw his eyes then. That's what I was focused on. I didn't have any time to notice the others. I'm sorry about that. I'm not very useful, am I? But *his* eyes were very dull – very defeated. Almost blank of emotion except that I did think, for a moment, that I detected a look of envy. It doesn't make sense, any of it. I'm sorry.'

Go on.

'I don't remember much more but one of the others had a spray can and I thought that was odd. I only saw his back but he spelt out LOCAL HOMES FOR LOCAL PEOPLE on the wall, the can hissing. He was in such a hurry you could hardly read it. Then they were gone.

'For a few minutes I just waited. At the time I told myself I was listening to see if they might come back. All I heard was the sea and some wood pigeons. I think that really, inside, I was hoping for a miracle, that when I did come out and stand in front of the window it would be complete. That the window of St John's would be untouched.

'I took the first step – not looking at the window at all – but I knew the truth because the glass was all over the floor. Each step I took it broke underfoot.

'To destroy such beauty is evil. I hope he finds his own hell, and that there's no colour, or light, or beauty there.'

Tape ends.

Shaw stood immediately, realizing he'd been holding himself totally still, so that his bones creaked as he stretched.

The corridor to their bedroom had bare polished boards, and the walls were panelled and painted white. On Lena's side he opened the bedside drawer and took out what he knew he'd find there: a Bible.

It took him a few minutes to find the right chapter.

Now Herod had arrested John and bound him and put him in prison because of Herodias, his brother Philip's wife, for John had been saying to him: 'It is not lawful for you to have her.' Herod wanted to kill John, but he was afraid of the people, because they considered John a prophet.

On Herod's birthday the daughter of Herodias danced for the guests and pleased Herod so much that he promised with an oath to give her whatever she asked. Prompted by her mother, she said, 'Give me here on a platter the head of John the Baptist.' The king was distressed, but because of his oaths and his dinner guests, he ordered that her request be granted and had John beheaded in the prison. His head was brought in on a platter and given to the girl, who carried it to her mother.

FORTY-SIX

S haw sat on the bed rereading the story of John the Baptist until the sound of fat raindrops made him look to the window. Outside the sun still shone, dashes of icy rain cutting through the beams. Running through the house, out on to the sands, he found Lena and Fran watching the storm at sea: thunder rolled, high-altitude winds tore the clouds into shreds. Warm air buffeted them, making their eardrums creak.

'This could be it – the end of the summer at last,' said Shaw.

'Look!' shouted Fran, pointing both arms out to sea.

A rainbow spanned the beach, the spectrum sharp and clear, including a vibrant green. Lena, laughing, shrugged herself out of her shorts and T-shirt to reveal a white bikini. Fran, already in her costume, joined her mother in a screaming run towards the water's edge.

Lena looked over her shoulder and shouted: 'Come on!'

Shaw realized he was still holding the Bible. Looking at the black cover, the gold-copperplate title, he sensed – a half second before it struck – the falling thunderbolt. The world turned silver, crackling like kindling, then the thunder cracked right over his head.

The coast, the dunes, the sky – all of it now appeared in black and white. Lena, clutching Fran in the shallows, shouted something he couldn't hear because his ears were still echo chambers of torn air. She pointed north, along the beach, then started to haul her daughter back out of the water.

Shaw looked where Lena had pointed and saw a narrow chimney of smoke rising from the dunes.

Lena arrived, Fran trying to pull her back. 'The lightning touched down, Peter. Along at Holme. There . . .'

'Let's get back in the water,' shouted Fran.

'Best stay out till the lightning moves on,' said Shaw.

'Beautiful too,' said Lena. 'The lightning that came down was blue, Peter. If I close my eyes I can still see it.'

Rain began to fall then turned to hail, and the air temperature plummeted. Ice pellets bounced on the roof of the shop and the café.

Lena covered Fran's head with her hands. 'We'll take cover,' she said.

'Go. Get warm. I'm going to check it out,' said Shaw, waving to Fran.

The force of the hailstones falling made him dip his head, but he ran on, through a grey world of hail, sand and dunes.

After ten minutes he climbed the nearest high dune. As he stood, soaked, hailstones in his hair, his heart creaking inside his ribcage, the storm edge passed overhead, a scrap of blue sky revealed in its wake.

Thirty seconds later the vista was complete, from the red and white cliffs at Hunstanton in the west to Holme Point and the pine woods to the east. The storm had cleared the beaches, except for a distant trio of horses being halter-led back to the stables. In the mid-distance, among the ridged dunes, a single figure knelt in one of the dry basins scooped out by the high tide. Something was lost, because the figure's hands were on the ground, mapping it out, feeling the surface. To one side, sticking out of the sand, was a spade.

Shaw was twenty feet away when he saw it was Sonia Murano, but by then she'd looked up and he couldn't have abandoned his approach, even if he'd wanted.

She didn't stand, but sat back on her heels. While she'd been working, searching the sand, her face had been animated, even joyful, but now there was no disguising the sudden rigidity, and a look of genuine, startled fear.

There was a dull echo of thunder from inland.

Beside Murano lay a rucksack, the top flap open, to reveal a pile of round stones. It was the final image that, combined with the rest, seemed to fuse into a picture with a single clap of intellectual lightning.

'I missed the obvious,' he said. 'I've always known its other name. Talk about in plain sight.'

He bent down and snapped off a sprig of woody samphire and held it up against the blue sky so that they could see the vivid green of the autumnal growth.

'Glasswort,' said Shaw. 'There's a plaque up in All Saints which spelt it out. The *salicornia* – the salty seaside plants used by glassmakers to produce lustrous, quality glass. The Venetians were famous for it, but I don't need to tell you that.'

She laid one hand flat on the sand. 'I can't find the spot. There was smoke, so there must be ash. But I can't find it.'

'The lightning strike?' asked Shaw, dropping to his knees, feeling the sand. 'I missed that too, but I won't be too hard on myself. Fulgurite is created by lightning turning sand into a silica mineral, otherwise known as glass, of course. God's glass. No oven required. How much is it worth?'

Her face unfroze, latching on to the question: 'A thousand pounds, maybe fifteen hundred. Rings are sought after, cut from the fronds of stone. Fire rings. And gem shops pay well, even for the rough mineral.'

'We shouldn't be talking, of course,' said Shaw, sitting. There was a gap in the dunes here and they could see the sea, the tide edging shorewards in a series of miniature white-water waves.

'I'm sorry,' she said. 'My father is overprotective. I simply said I wanted my privacy back. I was badly affected by the burglary. I'd only just got over Mum's death. He came up to be with me – I could hardly say no. He is my father, despite every-thing. He said that if he complained officially I'd be left in peace, and that's all I want. We thought it would do no harm, to put down a marker. A line.'

'In the sand,' offered Shaw.

She swung the bag of stones over her shoulder.

'What you really wanted was revenge, wasn't it?'

She stood, ruffling her blonde hair into shape.

'That's what your statement implies, I think. What were the precise words? "I hope he finds his own hell, and that there's no colour, or light, or beauty there."'

'The irony is that I wouldn't have read the statement if it wasn't for your father's complaint. I had no idea you were our witness. So I read it. Police work comes down to that so often. You have to make the time to read. Consider.'

She knelt on the sand.

'Why do you love glass?' he asked.

'It reminds me of my childhood, and Mum, and light, and being happy. It's like a magical key – it takes me there.'

'Is that why you killed Stefan Bedrich? Because he smashed the key?'

She had her head turned to the sea. 'I didn't kill him.' Her voice had lost its musical lilt.

'But you know who he is, obviously.'

She didn't answer.

'The motive's clear. It's the opportunity that I couldn't fathom. But then there's the samphire and the fulgurite. You collected samphire for the glass oven. There was a bed of it beyond Mitchell's Bank, so you must have known the marshes well. It had to be unpremeditated, because Bedrich was on the run from someone else who wanted him dead. He set out across the marshes, wounded, disorientated, his hands bound behind him.

'And he met you. Or, rather – you came upon him. And why were you out at night? You'd seen the lightning strike. From up at the house. It occurs to me you spend a lot of time there alone. Or do you sit out on the bench, your mother's bench? You'd have seen it from there.

'The lightning struck and you set out across the marshes towards Scolt Head Island, climbed over the ridge and found the spot, built your cairn, and were returning when you came upon poor Stefan. Had his energy given out? My guess is he couldn't free his leg from the rope and weight. Was he trapped in the mud, perhaps, lying there, sinking, crying for help? He wanted salvation and fate brought him you. Was recognition instant? He'd shaved off a lot of the hair – but you'd seen his eyes, his face. This was the man who had deliberately destroyed the beauty of the great window. The man you wanted to see in hell. So you sent him there.'

She'd stuck her spade into the sand and Shaw, kneeling beside it, examined the blade.

'One blow. You're a woman who works in a factory, after all – even if it is a glassworks. You have hidden strength. And he couldn't move, could he? Trapped in the mud. Did you consciously see the image then – of St John's head on the golden dish?'

She shook her head, fumbling for her mobile. 'I'm sorry, this is pure fantasy. I'm ringing Father. Clearly there needs to be a fresh complaint.'

'Do you always carry secateurs, or scissors, just in case you come upon some samphire? You knew the Polish migrant workers were trying to corner the local market. There'd been trouble at Morston – boats vandalized. So you sent us off on a false trail. That was quite a cold, premeditated action. That won't play well in front of a jury.'

Fingers shaking, she abandoned the attempt to use her phone and slipped it back in her pocket.

'What you don't know is why Bedrich did it, do you?' asked Shaw.

'He was a thief. He envies what others have. He violates the homes of innocent people . . .'

Her voice had risen but broke on the word *innocent*.

'Not so. There was a lot of beauty in Stefan Bedrich's life,' said Shaw.

His phone held several pictures he'd taken in the flat at Greenwood House, of the room decorated with the artwork of his wife, the exploding colours, the interlocking designs. He held one up for her to see.

'This was painted by his wife.'

He scrolled through the album: 'And this.'

He put the phone away. She'd abandoned any attempt to flee.

'We'll never know what was in his mind that night, of course,' said Shaw. 'It doesn't really matter. I think his story speaks for itself . . .'

Murano's face was perfectly composed but Shaw noted that it was wet with tears. 'Tell me.'

So he told Sonia Murano Stefan Bedrich's story: his marriage, his journey to the UK to earn money, the accident on the streets of Gdansk, the daughter – alone – cared for by grandparents. The devoted wife who'd sent him pictures to keep his spirits high.

One detail, he said, had convinced him of Stefan Bedrich's motives that night at Holme House, when he'd taken a crowbar to the splendour of the window of St John the Baptist. The burglary was on the night of the seventeenth of July. The Polish official at the Peterborough consulate who'd informed him of his wife's death had rung him – via the Lynn Polish Club – on the evening of the sixteenth.

When he'd told her everything he knew, they were both silent.

'I think the sight of the window was too much for him,' said Shaw eventually. 'It reminded him of the colour, the beauty, and of his wife, of what he'd lost. He couldn't be with her ever again so he destroyed it. Difficult to forgive, but not difficult to understand.'

'So not envy at all,' she said. 'Just despair.'

She didn't leave, despite the path which led away towards Holme.

'I don't think your father made his complaint because he was worried about what I'd find out,' said Shaw. 'I think he complained because he was terrified you'd tell me what really happened if I asked. It's what you want, isn't it? The relief of the confession. I'd give you time to think about that but I can't risk losing the forensic evidence. I need the spade, and the Barbour you're wearing, and the boots. So I'm going to have to ask you to walk back with me . . . to my house. Twenty minutes at most. I have to insist.'

She didn't speak at all.

They walked together, side by side, the advancing waves just to their right, the sunset too.

Shaw considered Murano's childhood at Holme House, the blissful years seen only with hindsight; and how misguided it was of her to seek to preserve such a distant happiness, and to think that it could be relived, while the future was denied. She'd compressed all her memories into a single object, an icon, until the window had *been* her childhood. But as Lena had pointed out, glass was such a brittle treasure.

As they came in sight of the Old Beach Café he saw that the holiday crowds, excited by the electric storm, had flooded out of Hunstanton to enjoy the blue skies which had opened overhead. Lena had reopened the café and Fran was clearing tables. The crowds ate, drank and watched the sunset. The café's tape of Beach Boys classics came just within earshot. He imagined the same scene at nightfall, the beach deserted, and for the first time since he'd moved back to the coast he felt that might be enough.

FORTY-SEVEN

Eight Months Later

A twenty-five-foot-high wind turbine turned lazily on its tower, throwing late afternoon shadows across the sands in front of Surf! – north Norfolk's newest bar/restaurant. It had been Fran's idea to paint the turbine blades in primary colours to mimic a child's beach mini-windmill. After a brief tussle with the local planning authority, which also objected to the decking for seating, permission was grudgingly given, although plans for a single neon sign, pulsing the word Surf!, were rejected without comment.

A banner proclaiming *GRAND OPENING* stretched between two volleyball posts. Children had been allocated a square, fifty feet by fifty feet, in which to enter the sandcastle competition. An entry ticket cost one pound and purchased you six square feet upon which to build a fairy-tale castle. Fran had joined forces with Lucilla, her new best friend, an alliance which had inevitably embraced Paulo and Cornelia. Duties had been assigned: Paulo had been sent off to collect lolly-sticks and any other useful 'found objects' from the high water mark, while Cornelia had been given the Sisyphean task of ferrying plastic buckets full of sea water to the moat around their creation – a scale model of Hogwarts.

A lifeguard on a high chair judged a junior surf competition in waves no higher than three feet, while a crowd of about two hundred milled around on the sand with drinks, or sat at the dozen circular metal tables. Lena supervised a team of ten waitresses, hired for the event. Leo D'Asti oversaw the kitchen and the bar, in between pressing the flesh of the VIP guest list: local councillors, press, environmental health and planning officers, and the entire staff of the local Tourist Information Centre. The café itself and every table outside was adorned with flowers sent up from Juliet D'Asti's shop on the King's Road.

D'Asti Senior had wandered into the café one Sunday morning a month after the arrest of Sonia Murano. His children had slurped hot chocolate while he'd offered a protracted, and sincere, thank you to Shaw – and the rest of the crew of the *Flyer* – for plucking them off Mitchell's Bank. D'Asti had gone on to explain that the family now lived permanently in Burnham Market and that Lucilla and Paulo would be attending the primary school for the new term, and that Cornelia would follow after nursery school. Fran and Lucilla would be in the same year. Meanwhile he would be a 'house husband', while Juliet commuted up from London for weekends, although he had his eyes open for a good local business opportunity.

Lena was away that day in London, seeing old friends, taking a break from the beach, so it had been Shaw who had broached the idea of D'Asti investing in the expansion of the Old Beach Café. As long as he could have his beach back at midnight, he was now more sanguine about the prospect of Lena creating a trendy 'oasis' on the lonely coast. His childhood memory of the spot, bathed in a golden sunshine that almost certainly never shone, was best kept inside his own head. Besides, Surf! would make Lena happy, and protect Fran from the crippling influence of boredom.

By the time Lena got back from London that night after dark D'Asti was prepared to invest £250,000 in the business for half the equity, following an independent audit of the accounts. Most of the cash was needed for the wind generator, a second 4×4, a sewerage and water plant, and alterations to the shop and cottage, including a ten-foot covered extension to the verandah. D'Asti wanted nothing to do with the day-to-day management of the business, although he was more than prepared to stand in behind the bar or even in the kitchen. While the kids were still young he wanted time to spend with them. However, he was prepared to take on advertising, purchasing, branding, and any of the paperwork needed if they took on full- or part-time staff.

The plans had become bricks, mortar and wood with almost indecent haste. And now the big day had arrived.

Shaw stood apart from the crowd, watching wind yachts speed silently along the sands. He didn't see Valentine until his DS was ten feet away. The raincoat and black slip-ons had been ditched

for a pair of chinos and a blue shirt, hardly Hawaii Five-O, but
an improvement nonetheless.

'George. Jan?'

'She's helping out in the kitchen. Frankly, this kind of thing
freaks her out. Me too.'

'Any news?' asked Shaw.

'Letters go out on the first of the month, but she's been tipped
the wink. I think she's in. Training starts at Hendon in October.'

'PC Clay, then. Blimey. You want to watch out, George. She
might outrank you one day.'

Valentine tried to hide his bare feet in the sand.

'Let me show you something by the bar,' said Shaw.

A minute later they both had drinks: Shaw the standard half
of Guinness, Valentine something red with an umbrella sticking
out of it. They were standing in front of a framed picture, an
abstract jigsaw of primary colours.

'I chose this one,' said Shaw. 'I reckoned two hundred and
fifty quid was a decent price. I used the money to frame three
others and sent them all to Interpol in Warsaw. They've passed
them on to the grandparents. One day the kid can have them.
She'll grow up with them anyway. It's something. Childhood
images are important.'

'Remind me of the name,' said Valentine.

'Kasia.'

The murder of Stefan Bedrich had left little Kasia an orphan.
Murano's trial for his murder was due to start at Peterborough
Crown Court in three weeks. She had made a full confession on
the evening Shaw had walked her back along the beach from
Holme. The court proceedings were expected to last less than a
day. The Director of Public Prosecutions had spent some time
evaluating the file on Pietro Murano, but had concluded that there
was little chance of securing a conviction for conspiracy. Neither
would give evidence against each other. There was little doubt
they were complicit after the fact, but complicit in what? It was
a waste of public money trying to find out.

'Hey up,' said Valentine, nodding over Shaw's shoulder.

Out on the edge of the crowd on the sand John Jack Stepney
stood with a glass of white wine.

'Cheeky fucker,' said Valentine.

'It's a free country, George. Surf!'s open to all. I think he likes to keep his enemies close. All very Al Pacino.'

Stepney was examining his mobile, no doubt bemused by the almost total absence of a signal.

'Latest?' asked Valentine.

'Not good,' said Shaw. The forensic sweeps of Stepney's house in Balamory, *Highlife*, and the Palace Arcade had drawn a blank. The licensed owner of the slot machines turned out to be a woman based in Brighton who ran three other arcades on the South Coast. The motorcycle gunman, Leslie James Hales, had made a slow recovery from his heart attack at Brandon Creek. Ballistics had identified the gun found in his leathers as that which had killed Shrimp Davies. Hales also had a pocket of loose change, among which were three fifty-pence coins, two ten-pence coins, a one-penny coin and a token from the Palace Arcade. The prints on the cellophane wallet containing the five thousand pounds were those of Emilia Stepney, John Jack's daughter. She had also been identified as a courier by Interpol, used by various Stepney associates, to ferry documents to and from a house in the hills above San Sebastian, La Gomera, in the Canary Islands, as well as three addresses in Poplar, East London.

'DPP says it's not enough,' said Shaw. 'We could get Stepney into the dock all right, but it won't stick, because we can't physically link Hales and Stepney and the cash. Hales will say anything Stepney's lawyers tell him to say. However, all is not lost, George . . .'

Shaw had spotted the arrival of the guest of honour: Max Warren, with his wife. The media coverage of the Chelsea Burglars had been low-key, their petty crimes overshadowed by the Mitchell's Bank killing, and the murder of Shrimp Davies. The only fly in the ointment was the county council's police committee. It had taken umbrage at not being informed of the news blackout ordered by the chief constable, and planned an in camera hearing. But the Home Office had expressed its gratitude to Warren, and eventually, inevitably, so would the Palace.

Half an hour later Shaw was able to sit the chief constable down in a canvas chair, alone, near the sandcastles. The bar staff had rustled up a glass of Glenfiddich with a little water, and

Warren was holding it up to the sun when Shaw told him that
he had been to see Leslie James Hales at HMP Wandsworth.

'I hope you haven't done anything stupid, Peter. I realize there
are unresolved aspects to this case, but life's not perfect. At least
mine never is, so I don't see why yours should be any different.
Hales will go down for life, but he'll be out in fifteen. So, as far
as I can see, job done. All right, I know he'll come out to a nice
little nest egg, care of Stepney and Co. But that's the way of the
world.'

'That's not quite how it looks from his point of view, sir. Hales
has a wife and three children – two boys and a baby girl. Medical
tests have revealed that he has a congenital heart defect. His life
expectancy has been put at between five and ten years. He might
be lucky, of course. But then he might be unlucky. He could
serve fifteen and then drop dead on his first day out.'

'So what?'

'He'd turn Queen's evidence, at least he says he would, *if* we
could offer witness protection. I'm sure you don't need me to
quote the precedent, sir. Serious Organized Crime and Police Act
2005 would be a good start. He wants a new identity now, to
serve time in a Scottish prison, then witness protection once he's
out, anonymity guaranteed. Witness protection for life.

'For that he'll tell the court how Stepney's brother made contact
in the first place about Davies, how he got instructions, and then
how he picked up the cash from Stepney in his office at the
Palace. The cellophane wallet was inside a brown A4 envelope.
Stepney handed him the envelope. I've taken him through it, and
my opinion is that he'd make an excellent witness. He's got a
good memory for detail.'

The chief constable looked out to sea. 'It's not going to happen,
Peter. Hales is the killer. He deserves to be behind bars. Have
you any idea of the cost of this kind of caper? Home Office has
to pay, I have to pay. The budget's two million under water now
– *now*, it's June, Peter. I am not handing my successor a police
service in debt. No way. The case is over for us. The courts have
got their man. They'll send him down. That's it.'

Shaw took a swig from a bottle of Estrella. The children had
formed a single chain and were running in and out of the various
sandcastles and moats.

'Have you given any thought to how to play the police committee hearing, sir?'

A ripple of laughter made them look back at the crowd, which had dwindled to fifty, all of whom were clutching champagne flutes as Lena circulated with a bottle of Prosecco.

'What the fuck is that supposed to mean?' Warren tried to sit up straight in the canvas chair but it refused to provide enough rigidity to counter his weight.

'In the normal course of events, in other words without a media blackout, we'd have used Murano to build up a picture of the burglar she saw at Holme House. That could have led to an arrest. An early arrest. More to the point, it could have led directly to us identifying Stefan Bedrich when we found him on Mitchell's Bank. Or – look at it another way. If we'd hauled her in to St James' to help construct a forensic ID she might not have taken a spade to Bedrich when she found him out on the sands. I'm just saying, it changes things. The media blackout; the media blackout you ordered, sir. And I opposed. In writing, if I recall, sir.'

Warren sniffed the malt. 'And you'd feel duty bound to share these concerns with the committee, would you, Peter?'

'In the present circumstances, sir.'

Warren began to struggle in the seat, which had sunk slightly into the sand. Shaw held out a hand and hauled the chief constable up on his feet.

Warren threw an inch of malt into the sand.

'All right, Peter. I'll write to the Home Office suggesting that we take a closer look at Hales. That he might be a candidate for witness protection.'

'I think they would value your opinion, sir. And that it would be most helpful if that opinion was that he would make a good candidate for the scheme.'

Warren looked right through Shaw's good eye. The new chief constable was due in post at Christmas. It was going to be a very uncomfortable few months.

'All right,' said Warren. 'That's the best I can do. I know Stepney's a low-life, but is he worth all this?'

Warren's wife joined them and they broke into smiles. Warren gave Shaw a fatherly pat on the shoulder and told them an old anecdote about his father, Jack Shaw, nicking a flasher on the beach on an August Bank Holiday.

Shaw escaped, took a fresh Prosecco bottle out of a bucket of ice in the café, and circulated the dwindling crowd. He found Stepney on the edge still, chatting to the council's head of environmental health. Shaw topped up his glass.

'Cheers,' said Stepney. 'Nice place. You'll make a fortune.'

'That's all down to Lena,' he said. 'She runs Surf! But I like to think it's my beach.'

'Is it?' said Stepney, raising an eyebrow, and sharing a sly smile with the council officer.

'Yeah,' said Shaw. 'It is.'